Redemption

OTHER BOOKS BY ASHLEY LUCERO

Absolution

THE AWAKENING SERIES

Redemption

ASHLEY LUCERO

Book design by Maureen Cutajar
www.gopublished.com

ISBN: 978-0997201604

She was chaos and beauty intertwined. A tornado of roses from divine.

—SHAKIEB ORGUNWALL

Prologue

The raindrops froze as they hit the windshield of the Escalade, eventually turning into thick snowflakes and blanketing everything around us. It was deathly silent as we made our way back to the city; everyone's thoughts seeming to be preoccupied with what they had witnessed earlier. I used to be an ordinary teenage girl before all of this. Just dealing with my parents' divorce, worrying about getting into a good college and what my Saturday nights would consist of. Now, I'm a hybrid; part angel, part fallen angel, but somewhere inside I'm still Alex Constance. Only I'm not sure how big that part of me is now.

There has never been a hybrid before who lived past infancy. Some of my female ancestors, those gifted with angel blood, had all been ordered to be killed before they could be used by fallen angels to open a portal to heaven and take over. My guardian angel disobeyed his orders to kill me when I was little and now I had been kidnapped and injected with fallen angel's blood, transforming me into the supernatural.

I could feel the edgy tension building inside the SUV with every breath I took. Everyone seemed uncomfortable in my presence, mostly because what I am isn't supposed to be possible, and also because I am presumably unpredictable. Absolutely no one, fallen angels and angels alike, knows what I am or am not capable of. And that terrifies me. But

1

because everyone else in the Escalade already lived in the realm which I have now entered, I suspect they know the potential power I possess and are perhaps more terrified than I am. I sense fear inside them; fear that's thick in the air around us; a vast unknowingness.

Nathaniel, my 'mentor,' had been instructed to eliminate me when I was a baby, but after defying those orders to kill me, was now a fallen angel and it had changed him to the point where he was going to get as far away from me as possible to keep me safe. He lost control of himself at times and suffered from minor short-term amnesia. Even his brother Uvall had killed Blyth, the love of his life when he changed. What did that mean for me? Would this new blood and body change me - or has it already - to the point where I would become a killer? How could I ever be normal after any of this? How was I supposed to keep my true identity a secret? Would I ever see Nathaniel again?

Pictures of Nathaniel and my family and friends danced across my vision relentlessly; then the words Ezekiel said thundered around me:

"Some are too lost to be saved right now... You're no longer a human; you need to tread carefully from here on out when you are around others. We'll be watching over you Alexandria; we'll be here if you need us."

I shuddered reflexively. Somewhere deep down I still had to be Alex Constance.

Chapter 1

A touch on my shoulder jolted me awake; instinctively I grabbed to remove it and was met with Luther's metallic eyes. I relaxed and released his hand as he stepped back and appraised me; uncertainty creasing the lines in his forehead.

"Sorry." I breathed as I looked around the room realizing we were in a hotel.

Luther answered my questions before I could ask.

"We thought it was best to get a place for the night; give you some time to recuperate before we have to take you back home," he said handing me a glass of water.

I happily accepted it and chugged it down in a few gulps.

"How long have I been out?" I asked, suddenly noticing the bright stream of yellow light hiding beneath the curtains on the window. Luther walked towards the windows then and pulled them back, allowing a bright illumination to fill the room. I squinted at first and then stood.

"Almost two days." He replied stepping back and watching me closely.

My eyes widened. "It's Sunday?!" I exclaimed. How had I managed to sleep a day and a half away without waking?

I would have to go home today. I would have to face my family, Kate, Trey and school and I wasn't even remotely ready. I frantically grabbed the clock on the nightstand that was facing the other way, and to my panic, it read 3:30PM. My dad would be picking me up from the airport today after my 'Washington D.C. school trip', which of course I never went on and I had no idea how I would even pretend to be 'OK.' I was anything but OK. Luther snapped me out of my panic.

"You should eat something; we don't have long before we have to take you back, but we can talk over breakfast. Seraphina brought your duffel bag as well," he stated as he exited the room and closed the door, allowing me my privacy.

I felt flustered as I got dressed and caught a glance at my reflection in a large mirror hanging next to a dresser. The girl that I had once known seemed vastly different from the figure staring back at me. My eyes were brighter; a brilliant emerald shining back hinting the same shine I had seen in Nathaniel's eyes before. My body and my hair also seemed to radiate a glow. I looked lively and fresh and I knew everyone would pick up on it; they just wouldn't know why I seemed so different.

I reached my hand over my head and tried to feel where giant wings had once protruded through my shoulder blades, but my fingers were met only with warm, smooth skin and two long thin scars. Otherwise, I looked completely normal. The sound of voices coming from the other room caught my attention and I turned away from the girl I didn't recognize to finish pulling on a long sleeved top and jeans. I found Caim and Lahash in the living room playing Texas Hold-em next to a giant rolling tray with all but one plate empty. Luther was on the balcony having a cigarette and Seraphina wasn't anywhere to be seen. I tried to take a seat across from Caim and Lahash silently, but my presence was noted instantly.

"We thought you were never going to wake up," Lahash stated, knocking his knuckles on the counter twice as they both locked eyes on me.

I fumbled my hands underneath the table, uncomfortably avoiding their gaze and his statement.

"Where's Seraphina?" I sensed she wasn't in the suite with us. The three were fallen angels who wanted to stop other fallen angels - perhaps evil ones - from taking over Heaven. They believed differently from others and had taken on the responsibility of further training me to develop my 'abilities.'

4

"She had some business to take care of. Everything's been crazy since Friday. You should hear the kinds of things everyone has been saying." Caim countered Lahash's move and finished Lahash's statement.

"No one knows what to do with a hybrid," he stated.

"What do you mean? What kinds of things?" I questioned, hoping to get some information on what had happened over the last 37 hours during my slumber. Caim replied.

"Everyone wants to know what you're capable of and some wild theories have surfaced about whose side you're on since you and Nathaniel..." Caim trailed off as Luther cleared his throat and shut the sliding glass door behind him. I turned to Luther expectantly for answers.

"What happens now? You can't seriously expect for me to go back to living my life as if nothing happened. What if I hurt someone? Or..." I trailed off as I felt a strange heat deep inside the pit of my chest stir. I swallowed. A nauseating feeling replaced the heat in my chest. Luther placed a plate of pancakes in front of me and took a seat next to Lahash and me.

"We don't really know what to do right now, but one thing is certain, if you don't return home your family and friends will know something is wrong. Things will become extremely more complicated than they already are. This will help give us some time to cool things off on both sides," he said keeping his eyes on me.

"What if something happens?" I asked, not liking the idea of this at all. "Is my family even safe around me? What about Uvall's people?" Caim and Lahash looked at Luther as I finished my question.

Luther gave me a small smile.

"They'll be just fine. Trust me; no one wants to tangle with a hybrid at the moment. Just like you, they have no idea what you're capable of. The safest place for you and your family right now is at home together."

I nodded feeling a little better knowing no one would be trying to kidnap me again.

"And Nathaniel? Have you heard from him?" I asked, trying not to sound hopeful.

Luther looked down for a moment before looking back at me and responding.

"He's off the grid. Last I heard he was called in to be initiated by fallen angels. I don't have any update right now."

"What does that mean? What type of initiation?"

Caim and Lahash shifted uncomfortably in their seats, pretending to be focused on their cards. Luther did not answer me, and the overall feeling in the room was not a warm one. Whatever *initiation* meant, it did not instill warm and fuzzy feelings. The silence in the room was almost painful. I took a bite out of my pancake, all my thoughts lingering on what was happening to Nathaniel. I set my fork down as nausea crept back.

"There are some things you should know about yourself before you go home," Luther declared as he motioned for me to continue to eat.

I fought the awful feeling in my stomach and forced myself to eat the pancake.

"Firstly, no one should ever see your wings. The last thing you need is to draw attention to yourself right now - from anyone. So, try and be as inconspicuous as possible. If they unfurl, relaxing will usually make them fold away again," he stated calmly and continued before I could interject.

"We don't know what your capabilities are just yet. They may be the same as angels or fallen angels or you may have other - unknown - abilities." He paused over the word 'unknown,' seemingly hesitant to imply whether that would be a good thing or a dangerous occurrence. He held his gaze on me for a moment perhaps searching for that 'unknown' something which he may have both feared and appreciated.

"As such, the last thing you want to do is get into a conflict with anyone. High emotions or stress could trigger your wings or set you off. You just need to tread lightly right now. We'll be checking in on you too to make sure you're alright."

"Set me off? Has anyone been to high school here!?" I yelled rubbing my temples. "I can name a list of things that were stressful on a daily basis when I was human, and you're telling me anything could set me off?!" I felt the flow of my blood quicken and my pulse race.

I trembled, shaking involuntarily as the emotions of what was happening and what had happened overwhelmed every pore. I held onto the table trying to steady myself, but before I could understand what was happening, I screamed, lurching forward. The room had gone quiet. I opened my clenched eyes and looked up. Everyone had moved far away from me. They were unmistakably tense and vigilant, and Luther, although straining to remain calm, looked ready to pounce.

"Alex, just breathe. Focus on your breathing," Luther called.

I glanced sideways at the dazzling pair of outstretched wings on either side of me. They took up much of the living room and had toppled over the food cart next to me.

A few tears escaped my eyes, and I squeezed them shut. After about five minutes of deep breathing, my wings retracted into my back again. The shaking slowly subsided as I kept my eyes closed and continued to take deep breaths. I could feel my pulse return to a steady beat, but deep down I was terrified. I knew I was different, like a science experiment that had gone terribly wrong. Whatever was mixed inside of me was lively and ready to explode outward at any moment. It's like it had a mind of its own. I took another deep breath.

"Luther, I can't...I can't do this. What did they do to me? Am I some sort of monster now?" I pleaded quietly for the answer from him.

He grabbed my hands and held them firmly as Caim and Lahash returned to their seats at the table.

"Look at me. None of us can even begin to understand what you're feeling or what you are going through right now, but nonetheless, we are here for you. Nathaniel wouldn't have gone without knowing that you would be well taken care of. You need to be strong right now. As hard as it is, this is what we're going to have to do for us to find out what you are really capable of. Understand?"

"Yeah." I muffled wiping the excess tears from my face with my palms.

"Good girl. I've got a few more calls to make, but Caim and Lahash are going to go over the basics of some of the feeding schedules and some of the things to expect, and they're not going to dwell on anything that won't help," he stated, shooting them both a look that I could only guess said *tell her anything that freaks her out, and I'll gut both of you.* Then he got up and exited the hotel room. Caim and Lahash looked knowingly at each other as Luther exited.

"Sooo... feeding schedules?" I asked with a raised eyebrow. I felt like a damn animal who had to be kept on a strict eating schedule so she wouldn't devour or hurt anyone.

Caim chuckled a little. "It's really not that bad, you know on average you'll save thousands each year not having to buy so much food."

Lahash and I stared at him for a moment wondering if he had just heard himself.

"What?! It's true!" Caim interjected after another moment of stony silence.

"Look, here are the things you need to know," he said, waving Caim off and holding up his fingers to count as he spoke.

"You still eat, but thanks to Google over here," jerking his head toward Lahash, "we know you won't nearly be eating like you used to. You should try to stick to some kind of a regular eating schedule though. Especially being new to all of this you'll get really weak if you don't remember to eat at some point. Angels and fallen angels are similar there. That goes for sleep, too. We all have to sleep eventually, count on every 30-36 hours sleeping and eating and you'll be fine."

"Oh and you probably won't get cold easily anymore," Caim chimed in.

Lahash nodded. "Yep, it'll take a lot more to get you hot or cold... and I think that's about it," Lahash stated, confirming with Caim who was nodding his head.

I shifted slightly. "What, that's it? That's all the 'need-to-knows'?" I still knew almost nothing about this new body, and they really hadn't been much help.

"Well, pretty much, yeah. You're different hun, sorry. Honestly, no one ever thought something like you could be made," Caim said shrugging apologetically.

Something like me. Even though he hadn't meant it, the words cut slightly.

"Right. Um, thanks," I stuttered as I slowly got up from the table.

"Hey, for what it's worth, we both think it's jacked up what happened. You need anything, and we're here," Lahash confirmed.

"Thanks. I think I'm gonna go get ready."

They each nodded, picking up their cards again and returning to their nearly silent poker game, but I could feel their attention on me even after

I left the room. They were nervous, and I couldn't blame them. After all, I'd lost control for just a second and...

I shut the door behind me quietly and laid my head against it closing my eyes. I stayed there listening to the sound of my breath for several minutes before grabbing my bag and heading for the shower. The droplets traced across my skin delicately as steam filled the small room, fogging the mirror. Even with the temperature turned all the way over to searing hot, my body remained a consistent, warm, temperature. I breathed the steam in, welcoming it as it circulated in and out of my lungs.

My hands ran over my arms and legs instinctively with a bar of soap but stopped when they ran over the bend in my right arm. I could still feel the slight prick where the needle containing the fallen angel blood had been injected. Flashes of the syringe and images of that horrible day blasted across my vision.

A knock sounded on the door bringing me back to the present.

"You OK? We'll be leaving once you've finished up." Luther's voice sounded from the other side.

"Yeah! Be out soon!" I called back running my finger over the spot one last time before shutting the water off. I pulled on some clothes, brushed through my hair and wiped the mirror off with a towel. A stranger stared back, radiant and lively.

"I am Alex Constance," I said quietly to the stranger, reconfirming it before taking a breath, tossing my bag over my shoulder and exiting.

Luther, Lahash, and Caim were waiting patiently by the door. The room had been cleaned spotless, leaving no sign of our stay.

"I'll take that," Luther said reaching for my duffel bag.

"I got it. It's not heavy."

Luther smiled and took the bag from my shoulders.

"I know. It's still polite where I come from."

The valet driver had pulled the Escalade to the front of the building by the time we reached the lobby. I climbed into the SUV with Caim and Lahash as Luther checked us out at the front desk. The ride, to my dismay, did not take long as the hotel we had stayed at had only been a few miles away.

I could lay low for a while, couldn't I? Maybe that was just what I needed. I tried reassuring myself as Luther pulled up to the 'pick up only' area. My hand rested on the door handle for a moment as we all exchanged glances.

"Will I see you soon?"

They nodded and smiled. I hugged each of them goodbye and muttered my thank you's for helping me through this. Luther handed me my phone back and told me to call him if I needed him. Lahash handed me a gift bag. I tilted my head in confusion.

"Souvenirs from your trip." He said with a wink before stepping out of the car to open my door.

I watched as the black Escalade faded out of sight. I felt alone, but the feeling was intensified as the vibrations of humans reverberated around me. There was no one else like me, and I felt it resonate as bodies hustled to their rides and cried for joy when seeing their loved ones. If I had felt alone before, I felt even more so now, like a spot of oil in water.

Plopping myself down on a bench, I set my bags down next to me. *Bbzzzz bbzzzz.* I opened the text announcing that my dad would be there in ten minutes and to look for him. I could do this. *I'll just lie low for a while, and everything will blow over,* I thought as I searched my phone for any messages or missed calls from Nathaniel. I chewed my thumbnail when I came up empty. Initiation. Right. He probably doesn't even have his phone. Thoughts on where Nathaniel was and what he was going through brushed across my mind and a cold feeling ran through me. I had to focus on something else, or I was going to go mad. I decided to dig through the bag Lahash had given me. My souvenirs consisted of a Washington D.C. shot glass, most likely for my brother, a pair of rhinestone earrings for my mom and a t-shirt for my dad that read FBI across it in giant letters. Not bad. I thought as I appraised Caim and Lahash's findings. For not knowing my family, they bought the same items I probably would have for them. A little while longer and the familiar outline of my dad's vehicle came into view. He hopped out of the driver's side and rushed over to me with open arms.

"How was your trip?"

"Hey! It was...great!" I said, not knowing how to respond, but genuinely glad to see him.

We embraced each other for a long minute. I couldn't help but let a tear or two escape. If he only knew.

"Missed you guys." I sniffled closing my eyes.

"He pulled back noticing the tears and hugged me again before helping me into the car.

"Awe, we missed you too! Was it a good trip though? You had fun?" he asked, confirming that everything was OK as he got in the driver's seat and pulled away from the curb.

"Yeah, I think I'm just tired from traveling. Ready to be home for a bit, you know?"

"I know that feeling."

"I feel like I've missed so much, what happened while I was gone?"

He chuckled slightly, but I could see the minor bags that clung under his eyes. He hadn't been sleeping too much lately. Was it stress? Was it Mom?

"Oh, I don't know if you missed much. We've been stretched thin on a project at work, so I've been working on that mostly. Ajax is dying to see you. He's been knocking over his water trough every day since you left, and Duck is a borderline stage five clinger." I laughed. Duck is my cat and has always had some serious issues.

"What about Mom and Derek?"

"Good. Good. We heard from Derek just after you left again. He misses everyone and said after this month they'll be letting him come back for a week or two."

I noticed he didn't comment any further on Mom other than, 'she's good,' but I didn't push the question. Instead, I talked about Derek.

"I miss him. Feels like it's been forever since we saw him."

"Me too. I know. Times flies and all of the sudden both of my kids are grown up," he reminisced.

"You look great! Was it really sunny out there? You may have even gotten a tan." He said smiling with raised eyebrows.

I laughed and swallowed hard.

"Ha! Yeah! Sunless tanners, Dad. Sunless tanners." I mentally slapped myself. Apparently, I'd be coming up with many more lies for everyone when it came to my new appearance.

He smiled. "There ya go."

I tried to avoid some of his questions about Washington D.C. besides the obvious things I knew that I had learned in school or from others who had been there. I wanted to tell my dad everything. To have him assure me that everything was going to be OK and that this was just a bump in the road or a lesson that would pass and help me grow into adulthood. I craved to hear those words from any of my family right now, but the truth left a bad taste in my mouth. As much as I wanted to, I wasn't sure it would ever be something I could tell them. They just wouldn't understand or believe me for that matter. I couldn't bear the thought of disappointing or scaring them like that. The truth could only do everyone harm, and I knew it. I would have to endure this alone, and that was that.

We pulled into the driveway. The farmhouse sat peacefully ahead of us, unchanged and serene. Gratefully, I exited the car with my dad and duffel bag. The wooden steps creaked slightly as my dad unlocked the front door. My nostrils were hit with the distinct smell of timeworn wood. I breathed in deeper letting everything hit me. The familiar barn smell of glycerin, leather and horse, the worn wood on the deck, and even my dad's familiar cologne brought me some slight comfort, but it would take some time to get used to this amplified sense of smell.

"I know you have school tomorrow, so I persuaded your mom, Renee and everyone else to let you just relax today, but I know they're both pretty excited to see you again. Renee made a chicken casserole that I figured we could have for dinner tonight."

"Yum," I replied monotonously.

I got 'The Look' in return.

"Right, sorry. Yum!" I replied ecstatically coupled with a sarcastic smile.

"Be nice." He replied smiling, but with a warning tone.

I rolled my eyes taking the hint and dashed upstairs with my duffel bag.

"Don't forget you're on horse duty later."

"Yep! Will do!" I called from the top of the stairs.

I jumped and fell backwards onto my bed. Oddly enough the fall triggered small convulsions that ran up my spine and into my shoulder blades. I sat up quickly and grabbed the comforter. I could feel something tingling at my back, itching to get out. It brushed against the skin inside my shoulder blades applying a slight pressure and causing me to catch my breath. It felt like a lifetime when I finally inhaled again and slowly I let my breath out. I remained planted until the movement inside my back became dormant once more. Was that my w-wings? It had to be. But it felt as if an alien was trying to pry its way out of me. I swallowed as I thought of the movies I used to watch with Derek where the aliens burrowed inside the chests of humans and I thought I was going to puke.

A text sounded on my phone and I eagerly reached for it.

OMG are you back yet?!! I need juicy detailssss!!! Can you meet now?

Kate is typing...

Scratch that. Meet tomorrow. 7am @ school library?

Kate is typing...

I hate chores!

;p :[:0

Alex is typing...

Yes! Bring coffee!

Kate is typing...

:D

Research. That was what I was going to do. And hopefully, I would be able to learn something about my new anatomy and how to deal with all of this.

Chapter 2

I was slightly woken by the sound of Duck meowing persistently in my ears. I chose to ignore him and instead, tried to hold onto the dream I was having. I was lying in a field filled with grass that brushed delicately against my skin as a cool breeze blew. The sun hung high in the sky above me filling me with warmth. I closed my eyes and breathed in deeply as the breeze carried the faint soothing voice of Nathaniel and the words, "I love you." I smiled.

Whack! Whack! Whack!

I was pawed from my pleasant slumber by an affection-deprived Duck who thrashed his tail back and forth as he watched me expectantly meowing. I would not get to enjoy the rest of that dream after all.

"OK. OK. I'm awake," I grumbled as I grabbed Duck and encased him in my chest smothering him with pets and kissing his head. He purred deeply in my arms and I could feel his small body go limp with pleasure. It was then that I realized I was on my rooftop and not in my bed. I stopped petting the cat and watched as Duck jumped out of my hands and back inside through my window. I sat with my jaw open, trying to remember why I had slept on the roof. *Um-mm? Seriously?* Was all I came up with after several minutes and no recollection. I climbed back into my bedroom feeling awkward and began to get ready, trying to blow it off. I swallowed hard and took out the braid from my hair. I ran my fingers through it letting the wavy curls fall to the sides of my face as I silently wondered how my first day back at school would go. My phone dinged on the nightstand letting me know that I needed to leave soon if I wanted to meet with Kate before class. I grabbed my book bag and dashed out the door.

I pulled into the school parking lot taking a deep breath. For a moment I sat quietly, and then quickly grabbed my bag and shoved the door open. A grunt sounded outside my door and I turned to see I had accidentally hit Trey with it.

"Oh, sorry! I didn't even see you," I said with a small smile.

He brushed it off quickly. "Sorry if I scared you. You look good. How was your trip to D.C.?"

"Um..." Was all I managed to squeak out before we were interrupted by a rambunctious Kate.

"Oh my God! Me first! Tell me everything!" She squealed with excitement pushing Trey aside.

"Wait, weren't you on the D.C. trip together, why would she..." Trey's face perked up then and looked at me wide-eyed.

"Alex!"

I grimaced as I got out of the car.

"Yeah, about that..." I said as the three of us made our way towards the school library.

"So if you weren't really on the D.C. trip where were you all weekend?" Trey pried as he eyed me suspiciously.

"I was with a friend..." I could barely get a full sentence out as they bickered between one another over my weekend.

"What friend?" he pressed, becoming wary.

"Dude, who do you think? Now spill it already. Did you guys kiss, fornicate, or what?"

Trey glowered at her in disgust and they both looked at me for a response.

"Fornicate? Um, no. We just sort of hung out all weekend," I said as I felt my cheeks flush just a tad.

"I'll bet," she snickered. "I guess his parents were there though, so I understand the whole no PDA in front of them, but did you guys at least have fun? You look like you got color, like your skin has a tan glow to it that we've never seen."

"Wait, we're talking about Nathaniel, right? That's who you were with this weekend?" Trey said in between Kate's barrage of questions.

The librarian pressed her pointer finger to her lips as the three of us entered. I headed directly towards the only section that could possibly hold some answers to my current state of being as Trey and Kate kept pace, only lowering their voices slightly.

"Yes, I was with Nathaniel, but can we try and just keep this between the three of us? My life may end if my parents find out I lied to them." I gave a pleading look to them both as we reached the aisle titled Religion. Scanning the bookshelf, I found a small section filled with books about angels and fallen angels.

"OK, OK, but you're coming with me tomorrow night to confession so you can give me details without nosy over here," Kate said pointing her chin towards Trey who rolled his eyes back.

"Wait, can I go to that?" I asked taken aback. I stopped reading book titles and turned to her with a questioning somewhat frightened look.

"Absolutely! Just because you're not baptized doesn't mean you can't go. Now, you can't go with me when I talk to the priest, but you can hang out in the church until I'm done. I dished quite a bit last week so I doubt I'll be in there for more than five or ten minutes."

I nodded and silently wondered if I would even be allowed inside. Wasn't I somewhat of an abomination that wasn't supposed to exist now? The thought made me shift uncomfortably and had my insides swirling. I immediately turned my attention back to the bookshelf and grabbed seven random titles that I was hoping had something useful in them.

My arms were full. Trey grabbed a few of the books I had dropped and we made our way to the nearest table.

"So you're coming then, right?" she said taking a seat with Trey across from me.

My stomach churned. "Yep," I said with a fake smile. *I guess that'll be test #1 – to see if I'm even allowed in* I thought.

"So you were with Nathaniel and his parents all weekend?" Trey asked setting the books I had dropped on the table.

I nodded.

"OK, seriously Alex babe, are you using a tanner or something? If so, I desperately need to know what, your skin looks amazing!"

"Do I really look that different?" I asked looking down at my arms.

Trey and Kate exchanged glances.

"Um, yes!" They both said at the same time.

"You look like you had a complete makeover. You've always looked good, but you're like..." Trey said scrutinizing me.

"Hot! Super gorgeous!" Kate yelled as the librarian shot us death glares.

I wasn't sure how to respond. After a moment of panicked silence, I blurted out an answer.

"Well, Nathaniel's mom used to be an esthetician. She gave me a little makeover over the weekend."

"I knew it!" Kate exclaimed

I smiled for a moment feeling grateful I had just dodged the ultimate revealing question about myself. I flipped open the first book in front of me.

"So when are you seeing him again?" Kate implored excitedly.

I shrugged my shoulders, fighting back the lump in my throat. "I don't know; he's going to call me. His family tends to...move around a lot," I said softly, wondering and anticipating the answer to that very question.

"What's with the research?" Trey asked picking up one of the books I had grabbed on the shelf and holding it up with a raised eyebrow.

"Um, our English paper, remember? The one that's due in a few weeks? I thought I'd get a head start on it." I couldn't help the lies that were rolling off my tongue so quickly; the only thing I hadn't lied about was Ms. Nethers' writing assignment.

I swallowed and kept scanning the interior of the book.

Trey's face fell as he remembered Ms. Nethers just announcing it on Friday.

"Crap! I still have to find a topic for that."

"Hockey, duh! You know like everything there is to know about hockey," Kate said rolling her eyes as she sipped her coffee.

We talked and laughed until the bell rang announcing we needed to get to class within five minutes or we would be late. I was glad when the conversation changed to everything but me for the remainder of our time in the library. It made me almost feel like just a seventeen-year-old girl if only for a minute. But the vibrations rippling from every human around reminded me this was not so. I could handle a few of them around me at once, but at the moment I wasn't sure how I would do in a throng of people. I was not used to feeling the movements and vibrations of others so vividly. As we made our way to English the vibrations of the students passing by crashed into me like waves causing me to catch my breath at times.

Kate bounced off to her economics class and Trey and I took our seats in Ms. Nethers' classroom. I took a deep breath, attempting to settle in.

"So, why'd you lie to your parents?" Trey asked confused as he leaned towards me.

I turned to him with a questioning look.

"I don't know; it seemed like the thing to do at the time I guess." I trailed off as I opened my books and averted my eyes from Trey's gaze. The vibrations of students pouring into our class and the others around me had me unnerved, to say the least, and I tried to distract myself.

"No way. I don't buy it. You're not the type to lie like that or about something like that." He said leaning back in his seat and crossing his arms in front of his chest.

"Maybe I'm beginning to act my age or something?" I said sarcastically with a small smile. I really just wanted this conversation to be over about my weekend and my transformation into the unreal.

"Are you wearing contacts?" Trey and I were distracted from our conversation when the petite brunette in front of me chimed in.

"What?" I asked, giving her a blank stare.

"Your eyes look super green, like only contact-possible green. What brand are they?"

I looked to Trey who seemed to try and get a good look at them as well.

"I thought you had perfect vision?" he questioned.

I could feel my stomach begin to stir slightly and I froze in my seat.

19

"I, um..."

"Lacy, please turn around and pay attention. I will not ask any of you again. The next person to disrupt class gets to stay with me after school." Ms. Nethers was not to be trifled with today. She pressed her quilt-like skirt as she grabbed the projector and after eyeing all of us once more, began her lecture.

I gave Lacy a 'sorry' look, but I was for once grateful of Ms. Nethers' chiding.

The rest of the class passed relatively quickly, and I felt my stomach settle some. The vibrations weren't as bad when the mass of students around me weren't moving.

By the time I made it to lunch I was ready to go home. The noises in the lunch room made me feel like I was at a live concert, which I wouldn't have minded so much if it weren't for the fact that every sound of a spoon falling or burst of commotion had me tense, alert and jumpy. Not to mention the fact that with so many students moving and sur-rounding me in one area, the vibrations made it nearly impossible for me to focus at times and as a result, I hardly ate anything at all. My anxiety was at an all-time high and Trey, and Kate more than once noted my un-usual behavior. When asked, I chalked it up to an oncoming cold and not really feeling like myself.

I could tell word of my 'makeover' had spread around the school by the time math class rolled around. Many took much greater notice of me than ever before. I probably would have been a little excited about this sudden burst of popularity had it not been for the fact that I wanted to crawl into a tiny hole and disappear.

I finally made it to Mr. Kritch's class and sat, opening one of the books I had checked out at the library. After about 30 seconds I closed it and shoved it back into my bag. I couldn't read here; it was far too dis-tracting. The tapping of another student's pencil was giving me a headache. I wanted to reach over and break it in half but resisted the urge. I desperately hoped this was only a phase of my transformation and that eventually, I'd get used to the movements of others around me.

"Everyone is asking me about you!" Kate said plopping down in her seat next to me.

"Great!" I said sarcastically. "I figured that when almost everyone I passed just stared at me."

She laughed. "You can't blame them though, even Trey and I had the same reactions. But seriously! Jesse said practically all of the football team has you on their radar now."

"Oh, God."

"Nathaniel better call you soon babe cause the sharks smell the blood in the water," she said with a grin.

I looked at the clock after about 45 minutes had passed. The tick of the big hand was embedded in my mind. Tick, tick, tick, tick. Ten more minutes. That was all I had to wait. I could go home and my first day back at school would be over. Just. Ten. More. Itty. Bitty. Minutes.

I twiddled my fingers for a bit and thought of Nathaniel. I still had no word from him. My stomach churned, and my mind raced with worry. I had to talk with Luther. I had to find out if Nathaniel was coming back soon. I needed him. I needed him to tell me it was going to be OK and to show me how this new body could be truly mine instead of feeling like a prison. A sharp prick stabbed at my upper back at that last thought. I straightened and froze, wide-eyed, looking at the front of the class. No, no, no. This was not happening now. Another dagger-like stab to the back made me lurch forward and catch my breath as it took nearly all of my strength from crying out. My wings were trying to push their way out of my back again. The heat in the pit of my stomach began to boil, and I tried taking deep breathes to calm myself. I looked at the clock on the wall. Three minutes. Oh, God.

I caught the attention of Kate who turned to me with a questioning look and mouthed "Are you OK?"

I wasn't even going to pretend I was OK. At any moment, my wings could burst from my back and, well, let's just say that would be the end of my social life or life in general. The cat would be out of the bag then. I had to make it out of the school without anybody seeing this happen. A tear escaped from one of my eyes. The pain was unrelenting, challenging my strength to keep it at bay. My breathing was jagged and uneven, and my nails drove into the underside of the desk as I fought internally with myself. Mr. Kritch eyed the clock and wiped a few beads of sweat from his brow as I held my breath.

Kate eyed me again and silently made a vomiting motion as I nodded fervently.

"OK class, this should be a good stopping point. Let's pick up from here tomorrow."

I didn't wait for any more of an invitation. I bolted from the classroom with my bag in tow, beating everyone out the door and making a break for the parking lot. Slamming my car door closed, I peeled out of the parking lot and headed towards home.

The pain in my back did not dissipate. Instead, it increased, slowly, breaking me down minute by minute. I panicked and pulled over near an empty football field letting the tears stream down my face. A searing pain hit me as my shoulder blades pierced through the skin and the wings unfurled, laying atop themselves, unable to spread to their full capacity, revealing a heavy down of plush white and black feathers, like a thick froth.

The car lurched. I was lucky my wings didn't break my windows. They seemed to be more powerful than I remembered, but elegant, and, this close up, more beautiful than I'd ever seen. If it weren't for the pain... I closed my eyes and laid my head against the steering wheel, exhausted from fighting it.

Two taps sounded on my driver's side window, and I shot my head in that direction. Luther was standing there with an apologetic look on his face. I couldn't exactly move in my current state, so I just rolled down the window.

"I came to see how your first day went," he said appraising me with concern.

He never asked what had happened or if I had revealed what I was. He just held my hand and silently rubbed my back, pushing some of the frothy feathers aside so he could do so until my sobbing subsided.

"How did you know I was here?" I asked pulling back to look at him and to wipe away the streams of tears.

He smiled. "I told you we'd be looking out for you. I got to the school a few minutes late and found you'd already left, but because you weren't too far away, I was able to follow your vibrations to find you. You'll eventually be able to do the same thing. It's not hard to track a hybrid when you're the only one."

I nodded. I was thankful he was here.

"Have you heard anything from Nathaniel?" I asked, hopeful and desperate.

He nodded and then took my hands.

"Listen, I don't think we will hear from Nathaniel for a while. The initiation process takes... quite a bit of time," he said, trying to help me understand.

"What do you mean? How long are we talking?" I asked. My wings twitched at the sound of his name.

Luther huffed out a breath. The smell of a freshly smoked cigarette lingered in his pores.

"Alex, my initiation and many other fallen angels' initiations lasted anywhere from six months to a year, and even then..."

"A year! You're telling me he could be gone a whole year!" This new information swarmed in my head, and my wings beat once causing the dried red blood on my back to crack again.

Luther's silent confirmation made me want to throw up. How was I supposed to survive that long without Nathaniel? How was I supposed to make it through another year of this alone?

"Let me drive you home, your wings should furl back in by then." He said putting the car into drive and pulling out of the football parking lot.

We were silent the rest of the way. There was no consoling me. I sat and thought about what I would do and how I would survive this.

I braced myself using the dashboard. My wings returning to their inner position was only slightly less painful than their emerging.

Luther pulled into the driveway, checking that no one was home first, and turned off the engine. I grimaced looking over my shoulder at the crusted blood on the back of my shirt and the two large holes where my wings had torn through. *So much for this shirt*, I thought, turning my attention back to the farmhouse as the car sat at idle in the driveway.

"I'm sorry Alex," he said. I nodded. There wasn't anything else to be said.

With a painful heart, I exited the car. I remembered my last moments with Nathaniel before driving away at Uvall's. Silently, I prayed he would come back sooner. He had to. We had pronounced our love for one another, and he had promised he'd come back for me. I had to hold onto that if that was all I had to hold onto.

Chapter 3

I had spent the night scouring pages and pages of books and scanning the Internet relentlessly, only to come up empty. I was nowhere nearer to finding out any helpful information and only came up with some disturbing information about demons or information I already knew.

The day had gone much like my first back at school, only this time I was only able to make it to science class until I had to run like a crazy person to the women's bathroom before my wings burst from my back. I had spent much of that class in the bathroom, locking the door so no one else could come in before they relaxed some and furled back into my shoulder blades. I was fortunate; I had brought an extra, long sleeve in my book bag to change into after cleaning up the small trails of blood off my back. At lunch, I had even talked Kate and Trey into all of us going and getting lunch so I wouldn't have to deal with the mass of people and their vibrations crashing into me in the lunchroom. For the most part, this worked. I was now counting down the final minutes of math class until I'd have to go with Kate to her church for confession. I was extremely nervous, to say the least. What would happen if I wasn't allowed in? I wondered if I'd somehow be struck with a lightning bolt for even attempting. Guess we're going to find out. I cringed at the thought.

I followed Kate in my SUV to the church and swallowed hard as I parked and took in the massive structure ahead of us. There was no doubt it was beautiful; large oval glass panes decorated with angels and cherubs glistened in green, blue, and yellow in the sun. The grand double doors leading in were solid and surrounded by stone that encased the entire church. It looked just as I had previously remembered, the numerous times I had gone with Kate and her family to Sunday church service, only this time, I felt uneasy. Like somehow, I was silently being judged. Kate waved for me to follow her in. I hesitated and got out of the car.

"OK I shouldn't be too long..." Kate's words began to drown out as we approached the doors of the church and I nodded as she turned and entered, leaving me holding the door open behind her and staring straight ahead. It was dead quiet as my hand rested on the large wooden door, with only the sound of my breathing as I paused. Taking a deep breath in, I stepped inside and closed my eyes tightly, awaiting my fate. Silence again. I opened one eye followed by the other and looked around for a minute. I jumped and stomped a foot and smiled until a voice shook me out of my surprised happiness.

"Ehem. Miss, are you here to see a priest?"

I froze and turned towards the voice.

"Um...what?"

"Confession. Are you here for confession?"

"NO! No. I'm just waiting for a friend."

He nodded but seemed distracted by my burst of a response. He refrained from saying anything further and motioned towards the pews.

I smiled, still nervous, and made my way over to the pews to take a seat and wait for Kate.

I was a little embarrassed about my childish display but I was also extremely relieved I had not gone up in flames upon entering the church. I mean, I know Ezekiel had said it wasn't my time to...'pass on' yet, after the whole sacrifice incident at Uvall's, but I was never supposed to make it past five year's old anyway. Given what I was now, it was comforting to know that I was welcome. Maybe there was still some hope for me after all?

A buzz shook my pocket. 'Unknown number' flashed across the front of my screen in giant letters. Without hesitating, I answered.

"Hello?" I couldn't hide the hopeful excitement in my voice.

"Hey! It's Renee!"

"Oh, hey, what's up?" The disappointment in my voice was noticeable I was sure.

"You sound like you were expecting someone else's call, I don't want to bother you if you need to go."

"Umm no, no what's up?"

"Well I know you're back from D.C. now and I just wanted to reach out and see if you wanted to go shopping with me for an hour or so tomorrow? I know we haven't really had a chance to hang out yet, but if you've got an hour, we could hit a few stores."

I hesitated. I really didn't want to deal with my dad's new girlfriend now, but I knew she'd only keep asking. That and maybe it would buy me some good graces with my dad in case I needed to miss a day or two of classes.

"Uh sure, it'll have to be after school tomorrow, but I could spare an hour."

"Great! Let's meet when you get off at the Four Corners outlets. See you then!"

"Sounds good."

I slipped my phone back into my pocket. I wasn't sure why I had just agreed to meet Renee, especially since I was trying to be stress-free these days. Kate came out of the back, her arms outstretched, throwing her head back.

"I feel great!" She exclaimed walking towards me.

I shook my head.

"What is it? You've got that face," she said as we began heading for the door.

"I'm meeting my dad's girlfriend tomorrow for an hour after school; we're going shopping."

Kate's eyes widened.

"Don't ask," I said putting my hand up in disbelief as well.

"Lawd give this girl strength!" Kate yelled, causing one of the priests to eye us as we exited laughing.

My hands braced the countertop firmly. You can do this Alex. Just like before, you just...

"Ahh!" My body lurched forward towards the mirror, nearly shattering it.

I breathed against the mirror, eyes closed trying to relax. This would pass, it had to. My class was nearly over, and I'd been stuck in the bathroom for some time now. I'd resorted to a bathroom hardly anyone ever used due to its location. The school had decided to remodel several classrooms nearby, and, as a result, the bathroom closest to those had practically been deserted due to the construction. I could feel a finger-like knife trail one of my shoulder blade scars and the sensation made me shudder. Eventually, the feeling subsided, and the final bell rang. So much for class. I'd have to go meet Renee now.

I threw some water on my face and wiped it off with a paper towel. *Just one more thing and you can go home. And stay there forever,* I pleaded with the girl in the mirror. I unlocked the bathroom and exited just as I received a text from Renee.

"Should be there soon! Excited 2 c u!"

I groaned getting into my car and slamming the door, almost too hard. I heard a crack. I took another breath and headed towards the mall to meet Renee. Pulling into the parking lot, I found her waiting for me by the entrance to a shop.

"Hey!" I said waiving and feeling stupid.

"Oh, good you made it! For a minute there I thought you'd ditched me," she said throwing her arms around me in a sudden hug. I froze for several reasons; her arms raked my fresh scars, I nearly growled, in addition to the fact that this was the woman who was voluntarily stepping in between my parents getting back together again, and now all of the sudden wanted to be besties. I gave a small awkward pat back desperate to create some distance.

Inside the store, my attention span landed entirely on my wings and as a result, I was nearly mute and dull. I kept throwing occasional, 'great' and 'yeah-s along with a nod or two when Renee brought me outfits that she wanted my opinion on, but I struggled to stay in conversation with her. I could tell she was getting frustrated and her tone short, but I simply couldn't take it anymore. Before I could stop myself, I was blurting out the words.

28

"Listen, this was great and all, but I've really got to go. I've just got a lot on my plate right now, and I think I just need to focus on it."

"Well. It's only been 20 minutes, but OK. Going shopping may not have been the best bet on a school night."

I smiled and told her we'd take a rain check, but left it at that while I bounded towards the door.

Later, back at home, I heard my dad's car pull into the drive and pretended to be doing something productive. Shutting the front door, I could hear him yell.

"20 minutes Alex!?"

Oh boy. Here we go.

"I've just got a lot going on right now dad. Sorry."

He dismissed my comment and flew to his next topic.

"I'll bet! Skipping classes must be exhausting! Your teachers have been calling your mother and me all week! What's going on with you?"

"I don't know." I lied.

"You'd better start figuring it out young lady! You were on such a good path for college and everything, and now, well now you're just going to throw it all out the window." He said dropping his work bag and tossing the keys on the counter furiously.

"You don't understand...I...it's not my fault!"

"Really? Whose fault is it? No, this is ALL you. Is this about that boy, are you still dating him, because if so, that's all about to change too..."

"No, dad! He left! And thanks for bringing it up!" I yelled storming up the stairs and slamming my door shut just in time for my wings to punch through my scars. I locked my door and slid to my knees sobbing. My life was thrown out the window. He was right. He just didn't know it wasn't my doing. When the tears faded, I looked towards my outstretched wings; they twitched as if noticing the attention. I let my fingers fall over the silky feathers and I began to practice feeling my wings through my shoulder blades. I had to try to start learning how to control them. Now was as good a time as any to start.

The first week of returning home had come and gone at a gruelingly slow pace, and after the fights with my parents over school, it'd become horrendous. One week of hiding my identity from everyone, pretending everything was OK, fighting with my parents about school and my unexplained absences and one more week of not hearing from Nathaniel at all – still. I knew Luther had said I wouldn't hear from him, but I couldn't believe it was true. In my heart, I loved him and I knew he'd come back for me. If it's going to take a whole year, so be it, but I have to believe he'll try to contact me sooner, initiation or no initiation.

Beyond finding out that I wouldn't burst into flames if I entered a holy place, the rest of my first week back at school was trying to say the least. I still struggled with focusing and containing my wings. After going with Kate to confession, the next day at school had me fleeing classes sporadically with hardly any control at all. I had lied to Kate and Trey and told them that I had caught the flu. It was believable for a bit but grew old quickly. And with practically skipping out on the shopping trip with Renee due to my unstableness, my dad's patience with me had snapped. My parents were now concerned with me missing too much homework and falling behind so I'd been forced to attend since. I'd even been tossed some extra chores for the whole thing with Renee to top it all off. Which only made me regret agreeing to go with her in the first place. Now wasn't the time for me to deal with that anyway.

I crouched atop a boulder, my eyes closed, listening to the quiet sounds of birds and wildlife around me. I could feel the crisp wind flow between my wings. They twitched in response to the sensation, longing for the chance to fly freely, a luxury they had never been given. A light snowfall had started to season the already frozen earth around me. During this past week, it had begun to dip into the single digits and brief snow showers had come and gone creating a cold, desolate scenery. This place had been my sanctuary since returning home, after re-discovering it over the weekend. A place to collect my scattered thoughts and a place I felt somewhat normal and was at least quiet. No crowds of humans and no vibrations to worry about, just me.

The ruins lay deathly silent ahead of me. I never knew why I had begun coming to this place again after I had come back home; the place Nathaniel had brought me shortly after we had first met. Was it because I still longed for him to return? Perhaps I worried I would forget he ever existed? Or maybe it was because it had been the only place where I could find solace and try to understand what to do with my life now, with these abilities. I wasn't entirely sure why, but I had accidentally stumbled upon it on a ride with Ajax and I had continued to return each morning since and occasionally at night as if it called me back.

I had discovered some more of my abilities as well, though I was certain I was only scratching the surface. I looked down at my skin, a vibrant caramel color radiating heat. Caim and Lahash were right. The temperature no longer affected me. My skin seemed to act as a repellent towards the blazing heat or cold, allowing me to still feel the sensation, but somehow, I was extremely resilient to the weather conditions now. On days like these, with the temperature averaging around nine degrees Fahrenheit, I could be completely naked outside for hours before I would begin to feel a slight chill.

I continued to struggle with my new eating and sleeping habits. It was strange to get used to, and I tried monitoring it more and getting on a consistent schedule, but there were times I still forgot to eat or sleep, causing me to feel weaker and drained or less in control. I no longer needed eight hours of sleep, but a modest two, and my food consumption was roughly every 30 hours, just as expected. My instincts and senses were stronger now as well. Touch was an intensified sensation, and my hearing and smell would have made any bloodhound jealous.

I let another deep breath of the crisp air fill my lungs and then set off back home to get ready for class. I let my wings extend and flap and they begged me to let them carry me over boulders and around trees, but the risk was too great. I was constantly being reminded to never fly above any tree line, exposing myself. The national forest had been one of the only places I had found where I could discretely unfurl my wings and occasionally let them raise my feet off the ground slightly, if only for a short time. I still had a lot of learning to do. I was by no means fly-ready, but I wished for the opportunity to fly one day. If I was stuck as I was forever, I might as well enjoy the biggest perk of all right? I relished the freedom it brought me letting my wings unfurl and spread wide. That freedom always ended too quickly as I approached the farmhouse and civilization again. Over the past week, my wings had become more and more familiar

31

to me, they were strange and alien at first and they demanded to be unfurled, but now, they were slightly easier to control since I'd been
unfurling them whenever I could and working with them more frequently. I stopped and stretched the beautiful black and white wings out once
more and regained my balance as I felt them fold and tuck away beneath
my skin. I was still getting used to unfurling my wings and furling them
on command. It still hurt like hell every time I did it, and it wasn't pretty,
nor was I an expert, not by a long shot, but the advice Luther had given
me on relaxing seemed to work a decent portion of the time. Sometimes,
however, they seemed to have a mind of their own and no matter how
much I relaxed, they remained open and immaculate.

I crossed the pasture to the house quickly and quietly before slipping in
through my bedroom window. I checked to make sure my door was closed,
knowing full well my father's alarm would be going off any minute now. I
turned on my bedside table lamp and paused for a moment before address-
ing Luther. "Checking in on me again?" I chided quietly. Luther stepped
forward from the shadows across the room; the light bounced off his features. I had been getting semi-frequent visits from Luther unexpectedly since
I had been sent home. Our visits typically consisted of him asking me how I
was doing and making sure I was obeying all the new 'rules.' I was quickly
beginning to sense when he was around each time we met. In addition to
being able to sense the vibrations of humans, I was endowed with being able
to sense other angels and fallen angels. I could pick up the low frequencies
his body, and other fallen angels emitted. They were different rhythms compared to those of humans or angels. Likewise, angels' vibrations seemed to
have a higher pitched frequency than that of fallen angels. I wasn't prefect
yet, but I was starting to find a rhythm with it. I had to begin to trust and
rely on my senses more instead of my eyes.

"Any news?" I asked hopefully.

He shook his head knowing I was referring to Nathaniel. I pretended
to brush it off. No news was good news, right?

"I haven't told anyone about me, angels or fallen angels," I said leaning on my dresser and turning to face him.

He nodded but hesitated before he spoke again. "How are you doing?" He asked scrutinizing me.

I rolled my eyes and flopped myself on my bed.

"This is a wellness visit? Well, I'm in hell if you really want to know," I said sitting up again when I heard my dad's footsteps in the other room. My tone softening.

Luther nodded understandingly.

"I feel like I'm suffocating, I can't focus in my classes or at school...I don't know how much longer I can go on pretending that I can do this," I said finally, looking back at him.

It was true. Ever since I had been back I had felt like an outcast and even though no one at school or my family knew I was a hybrid, rumors at school flew around like crazy; even Beth Ryder and her posse had tried to get the truth from me on why I was so different. Which made me even more uncomfortable as people outwardly announced to me that they knew something was off. Even Kate and Trey acted suspicious when I had randomly canceled on them to hang out a few times. I felt bad. I wanted to tell Kate so badly and Trey for that matter, but how could they even begin to possibly understand? I had also attempted to make up the homework after missing several days of school last week, but my lack of focus had made my grades almost instantly drop in each of my classes as tardy after tardy and late homework or missing assignments piled up.

The thought of school just didn't seem to matter anymore. I was an angel/fallen angel hybrid now at 17 years old. Whatever I was supposed to do, now, wasn't sitting in a desk for eight hours a day at a high school. Besides, I couldn't possibly get used to this 'new me' if I couldn't even focus long enough to get used to my not so normal senses. I had sifted through every book in the library and none had given me the answers I'd hoped for. I had to learn everything on my own or from others, not in a human classroom, and it wasn't like I had any 'others' on speed dial. I still remembered the look on Trey and Kate's faces when I literally turned animalistic over a cheeseburger after not having eaten in over 53 hours. *Whoops.*

Kate and my parents consistently asked about the non-existent Nathaniel and I wasn't sure what else to say besides telling them that he had moved out of state with his family again. They had questions, many questions, but that was all I could tell them. For now, he was gone.

Luther broke me from my thoughts.

"What if I told you that you there may be an opportunity to go some-place where you'd be free to be yourself?" Luther asked bringing my attention back to him.

"What do you mean? Where could I possibly go?" I asked wondering what dreamland he was thinking of.

"Well, you know you're special Alex. I was visited recently by a few high-ranking archangels. They asked me to persuade you to attend their school for angels." He paused as I gave him my full undivided attention before he continued.

"They'll give you a room and you will be able to attend some of their classes."

I tilted my head a little in confusion.

"There is a school for angels?" I asked in disbelief.

Luther nodded in response before continuing.

"It's a prep school of sorts, or at least that's what everyone else has been lead to believe. It's more of a training camp for guardian angels and angels before they are initiated. They attend the classes to learn about their abilities, duties, and rules before being assigned to their full-time jobs. It's called Crest Prep School."

I couldn't help but feel my heart flutter at the chance to get out of the monotony of my daily life. To feel free to be what I was, or at least learn more about myself. It did seem strange though to be asked to join angels at one of their schools, and even more peculiar that angels would want an unpredictable hybrid skulking around on their campus.

"Why would angels want a hybrid around? I mean, what's the catch?" I said, eyebrows furrowing.

Luther shifted slightly against the wall.

"Yes, I thought the same thing. I'm not sure if they have ulterior motives, to be honest. But Crest would be the best place for you now. They may be able to help you learn how to control some of your new abilities and help you discover any new talents you may have that you – we – are currently un-aware of. You are the only hybrid out there so naturally, they're curious, as are the rest of us. But, I think they have good intentions. I wouldn't have brought it up otherwise," Luther stated confidently.

I knew Luther had my best interests at heart and I did trust him, but I couldn't help but feel as though my lack of knowledge in this world could seriously get me in trouble, and let's face it, I barely knew anything at all right now.

"And I can leave whenever I like? If it doesn't work out?" I asked finally.

The radiating heat inside me stirred. Its presence was becoming all too familiar but still had me on edge.

"Yes. If you change your mind or if you need to get away, you are free to come and go as much as you like. There are some basic rules in place which you will need to follow. But you're not obligated in any way to stay."

I bit the inside of my lip while quickly running through the pros and cons in my head again.

"What would we tell my parents?" I questioned.

A small smile formed on Luther's face.

"Your grades have been dropping consistently across the board ever since you have been back home. They will think they are sending you to a prep school in the mountains where you can re-focus and have more opportunities available to you."

"How do you know my grades have dropped?" I asked feeling an immediate invasion of privacy.

Luther continued to smile at me for a moment.

"I was told to keep an eye on you. That means knowing everything that goes on. So shall I make the arrangements? We can have you out of here by tomorrow." He said while eying me carefully.

I thought about it again. It really did seem like my best option, at least, that's what I kept telling myself. A place I could be somewhat normal, plus being surrounded by other angels for a while didn't sound half bad. I wouldn't have to hide my wings or have to run to the nearest bathroom at school because I couldn't control them. Right? It would give me a little more freedom, and at this point, that was worth everything to me. I couldn't be caged like like this forever.

I nodded, giving him my approval as he walked towards me and grinned slightly, handing me a pamphlet that read:

"Crest Prep School: The place where students can re-charge & re-focus their energies to better their future opportunities."

Then he turned and disappeared into the shadows and out my window. OK, I thought. *Angel prep school it is.*

Chapter 4

Abraxos and Eloa remained in the office, silent until the sounds of passersby quieted.

"You're giving me *that* look again."

"I'm not...I just want to make sure we're doing the right thing here. We don't exactly know her, even though Luther vouches for her seamlessly." She seemed to drift and get lost in her own thoughts.

"I'll be her judge. No offense to Luther, of course." Abraxos was agitated.

"Besides," he said, shifting his right ankle so it was resting on his opposite knee. "Isn't it better to keep our enemies closer, if that is indeed what she is? If she turns out not to be, then the better it is for us. She's moldable right now. Pliable. We need someone like her to be on our side."

"Yes, I suppose. There've been many rumors already spreading about her. The students are going to have a field day once they realize we've welcomed her onto our training grounds."

"Maybe so." He leaned in over her desk and let his hands fold together tightly.

"But this needs to happen. We need something – someone with her qualities to be obedient if we want to see ourselves survive."

Eloa breathed out a large sigh and nodded respectfully. She knew what the other side was capable of. They'd been trying things for years. Inside, she feared if they were taking things too far – molding a fresh hybrid, part human, to tip the scale to their side. It wasn't exactly what she'd had in mind. On the other hand, what if the fallen were attempting to accomplish the same?

I took my seat next to Trey in English class and sighed when I realized I had left my textbook at the house again. Ms. Nethers wasted no time in clapping her hands and having the students in the room open their books to a reading activity. I looked to Trey, he smiled shaking his head and motioning for me to scoot closer to him so I could read off of his. I flashed him a 'thank you' smile and pushed our desks closer together.

"So, you OK? Ever since you got back, you've been sick and now just seem kinda..." He seemed to search for the right word. "Spacey."

I wanted to avoid his questions, but honestly, I was getting tired of lying to everyone about everything, and he was spot on with the spaciness. I was never the type to forget homework assignments or due dates, but my academic abilities seem to have faltered quite a bit.

"I'm alright, just haven't really felt like myself lately."

He nodded.

"You sure you're OK though?"

"Pretty sure," I said, smiling a little before continuing. "I don't know, I guess my parents may be sending me to some prep school for the rest of the semester because of my grades," I said, gauging his reaction. His eyebrows furrowed hearing my words.

"Mine too. They said it would be good for my character-building skills for the family business," he said, sounding somewhat irritated at the statement, and surprised to hear that I was being shipped away as well.

"Where are they sending you?" he asked.

"It's called Crest Prep School I guess," I said, still shocked to hear his parents were sending him to another school also.

A grin formed at the side of his mouth then.

"Looks like we'll be stuck together then," he said leaning back in his chair.

My eyes darted to his.

"Wh... what? You can't be going to that one too?" I asked him in disbelief.

Trey was not an angel. I knew because I could sense angels and the vibrations they gave off. His were human and human only. So why were his parents sending him to an undercover angel training camp?

"What about your hockey and everything here?" I asked in disbelief.

"Apparently, they have a rink there and a team that's already accepted me. Kinda sucks. I'll be leaving the guys here, but may open up some other opportunities for me with talent scouts." I just looked at him dumbfounded.

He smiled at the look on my face.

"Crest Prep School. The place where students can recharge and refocus their energies to better their future opportunities." He recited the school informational pamphlet I had received this morning from Luther like he had studied it relentlessly.

Holy crap! He WAS going to Crest.

"You seem thrilled to have a buddy," he said still smiling back at me after I didn't say anything.

I closed my mouth and attempted a response.

"No, it's not that, I'm just really shocked is all. I thought your grades were fine?"

He nodded.

"They are. They must be with hockey, but my parents are sending me there so that I'll be ready to take over the family business one day. They say it'll help me build character and that I'll be ready to work for them starting this spring if I go and do well. So much for choosing my own career path, right?" he said sarcastically.

Ms. Nethers shot a warning glance our way, and we turned our attention back to the textbook so we wouldn't get in trouble. I thought back to what Trey's parents did for a living. From what I knew, his father, Luke Banoff, was a businessman. He owned and operated an investment company designed to help customers find their ideal personal investments and manage them. Trey's mother, Sarah Banoff, was a real estate agent who also worked alongside her husband at their company, New Creation

Investment Group. I couldn't put my finger on it. They were completely normal, and I'd known them for as long as I had known Trey. And there were tons of other prep schools closer to home that help refocus students. It seemed a little weird that they would have chosen that one. Maybe all they really wanted was for their son to go to the best school? They continually attempted to mold him into the perfect prodigy to take over their family business.

I wondered how Trey would even be allowed on campus since he was a human. Was it only partially an angel training camp? How could it be an angels' training camp if humans were allowed there as well? Wouldn't that be breaking the number one cardinal rule of never revealing yourself to a human? I was so confused, but I couldn't take my mind off of Trey and OUR new school.

The remainder of the school day went quickly, during lunch, Trey and I confessed to Kate that we would be going to Crest Prep School for the remaining school year. Needless to say, she threw a fit.

"How am I supposed to hang out with my best friend!?" she screeched.

Apologetically, we tried to console her.

"You can still visit whenever you like. Not only that, I'll still be around on the weekends so we can hang out. Just think of it like my house moved just a smidge father away," I said. To be honest, it was going to be strange. Not going to school with my best friend was absolutely not on my list of things that I wanted to happen right now, or ever, but the truth was, I couldn't confide in her. With anyone for that matter. I had to do this for myself, no matter how much it sucked.

"You're like two hours away now. I'd hardly call that a smidge," she said raising her eyebrows.

Trey and I gave her a frown face, and she set her phone down.

"Fine, fine. I don't know how I'm going to forgive you both for leaving me here. And I'm going to have a serious discussion with each of your parents. We better still hang out," she said determinately. I smiled. She'd taken it much better than I'd expected.

Math class came and went, and I miraculously held myself together. My wings did not try to pry their way out, and I didn't have to run to the bathroom like a crazy person. Success! At least until I got home, that was.

I just managed to get inside the house, and they burst open unexpectedly! Why? I wasn't under stress or panicking over anything. I dropped my head back and groaned, dumping my bags at the door. Seriously? I thought about buying shirts from the dollar store until I could control my wings. It'd be a hell of a lot cheaper that was for sure. My dad had already asked me where all my new clothes were disappearing to and I had to make some quick excuses - left this in DC, tore that in gym class, spilled something stain-worthy on another.

I trudged my way into the kitchen, my wings delicately brushing everything I passed, and I opened the pantry. I closed my eyes and took a deep breath. Letting my hand graze over the different foods. I stopped abruptly and grasped a bag of thin mints. I was completely engrossed in them - that was until I felt a slight prickle on the back of my neck and felt the vibrations. I dropped the cookies and was startled to see Luther standing in the kitchen staring at me.

"You seem to be doing better," he said smiling.

"God! Can't you people announce yourself or something?" I yelled and braced both hands on the counter. The short adrenaline burst was nothing like I had encountered before. Compared to a human's it was much more extreme. My body shook slightly, and I leaned harder on the counter.

"Seriously, Luther. We don't even know all of what I can do yet, and you think it's a good idea to scare me?" I said, shaking my head at him as I attempted to control the spasms.

He put his hands up in defense.

"Hey, I just came to bring some news. Calm down and eat your cookies."

I semi-glared at him, shakily picking up the cookies and motioning for him to continue.

"Is this about the prep school? Did you know Trey is going there too?"

He paused for a minute, weighing this new information.

"He is. That's not why I came here."

"Wait, so you knew he was going? Why didn't you say anything?" I was suddenly angry like this information should have been provided when he knew about it. Why keep it from me?

"Alex, you need to hear this." Luther stopped me from asking anything further and set his phone on the counter hitting play.

His demeanor made me uneasy, so I swallowed my frustration and listened.

"*What girl?*" *The voice asked, smooth and dark-like.*

My heart beat a little quicker at the sound of the voice.

"*You know which one. The hybrid. You killed some of your own for her.*"

"*I left her. We have no ties.*"

There was some shuffling in the background and then silence for another moment.

"*You're saying you don't love her?*"

Silence again.

"*Don't play games Nathaniel,*" *The other voice threatened.*

"*She means nothing. I thought I proved that already.*"

"*Mmm, but did you? Our recent, 'incident' had nothing to do with you?*"

A shout rang out causing me to jump.

"*She's an abomination! Something for us to use or dispose of!*"

Glass shattered violently in the background.

"*Easy Nathaniel, I was just...*"

"*Enough!*" Nathaniel's voice ripped out stopping the other man completely.

"*We are done here. Bring this up again, and I'll personally dispose of you too.*"

I didn't move when Luther grabbed the phone and put it back in his pocket. Nor did I say a word, but inside I felt a piece of my heart slowly catch fire and incinerate. I sucked in a breath and stooped towards the counter as my wings furled back into my shoulder blades. I winced at the sharp pain as they retreated, never making a sound, I just stared at the kitchen counter-top as if in disbelief.

Luther shifted uncomfortably.

"Why did you play that for me?" My voice was monotonous and quiet.

"You should know he is not the same person anymore. He's on the fast path to completing his initiation, but he's not who we remember him to be."

"Remember him to be? I've only been home for one week; he's only been gone for one week! You make it sound as if it's been months! Years!"

"It might as well have been. He's not the same Alex, and he's probably not coming back. You just need to know that."

Luther's tone was serious and flat.

I couldn't believe what I was hearing. The rush of emotions flooded my body and hit me like a whirlwind.

"So that's it?" My voice broke a little. Was what Nathaniel and I had to be over so quickly? Was I really *nothing* to him?

Luther nodded.

"You need to focus on yourself right now Alex. You need to start preparing for Nathaniel *not* returning. I didn't just come here to have you listen to that recording. I came here to see what your decision was with Crest Prep School. I need to get you in now if it's what you choose."

I gulped feeling my head throb as the boiling in my stomach sloshed like a raging storm inside me. What was I *supposed* to do? The words from the recording reverberated in my eardrum. I couldn't stay here.

"I'll go."

Luther relaxed slightly.

"Good. I'll make the arrangements, and we can get your parents' approvals." He stood.

"It's going to be OK Alex. I think this is the best decision for you right now."

I nodded and watched him leave, feeling the world come crashing down around me along with the brittle pieces of my heart.

It had only been a few hours since hearing the heart-shattering recording from Luther. I had taken Ajax for a long ride in the woods, just trying to piece together why I had let Nathaniel into my life and how I could have been so blind to not see the truth. I couldn't comprehend it. Deep down I wished none of it had ever happened; if I had never met Nathaniel, then I wouldn't be heartbroken now. I had trusted him; I had opened my heart only to have it destroyed. Ajax and I wandered back into the barn. I unsaddled him and put him back in his stall giving him a few peanut butter cookies in the process.

A tingle tickled its way up my spine, and I closed my eyes for a minute, concentrating on the bodies inside the house and the vibrations I felt. I knew my mom had come over after my dad had gotten home from work. Two were human vibrations, but one stood out. It was the vibration of a fallen angel. The hairs on the back of my neck rose slightly, and I made my way back towards the house, uncertain of who else was inside. The back door creaked loudly as I opened it, and I made my way to the kitchen. The look on my face changed from one of alarm and uncertainty to one of shock. Luther was in the kitchen with a name tag pinned to his jet-black suit and information pamphlets from Crest Prep School lay strewn about on the table in front of him and my parents.

"Alex, we're glad you're back. This is Luther; he is from Crest Prep School. He said they visited your school and you showed some interest in attending their campus for the rest of the semester to help get your grades up," my dad said, searching for my confirmation.

I nodded and put a fake smile on my face, shaking Luther's outstretched hand. I hadn't expected that we'd be telling my parents so quickly, but part of me was glad.

"It's good to see you again Alex, I was telling your parents how we could enroll you and you could continue taking the classes you currently have. You'd be able to start as soon as Thursday with classes, but could get you moved and settled in starting tomorrow," Luther explained convincingly.

"Thursday? That's very soon. Are you sure you really want to do this Alex? I mean, it's kind of far... and you have Ajax to worry about." Mom said.

"I think it could be good for me. My grades have fallen, and this would help get me back on track for getting into a good college," I admitted, knowing it wasn't all a lie.

Luther added to my statement. "Yes, it will definitely help her get back on track, and what's great about Crest is that we enroll students all year long, allowing them to pick up where they left off and return home when the normal school semester ends. Also, we have an equestrian center that could house Ajax, and if Alex's attendance is met, housing for Ajax is free."

My parents nodded their heads and exchanged a few looks between each other. I could tell they were a little surprised to find I wanted to go to this school, but they couldn't help but look over my grades in panic. They knew I needed some help quick if I was going to get into a good college. What worried them the most is this was the first time they'd ever seen me struggling with homework and attendance, and they didn't know what to make of it.

Luther and I spent the next hour and a half discussing the pros and cons and details with my parents before they each eventually signed off on my enrollment. Anticipation slithered through my veins. It was official. I was going to Crest.

Luther thanked everyone and announced that a driver would be by the next day to pick me up and help move Ajax and some of my belongings. My parents nodded in confirmation, but still struggled with how fast I'd been enrolled and accepted. They were pleased that I was suddenly taking my studies seriously and that I was concerned with college and my future, and that's what eventually won them over. They ultimately wanted nothing but the best for me.

After dinner, I went back upstairs and closed my bedroom door. I laid on my bed and tried to imagine Crest and what it would be like. Other than what the pamphlet said, I really didn't know much except that it was somehow a secret angel's training camp. Even with the distraction of going to Crest, however, I couldn't pry my thoughts away from Nathaniel. We had declared our love for one another, and I had found out it was all a lie. Was it always about just helping him get his wings back? He had to have been using me from the start. Salty tears kissed my face as they poured from my eyes. Nothing made sense. I had been lied to, and none of it was real. My 'new abilities' seemed to be a constant reminder to me that any of it ever really happened. I fought to repress the memories of him again. I didn't need Nathaniel. He had used me, and I was nothing to him. Luther was right, all I needed right now was to focus on myself and forget about everything Nathaniel.

I fought the invisible weights on my eyelids, trying to stay awake until sleep eventually won out and I began to dream. The feeling of eyes boring into me was utterly apparent to every pore in my body. I walked through the fluffy untouched blanket of snow towards the familiar rubble of ruins. The giant boulder I had visited just this morning and every morning since returning home had been partially covered in fresh powder. Nothing looked different or out of the ordinary, but I could tell I was not alone. A chilling wind gripped my skin tightly as I closed my eyes and tried to focus on the vibrations coming from my onlooker, hoping to pinpoint their exact location.

Whoever was there moved sporadically, making it difficult for me to pinpoint their location, but I could pick up on distinct fallen angel vibrations. That they could not hide.

"Luther?" I called out cautiously hearing the howl of the arctic wind rush through the pine trees surrounding the ruins.

No response. It was not Luther. The hairs on the back of my neck prickled to life, sensing danger, but deep down, another part of me burned. Yearning for the individual to come forth from the shadows and reveal themselves. That part of me was not nervous. I felt confused and tried shifting through the distorted thoughts and feelings I was experiencing.

"Don't go to Crest." A familiar male voice rang out in the tree line.

That voice was haunting to me now. I stood frozen for a moment wondering if I had imagined it.

"Nathaniel?" I managed to breathe out slowly. The sound of his name sent a series of painful surges through my body.

Silence filled the air again, and the burning in the pit of my stomach began to swell and ache. It was him. I felt his breath slide across the back of my neck. I could hear his velvety melodic voice whispering my name in my ear and yet silence still clung to the frigid air around me. Was I imagining these sensations? These memories? I wasn't sure, but it was the first contact I had had with him, and deep down it felt more than real.

"Don't go." He spoke once more, pleadingly.

I began to search the forest around the ruins for him. I was desperate to see him.

"Where are you? Why haven't you returned?" I questioned trying to pinpoint the direction of the vibrations again.

South of me, no North. He was all around me and yet nowhere. Frustrated and despondent, I sat on the boulder feeling as if the scorching heat coming from the pit of my stomach would burn a hole straight through me. I couldn't stop a few tears from escaping my eyes. I had felt so lost since this transformation, and the one person I believed could end that torment for me had lied and was now going to play games with me.

Sniffling the rest of my tears, I decided I wouldn't cry. Whatever this was that Nathaniel was doing I wasn't going to be involved. He had already lied about loving me and abandoned me in my time of need. I wasn't about to let him play with my emotions again. I couldn't. I stood up from the boulder and felt the heat in my stomach rise, filling my chest cavity completely.

"You lied. Don't try and contact me again." The words burned as they came out. I hadn't noticed my wings had unfurled. I ignored the sensations and warnings thrown at me then and shut everything out closing my eyes tightly. I opened them again when I could no longer hear his velvety voice, nor smell the earthy mint his scent left that I loved so much. I lifted myself from my bed. I was alone, and whether the dream I had had was real or imagined, one thing was for sure; I was going to Crest Prep School no matter what.

"Sorry sir, but you want me to do what? Train a hybrid?"

"You've been the top of your class; shouldn't be too difficult."

"We know nothing about her, and you're just going to allow her on campus?"

Abraxos put his hand up, depleting Jared's argument entirely.

"This isn't a debate. You've been charged with this task, and if you want to become a guardian you're going to take this on; otherwise, you can kiss all hopes of following in your father's footsteps goodbye. I imagine he'll be thrilled to hear how you turned down your only opportunity."

Jared remained silent.

"Now that we got that out of the way. You will find out about her, get to know her, the way she thinks, what triggers her anger, who she cares about the most, and most importantly, where her allegiances lie. If they lie elsewhere, it's up to you to correct them. Make her see us and make her see them for what they truly are," he said motioning towards a fallen angel's picture in his stack of papers. Train her and get her following Angels' orders. That's your job until otherwise noted."

"Yes, sir. I'll meet her when she arrives," Jared replied between gritted teeth.

"Good. Start familiarizing yourself now."

He tossed a manila envelope to him with a picture of a girl paper-clipped to the front and a name scribbled underneath:

Alexandria Constance.

Shit, Jared thought as he walked back towards his dorm and recognized the tall, stiffened figure standing just outside of his building. *His father would be so kind as to pay him a visit today, no doubt he'd already been in contact with Abraxos about his 'assignment.'* They'd been close once, his dad and him when he was younger, but then it all became clear. They'd been shaping him to be exactly like his father the whole time. To follow in his father's footsteps and make the family proud. It wouldn't have been so bad being like his dad. His dad was respected among many, he was strong, someone you could look up to, but what killed their relationship was the constant pushing to be the best and do the best, to live his life exactly how his parents thought he should live it, even right down to making his decisions for him. It had worn thin on him over the years, and the helpful steering had quickly turned into the manhandling of his life by his parents. Sure, he wanted to be like his dad, a guardian, but he wanted to do it on his own terms, not the terms of his parents, and that simply was an afterthought, if a thought at all. What made it worse, was that he knew his parents wanted nothing but good things for him, and there were times it felt as if they were beginning to bridge the gigantic gap between them finally, but those moments were fleeting, tumbling down like a domino effect right back to where they had started.

"Dad."

"Jared. Your mother and I thought it was best if I came to make sure you approach this new task properly."

"Abraxos gave me the details on what I need to do, and..." he waved the file in his hand.

"I've got everything I need in here. Thanks though."

"Yes, a file can tell you about someone, but it can't tell you what it doesn't know. You need to be wary of this hybrid. Your future counts on it."

"I know. I will."

"Good. Stay focused."

I nodded and watched as he left without saying anything more.

"Alright Alex Constance, let's get to know you," he said flipping open the file.

Chapter 5

The next few days had passed in a blur of activities and, just as Luther had said, a driver had come to the house and trailered Ajax to the equestrian building at Crest along with most of my clothes and a few backpacks of books and other school materials. Kate and my parents had even managed to host a small going away dinner for me. I had to keep reminding everyone I was only just a few hours away and not in another state. Derek had called as well after hearing that I was going to Crest and we talked for some time, catching up on each other's lives and activities. I tried to focus on what was new with him as the reality of my life was in shambles, and my relationship with Nathaniel had been a sham. He had tried to pry many times about what had happened between us. He could tell I was hurt, but there was nothing I could tell him. I was putting Nathaniel behind me and going to Crest. Hearing Derek's uplifting words helped instill that I was making the right decision by going.

The weather outside was strangely warm, with only a lingering hint of the frigid weather we had been getting. Today, Luther was taking me to Crest, and I couldn't wait. I was anxious and unsettled, but I was set on going, nothing was going to change my mind. I was bound and determined to do anything and go anywhere that would help keep my mind off Nathaniel, and after last night's dream, I was more than insistent on going.

The familiar black Escalade pulled into the drive, the tires crunching on the gravel. Luther put it into park and got out to grab my bag. He had wanted to make sure I was 'settled in' properly and to introduce me to a few friendly faces when we got there just in case I needed anything.

We didn't speak much on the ride there and I didn't mind completely. I was immersed in an ocean of thoughts. After a two-hour drive through winding canyon roads we eventually came upon two giant wrought-iron gates that automatically parted for us as we approached, allowing us to enter. An intricate metal sign hung above the gates that read Crest Prep School in stone letters.

A paved road led us straight towards a set of seven separate stone buildings. The campus looked more like a giant university than anything. It sat in the middle of roughly 40 acres and looked to be well taken care of. Benches, giant maples, aspens and pine trees dotted the manicured landscape almost making me believe that this was an actual school and not an undercover angel training facility. The mountain's front range lay beyond the school's perimeter, creating a fishbowl effect with the school situated in the middle. I was taken aback by the beauty of the campus for a moment, with the snow still covering the ground. Even with the colder dreary weather due to the location's elevation, the school seemed bright somehow. Picturesque and inviting. Whatever this place was, it had a peaceful feeling that I absorbed almost immediately.

I smiled as the view of the Equestrian Center came into focus on the Southwest side of the campus. Ajax would undoubtedly be loving his temporary home here. Luther's voice snapped me out of my thoughts.

"Like what you see so far?" he said, appraising my astonished look with a small smile before lighting a cigarette and snapping shut the Zippo. I nodded, unable to reply at first. The smell of smoke filled the air like a thick paste.

"It's not what I expected," I managed to say, feeling a little unnerved from the hundreds of angel vibrations that reverberated towards me. A large part of me was excited. Like a dog excited to play at the park with other dogs, my wings stirred with excitement and anticipation beneath my shoulder blades as I sensed the angel vibrations. Another part of me felt restless and uncertain. It had me wondering what I was doing there as if I were in danger.

I quieted my unease, pushing it far into the back of my mind. This was my choice to come here, and it already felt better than home, sort of. I would just have to get used to some things. The unfamiliarity of the school is why I felt uncertain, I gathered, but my heart flipflopped at the idea of having a little more freedom here.

Luther pulled in front of a building with giant gold letters that read 'U-Building #1-37' and turned off the engine.

"This is where your dorm is located. Your room is number: U-37." He said as he dropped a plain bronze key into my hand.

Luther and I grabbed my bags and entered the building through its arched, wooden, castle-like door. We followed the signs to floor seven, which also happened to be the top floor. There were no elevators in the building, only thick concrete steps leading up and down. I was thankful for my new strength and stamina and wasn't even winded when we finally made it to my designated room. If I had still been human, I would have still been on floor three. At least I had something to laugh about. My cardio problems seemed to be over.

Black metal numbers U-37 hung across the arched doorway, and I slid the key into the lock expectantly. A loud click sounded, and the heavy door creaked open with ease, showcasing a quaint 500 square foot room complete with a bed, a small bathroom in the back, vaulted attic-like ceilings, an intricately carved wood desk and chair, and a quaint kitchen with minimal necessities. One giant old-fashioned window filled the room with light. I dropped my bags and took in the surroundings of my new home. It smelled as if it had not been lived in for quite a while, but it was my own private space. I didn't have a roommate from what it looked like, and it was more than I could have imagined. It was perfect. Here, I could just be Alex Constance, whoever that was. I couldn't contain my excitement, I turned and practically jumped onto Luther engulfing him in a bear hug.

"Thank you!" I exclaimed. He laughed a little, almost choking on his cigarette before grabbing it with one hand and helping me off him with the other, surprised by my sudden outburst of affection.

"I managed to pull a few strings," he said, winking and returning the cigarette to his mouth, taking in a long drag as if remembering just how many strings he had to pull to get me here.

Hushed tones rang out from beyond my open door. My eyebrows furrowed as I watched a few passersby peer into the room cautiously, then continue to briskly walk away, as if they had seen something forbidden in their building. Luther grabbed my attention.

"Ignore them. Keep in mind they can sense that you're not a full angel. It may freak them out for a bit, but they will get used to it. They're probably just as shocked to see a full fallen angel on campus," he said, motioning towards himself. Luther seemed uncomfortable as he took drag after drag of his cigarette, letting the smoke consume and comfort him.

He was probably right. I was sure everyone would be just as shocked as I was, but I couldn't help but feel a small pang of sadness hit me when I realized I would always be somewhat of an outcast no matter where I went. Regardless of who I was inside, I was different from everyone else, and that made most people nervous. Hell, it made me nervous around most people, too. I couldn't blame them, but at the same time, I couldn't help but want to be accepted.

After dropping my belongings off in my room, Luther escorted me outside across a snow-caked yard and into another stone building named 'Atrium/Main Office.' Inside, we signed in with the receptionist, an older woman with short curly gray hair who reminded me of Kate's grandma, only much less friendly. She eyed me with her brown orbs, seeming to judge my character, before nodding and strutting off through tall glass double doors into another room. I could sense she was an angel and figured she was trying to wrap her head around what I was and why I was there.

I looked up and realized the ceiling of the building was an enormous atrium, hence the name. Bright natural light spilled over the interior walls creating a warmth inside. Moments later a woman appeared through the tall glass double doors, her arms outspread welcoming us and a pleased smile shining across her face. She wore a cream pencil skirt and a pink and white blouse that complemented her taller but petite frame. She had light blue eyes and curled champagne colored hair that bounced slightly as she walked and shined brilliantly in the light of the atrium. Her dark red lipstick contrasted her paler complexion, and I noticed Luther had dumped his cigarette quickly.

"Luther! Oh, my! It is so good to see you! I am so glad we could make this happen and give the proper arrangements to our new student," she said gleaming back at me as she embraced him.

It was obvious they had history together. The way he held her for a few seconds longer than usual and the slight pink blush forming in Luther's cheeks told me they had not simply met on campus. The woman's eyes peered back into Luther's and held his gaze for a moment as if reliving a moment between them that was lost in time.

"Madam Eloa, it is always, always a pleasure to see you," Luther said smiling.

It was the only time I had seen him light up and it reminded me of a child opening a gift; He seemed completely enamored with Madam Eloa.

"I'd like to introduce you to Alexandria Constance. Alex, this is El. She is going to help you get settled here with your classes and with anything you may need here." His eyes lingered on her with a sense of longing.

Before I could respond, a loud masculine voice sounded from across the atrium, startling all of us from our thoughts. A tall man dressed in a gray and white suit with similar build and age to Luther strutted across the mosaic floor towards us. He appraised me considerably before looking back to Luther.

"I thought I sensed a familiar presence on campus." He straightened his back as he eyed Luther and Madam Eloa.

Before anyone could respond, he directed his attention to me abruptly.

"And this must be Alexandria. What a beautiful creature you are my dear." He said glancing back at El.

Luther tensed noticeably. I could feel it. His tension seeped into my chest cavity and made me nervous. Call it fallen angel telekinesis, but whatever it was Luther didn't like about this man I was quick to pick up on it and I felt the same heat of uncertainty and distrust flare within me.

"Abraxos. I didn't realize you were working here now," Luther replied in a cool sarcastic tone.

Abraxos smiled slightly, but it was a forced rigid smile with no hint of being friendly.

"I like to stop by now and then to check in on the initiated students. It's more of a commitment to the future than an occupation." he stated confidently, ignoring Luther's sarcastic tone.

"I want you to feel comfortable coming to me for anything you need Alexandria." He slid a gold metal card from his pocket and passed it to me.

I accepted the gold card, feeling the solid cold metal in my hand, and met Abraxos's gaze. His hazel eyes, well-trimmed dirty blonde hair, and firmly pressed suit made him appear businesslike and approachable despite the vibe I was getting from Luther.

"Please don't hesitate to call me for anything you may need or if you have any questions or concerns. I'm sure it will take some time getting used to your new surroundings." With that, he smiled and nodded to El then Luther and strutted out of the building lobby.

Luther relaxed some as soon as he was gone and El began to give us details of the campus. I kept noticing the steely glances El and Luther made between one another along our tour, yet neither one spoke intimately to the other. After a tour of the campus library, cafeteria and grounds, Luther and I parted ways with El, and he walked me back to my dorm room. I wanted to ask him how he knew Madam Eloa and why they looked as if there was so much left unsaid between the two of them, but I decided to respect their privacy. Deep down, I wondered if somehow that was the future of Nathaniel and my relationship. Was it only to be steely glances and unspoken words between us? The thought made my heart sink. He didn't love me. I wasn't sure if he ever really had and somehow, I just had to get over it. I'd never had an attachment or pull towards anyone as I did with Nathaniel, but I needed all the thoughts of him and me to disappear. Easier said than done to my dismay.

Back in my new dorm room, I said goodbye and thank you to Luther, and he left me to get settled in, confirming that he would check in on me again soon and giving me a number to call in case I needed him.

I shut the door, locking it in the process, and turned to look at my new little home. Closing my eyes, I breathed in deeply. I could feel the other angel vibrations close by in their dorm rooms, but many of them were quiet and weren't moving around too much. Probably studying I guessed. It felt somewhat safe here; regardless of how uncomfortable a piece of me felt in this new environment surrounded by so many angels, I felt like I could breathe more.

I peered at my cell phone perched on the corner of the desk. It sat ominously, daring me to do what I dreaded. I would not call him or text him. I would not; I thought determinedly as I went to the kitchen and poured a glass of water, chugging it. Eventually my willpower was defeated, however, and my fingers had taken over and were dialing Nathaniel's number. My hands trembled slightly as I put the phone to my ear and listened to the first ring, then the second, then the third. My anxiety worsened with the sound of each ring until the voicemail picked up. Wow. So it was true? My anger flared, and I didn't stop myself from leaving a voicemail – letting my anger take over and get the best of me.

"So that's it then? You're unbelievable. Thanks for making it clear!" I yelled sarcastically.

The moment I hung up and tossed the phone down, I regretted leaving the message; if anything, it made me feel stupid. However childish it may have been, I brushed it off not caring, at least I got the last word in, an attempt to make the hurt go away.

I huffed loudly in aggravation and decided to occupy my mind with something else before I went mad. I flicked the desk lamp on and sent a text to my parents, Derek and Kate to let them know I was getting settled in, loved the new dorm room and that I would call them soon with more updates.

Afterwards, I changed into my pajamas and slid under the full-sized, milky white comforter and sheets. Just as I was about to drift off for a few hours, a loud pound sounded at my door. I sat up feeling my pulse quicken and my senses heighten. It was an angel I gathered after focusing my attention on the soft but deliberate high-frequency hums vibrating through the arched doorway. The pound sounded again, and I rose from my bed, hesitantly making my way over to the door. Before they could pound on the door a third time, I cracked it open quickly.

I was surprised when I found a tall, masculine guy a bit older than I was staring back. His light brown hair was messy and long enough to partially conceal one of his sea-green eyes. He seemed unimpressed by my presence and smiled, but his smile was more calculating than happy.

"Can I help you with something?" I questioned warily, thrown off by his sudden presence.

"I thought you'd be taller," he said. He smirked down at me in amusement.

My eyebrows furrowed. The last thing I needed was a 'funny guy' at my door right now.

"Excuse me, I am tall and just who do you think you are?" I said feeling uneasy with some stranger evaluating me in my doorway and aggravating me.

He blew off my comment and continued.

"I'm your new training partner. Show up here tomorrow and don't be late." He said shoving a slip of paper in my hand before striding off.

"Wait, my new...what?!" I called after him in the hallway, confusion dripping across my words, but he didn't turn to respond. A few doors opened, and eyes peered out into the hallway at me. Annoyed and embarrassed, I disappeared back into my room with the slip of paper.

What did he mean he was my new training partner? Just who did this guy think he was? I was irritated and felt a burning heat well up in my stomach. I knew my wings were close to unfurling from the stress of my emotions, so I decided to blow it off and deal with it tomorrow. The poor guy probably had the wrong person anyway. Pulling the milky white sheets up to my chest again, I let sleep envelop me.

Chapter 6

I awoke to a series of unfamiliar sounds. Keeping my eyes closed, I listened to the sounds of initiated angels in the hallway shuffling to and from their rooms. I opened my eyes, but blackness consumed the room. The sun wasn't up yet. I turned over, steadily becoming more alert, and read the clock on the desk across the room. 4AM. I stretched and leapt out of bed throwing on my black riding pants and boots along with a long-sleeved top. I felt a spurt of freedom hit me; no school, no running to the bathroom during class to hide my wings and no hiding who I was. My first taste of freedom had me on cloud nine.

I was going to see Ajax this morning to make sure he was doing well here and to get a morning ride in. I peeked out of my room, stepping out and locking the door behind me. I slid the key into my pocket and hastily crossed the hallway to the stairs, ignoring the other students as best I could. I received quite a few stares leaving the building, some angels stopped entirely, but I was relieved to find only a few other angels outside.

I made my way along a concrete path bordered by large, snow-covered, blue spruce and aspens, the snow crunching beneath my feet as I walked. It was a brisk morning, a frosty wind nipped through the strands of my hair. Although I seemed to be near impervious to the weather now, I still could feel a cold sensation. The stars glinted, so many lay scattered above that it looked as if a cosmic explosion was happening just overhead. The stars here put the stars at the farmhouse to shame. Without a city's lights nearby, a beautiful illumination of stars glowed above.

I made it to the barn and opened the side door, more than pleased to find a rustic wooden barn interior with modern amenities. I saw a gigantic, freshly raked indoor arena, spacious tack room, complete with my own saddle rack, and roomy stalls with new bed shavings. It had to be five times the size of the barn back at home, with quite a few horses housed in it as well. I searched the rows of stalls until Ajax, and his stall name-tag came into view.

After some tedious tail brushing and grooming, I saddled Ajax and led him into the indoor area. Ajax had noticed my change as much as everyone else. At first, he was nervous around me, jumpy when I moved too quickly, but as I spent more time with him, he seemed to ease into the familiarity of the *new* me.

The feeling of galloping helped to clear my head, eventually fading out any thoughts and easing me until I was just riding. I focused on Ajax's smooth stride and let my mind clear, gliding along with his strides. The more I relaxed and concentrated on his strides, the more I became aware of myself with complete clarity. I smiled as we floated effortlessly along. Closing my eyes, I concentrated on my shoulder blades. They itched slightly, twitching to unfurl, feeling the wind brush against my skin as Ajax and I galloped. I tried to hold them back at first, but their persistence was unrelenting, and they pried their way out from my back anyway. I hadn't quite figured out their triggers yet. It seemed anytime adrenaline ran through my body, like when I felt threatened or when I was riding or running, they wanted to unfurl and fly. I guessed it was anytime they felt like it really. Bottom line, they wanted to take flight desperately, and they had a way of getting what they wanted. I sighed, knowing my wings had torn two perfectly round holes in the back of my newest long sleeve, the one I had bought to replace the last ruined one. I guess that was the truth with practically all my shirts at this point. I was beginning to run extremely low on undamaged shirts.

A vibration brought me back to my surroundings, and I turned to face it immediately. The same tall, athletically well-built guy who had visited my dorm room last night stood leaning against the spectator railing watching me intently. He smiled as he observed the brilliance of my wings. My eyebrows furrowed and I galloped Ajax over to the railing, irritated by his presence and uncomfortable with him appraising my wings. I hadn't shown anyone my wings yet, besides those who witnessed them that day Nathaniel left, and I wasn't sure how comfortable I was with a complete stranger's beady eyes on them.

"What are you doing here? Are you following me or something?" I questioned as Ajax snorted, sensing my uncertainty and anger.

He straightened himself but kept a sly smirk plastered on his face.

"You missed our meeting this morning, so I had to come find you," he said matter-of-factly.

My wings flapped at his response causing Ajax to snort and stir restlessly.

"About that, I think you've got the wrong person." I slid off Ajax and tucked my wings close to my body so as not to spook him. I tried getting them to furl back into my shoulders, but they weren't having it.

Frustrated, I gripped the reins and began to lead Ajax back to his stall to unsaddle him. To my dismay, the stranger followed.

"You're Alex Constance are you not?" he asked, knowing the answer already and sounding slightly bored.

When I didn't respond, he continued.

"I've got orders. You've been assigned under me, and we're to train together. It's not optional Alex," he said, seeming to read my mind as he helped take Ajax's saddle off.

We exchanged a look; his was of satisfaction while mine was filled with uncertainty and defiance.

"I don't even know your name, and I just got here," I said, still skeptical, taking the saddle from him.

"Jared and the first lesson you're getting is how to make your wings furl and unfurl on your command." He followed me into the tack room with Ajax's bridal.

I was uneasy being cornered in a small space with a stranger and the hairs on my neck stood at full attention. He blocked the doorway after hanging the bridle, and my wings fluttered spastically.

"Move," I ordered rather than asked, hoping he didn't sense the slight nervousness in my tone.

"You need to relax. You're uneasy, which won't make your wings retract," he said, folding his arms across his chest refusing to move out of the way.

I was vexed by his calmness but knew he was right.

"Please, tell me how I can do that," I asked defensively, gaging his movements as he walked towards me calmly. He moved towards my back, and I instinctively tried to counter his move. His hand met my shoulder, but it wasn't aggressive, it was gentle and non-threatening, with only enough force to hold me in my place.

"Just relax for a minute," he said gently, his voice sending a small electric shock through my body. I felt his hand touch my shoulder blade and a tingling sensation flew up my spine causing goose bumps to rise on my arms. A moment later, my wings rose delicately and retracted themselves smoothly into my back once again. Jared's hand went to linger over the thin shoulder blade wing scars, but he pulled it away and removed his hand, moving in front of me again. I faced him with surprise and slight suspicion. How was he able to make my wings retract practically on command with his touch? I had to admit, his calmness and how easy he made it look made me slightly jealous.

"How did you do that?" I asked, feeling the holes in the back of my shirt where my wings used to be.

He seemed pleased with himself.

"It's all in the touch. Now, are you coming with me to our training? I'm curious what skills a hybrid has," he stated, watching me curiously.

"That makes two of us," I replied, still intimidated by the stranger as I brushed past him and led the way out of the tack room. I tossed some hay in with Ajax and left the barn.

We walked along the concrete pathway until we reached a stone building labeled 'Gym/Rec Room.' The building resembled that of a typical gym, complete with a pool, running track, weight area, and treadmill area. A small round lounge sat directly in the center of the building. I was surprised to find a lot of angels in the gym, and all of them seemed to watch as Jared led me up the stairs and through a hallway that ended near the restrooms. I was impatient and cautious. Call it my previous kidnappings, but, yes, I was now very paranoid about following strangers to unknown places. We passed the restrooms and ahead of us stood a normal green painted door with a keypad labeled 'Janitor's Closet.'

I watched as Jared typed seven numbers into the keypad and the door clicked, unlocking. I hesitated as Jared waved me in.

"What is this?" I questioned, hearing my own panic in my words.

Jared studied me for a second as it finally dawned on him that I was uncomfortable.

"This is where we train, I'm not like...going to take advantage of you or anything," he said trying to find the right words. It was the first time I had noticed him shuffle for the right words to say since I had met him, but still. He was a stranger. I had met plenty of those over the past month, and I did not know what he was doing or where he was taking me. Up until this morning, I hadn't even known I had been assigned a trainer. I swallowed the lump in my throat as I gave him an unconvinced look.

"Here, the code to get in and out is 7876457." He said typing it in. I heard the click, and the door unlocked again; he turned to look at me innocently.

"See? You can get in and out."

I felt my feet glued to the carpet where I stood. I had the code and it was legit, he'd proved that plus, I'm a big bad hybrid now right? I knew I would probably be OK, but I couldn't help the slight post-traumatic stress haunting the back of my mind. It took all I had to ignore the alarm bells sounding in my head. I huffed and stepped inside, hoping my fears were wrong and that I wouldn't regret my decision.

Inside, the facade of the janitor's closet led to a giant open gym floor and training area. The lights automatically flicked on in our presence, and he shut the door behind me. There was quite a bit of miscellaneous equipment in the corners of the room, and the floor was made of wrestling mats. It dawned on me that this might be what Luther was talking about when he mentioned this being an undercover angel training camp. It was just hidden from view apparently.

"So this is where the angels train?" I asked curiously, wanting to confirm my suspicions.

There were boxing bags, some treadmills, and rope climbing equipment encircling a giant open space in the center of the room. The ceiling was also much taller in this room, probably so trainees could fly and train if needed, I guessed. He smiled some at my remark.

"This is *one* of the training spaces offered on campus; there are about 12 others. We got lucky, this one has been strictly dedicated to your training. You won't have to worry about anyone else in here. It's just us." He pulled off his hoodie revealing a well-sculpted chest and arms under a form-fitting tank top.

I looked away as a little blood flushed through my cheeks. Peering down at my riding boots, I wished I had changed before following Jared here. I smelled like...barn. Seeming to read my thoughts, Jared motioned to a small door on the other side of the room.

"There is a locker room in there where you can change. I took the liberty of bringing some clothes from your dorm for you to train in," he said, taking a drink of water from his water bottle.

"You went through my clothes?" I asked, perturbed and shocked. "What the hell? How did you get in?" I said hotly as anger rose inside me. Just *who* did this guy think he was!?

He grinned at me.

"Don't worry; I didn't look at anything I wasn't supposed to. Oh, and I used your key," he said pulling the bronze key out of his pocket and tossing it to me from across the room.

"You stole my key!?" I accused. I was bewildered at how he had even taken it in the first place.

"Get changed, and we'll talk about it." He seemed unaffected by the irritation in my voice. In fact, he seemed amused. Amused! I shot him a deadly glare, huffing and storming off into the locker room as the heat in my face seared. The first thing I was going to have to discuss with Jared was personal boundaries. Like, for example, don't go into my dorm room unless I say so and stop stealing from me were all good starting points. I didn't even know this guy, and he had already gone through my underwear drawer. *You've got to be kidding me!* I was utterly embarrassed and flustered. Nathaniel hadn't even gone through my underwear when I was forced to be his fake girlfriend! Well, at least I was pretty sure he hadn't.

I pushed Nathaniel from my thoughts as I recognized my small duffel bag on the bench and opened it. Inside, there was only a sports bra, black yoga Capri pants, tennis shoes and socks. I scowled at the sports bra angrily. I had plenty of other shirts in my closet, and he chose this. Lovely. I didn't even know this guy, and I was going to murder him. I repulsively cursed and changed clothes, tied my hair back and left the locker room. Jared was stretching his arms when I came out. He turned towards me immediately smiling as he appraised his outfit of choice.

"Ready?" he asked, pleased with himself.

"Apparently you missed the entire row of shirts in my closet!" I said sarcastically, nearly shouting at him in a fury.

He laughed a little.

"I just didn't want you to ruin another shirt if your wings unfurled again," he said smirking back at me.

"Mmm hmm, and for the record, do not ever go into my room again or rifle your hands through my clothes," I said furiously, knowing he had clearly taken the time to rummage through my clothes to see all of the holes in them.

"I thought angels were supposed to be all saintly and good. So far, all I know about you is your name, that you're a thief, and that you are most definitely a pervert," I stated flatly as he strapped some punching mitts on his hands and motioned for me to follow him to the center of the mats.

He smiled and rolled his eyes at my melodramatic statement.

"I promise I'm not a pervert," he said. With that, he hit his hands together and signaled for me to start throwing punches at his mitts.

I squared up and threw a punch before responding.

"Could have fooled me! Besides, isn't that what all perverts say?"

He laughed and moved a mitt before I could hit it, changing it up and only causing my blood to boil more.

"I don't know, but I'm not a pervert. And angels aren't all angelic either. I'm still a dude; we're just superhuman with mostly good intentions." I stopped hitting his mitts for a moment.

"And stealing is an acquired skill some angels learn?" I said sarcastically, eyeing him.

I was utterly annoyed with Jared, but I was curious about him. That, or I was incessantly paranoid, I couldn't be sure. Either way, I couldn't help but practically play the 21 questions game with him. He dodged my questions, but not because he was trying to hide anything, instead, he seemed bemused by them.

"Do you always ask so many questions when you first meet someone?" he said, raising his eyebrow.

"Maybe I'd just like to know who I'm training with. And confirm that you're really *not* a pervert or something," I replied in self-defense.

"Or one could say that you have trust issues, like *major* trust issues," he retorted, grinning.

I furrowed my eyebrows at him and punched the mitt harder. That hit a nerve. Who was *he* to start judging *me?* Maybe I had trust issues because I had been kidnapped and lied to, or maybe because of everything with Nathaniel; either way, it was *none* of his business!

"Ow," Jared nonchalantly said out loud.

It snapped me from my rage, and I lightened up my punch some. If only a little.

"So...who was he?" Jared continued after a brief period of silence.

"What? Who was who?" I asked confused, trying to figure him out as I stopped to take a swig of water from my water bottle.

"Who was the guy that you left, or the idiot that left you?" he asked flatly. His sea green eyes searched for something in mine.

I felt like I wanted to scream. Was it really that obvious that I was in a 'complicated' relationship or damaged goods? Wow, I really was beginning to feel like this was more of a therapy session with a shrink rather than a training session.

"That's *none* of your business." My voice was flat and deadly, warning him not to push the subject.

He held his hands up in defense.

"I was just trying to get to know my trainee."

Using the same excuse he had previously, I tried to change the subject.

"Do you always ask such personal questions when you just meet someone?" I replied sarcastically.

He smiled.

"You're right, how rude of me. Dinner then?" He smirked at my bewildered expression.

I stood dumbfounded at his words. Was he really asking me out?

"It's either dinner, or you tell me who the guy was that you're practically mourning over." Yep, he crossed the line.

I threw the mitts at his face and turned to leave, my mouth forming a tight thin line of disgust and disbelief at his words. I felt a hand on my wrist and, without thinking, I grabbed his hand to twist it behind his back. When he countered my move, my wings unfurled. I was infuriated. I felt my feet lift off the ground. It was almost as if I was taking a backseat to the entire movement. My wings flapped vigorously once towards him causing him to fly backwards and hit the wall on the other side of the room. I heard the breath leave his chest and for a moment he stayed down. Then he knelt and looked up at me pleased.

My feet precisely landed on the mat once more as I took back control of my body, my mouth hanging agape in sheer surprise at what had happened.

"Did I just do that?" I said out loud more to myself than to him.

I had no idea how I had, but somehow my body had taken over for me and protected itself.

He didn't answer my question, but I watched as two creamy white wings had spread out fully to each side of his body. They glowed slightly and relaxed more as he stood.

"That was good," he said, smiling.

I was mesmerized by his wings almost as much as I had been by my own. I had never seen anyone else's wings before. It was the first time I was able to take in just how different they really were. His were longer than mine and slightly narrower, whereas mine were of a fuller shape and fluffier. There was no trace of any black on his wings whatsoever either.

"You're not the only one with wings here you know." He smirked at my wide-eyed gaze.

I couldn't help but grin slightly. *I wasn't the only one with wings.* I repeated internally. The thought made me smile wider.

We continued to train for two hours. Finding out my new abilities over-powered my urge to walk out. After some time in the gym, we had practiced new techniques and defense mechanisms I didn't know I was capable of. We sat for a moment, our wings still at our sides and chugged down some more water. I had discovered a little more about Jared during our training session, too. He had been initiated three years ago, and his little sister was well on her way to following his footsteps. His parents, specifically the way he spoke coldly about his dad, made me think they didn't have the best relationship, rather more of a strict one. Apparently, he is scheduled to be finished with his training this year and would be moving on to become a guardian, once he completed his final tasks. I got the feeling he was one of the top in his class which was why he was asked to help me with my training. That, and he seemed well trained. I had just met him, but it was actually nice to talk to someone who was sort of similar to me. Aside from our first interactions together, talking to him made me forget about Nathaniel. And that was worth its weight in gold right now.

I was surprised to find that when asked a question, he answered. He was shockingly generous with sharing information about himself, extremely blunt and unorthodox at times, but he was the first person through all of this that willingly wanted me to know everything about him. I had to admit it was refreshing after dealing with the hidden secrets I was used to scraping together and practically beating answers out of Nathaniel.

"So, you know a lot about me already, but I still don't know anything about you. I know basic information from your file, but nothing about how," he motioned towards my wings, "those happened, besides what the rumors say anyways." I shifted a little on the mat and my back straightened.

I had built up thick walls, to say the least, to surround me after my kidnapping and transformation. Even though I had wanted to tell my loved ones, I refused, knowing rejection was the only possible outcome from my honesty. The fact that a complete – well maybe not complete – stranger was asking me to divulge the worst day of my life was not something I was quick or even willing to jump on. And how was there a file on me here already? Anxiety caused my wings to twitch open and closed. I didn't respond, but his sea green eyes remained calm and patiently awaited an answer. Uncomfortable under his gaze, I said the only thing I could think of to drop the subject. My wall would not be torn down. It was solid, hiding my innermost secrets, my vulnerabilities, my fears and I wasn't about to let anyone in. As far as I was concerned, I'd buried that day, and I'd keep it buried for as long as I could.

"It's complicated; I'd rather not talk about it." I looked away, and my wings retracted on their own.

The pain my wings inflicted every time they furled and unfurled was getting much easier to bear, but it still didn't feel pleasant as the scars on my back remained fresh. Jared's wings retracted as well, and he gripped my wrist gently before I moved to stand up. Our eyes met, and I wondered if he saw the same torment behind my eyes that I had seen in Nathaniel's when I asked about his past. Whatever he saw, Jared's eyes did not give it away; they bore into me sincerely and with intent.

"For what it's worth, I'm sorry for what they did to you," he said softly, releasing my wrist and standing, not breaking his gaze.

I didn't respond, but his words felt genuine.

"With my help though, you'll be able to defend yourself so no one can hurt you again," he said reassuringly, letting a grin take over his features. My eyes appraised his boyish but manly facial features intricately. The sound of his words brought a fire burning within me to my attention. I would *never* let anyone hurt me again. That was a promise.

Chapter 7

I showered and afterwards changed into a pair of jeans and a t-shirt that Jared had tossed on top of my duffel bag. Apparently, Jared had snatched them from my dorm earlier and only decided to present them to me now. Sighing, I pushed the irritation from my mind. At least I had something else to wear. Shoving the rest of my clothes inside my duffel bag, I stepped out of the bathroom and found Jared waiting for me. He was leaning against the wall and straightened himself when I emerged.

"So, what exactly does being my trainer entail?" I asked raising my eyebrow. I was perturbed, sensing that meant I would have a shadow from now on.

He grinned.

"It means it's my job to make sure you are trained properly, we establish any new abilities you have, and I get to check in on your overall wellbeing."

We emerged from the hidden room and into the regular gym area.

Lovely, so I *do* have a shadow now.

"Speaking of your wellbeing, you never answered my question before."

Other angels exchanged a few glances between one another as we passed. I wasn't sure where he was going with this. I had just met this guy, and he was already prying for very personal information.

"Your question?" I was a bit confused as to which question he meant.

"About dinner," he confirmed.

Wow. He was boyishly handsome, sure, but a total stranger. Besides, boys were definitely not on my list of things to chase right now and neither were strangers. My life was officially already too complicated.

"Listen, Jared is it?" I began but was cut off before I could finish.

"OK, no dinner, a club then? You don't even have to talk to me or anyone in a club," he grinned.

His persistence made that tiny bit of the old Alex want to laugh, but inwardly...

"Listen, I just met you, you've apparently been assigned as my trainer, something, by the way, which I will discuss with Eloa, and..." I struggled to try and explain myself and how I wasn't looking for another guy to come into my life and mess with my emotions again. Was I being presumptuous or was this just Jared being Jared? I fought for the right words as this literal stranger continued to watch me. Why hadn't Luther told me about him - this?

"Look, it'll help you convince me that you're not still hung up on some idiot."

What is it with this guy? I wonder how old he is... Is there such a thing as angel years?

I glared at him and retorted angrily, narrowing my eyes.

"Is this normally how you get girls to go out with you? I was wrong. You're not a pervert; you're a potential stalker. And, FYI, he's far from being an idiot. Do you actually know him? Is that what you think entitles you to an opinion? And whether or not I ever was, am, or am *not* hung up on him is none of your business! Not now, maybe not ever. I don't know. I'm new at this!"

This seemed to amuse Jared even more.

"So there was a 'he' then? And I'm not a stalker either," he snickered. It seemed as though all I could do was furrow my brow and shake my head in disbelief. Speaking of idiots. I was already walking down the path to my dorm and quickened my pace.

"So what happened?" he persisted, matching my pace.

"OMG, you're relentless! No means No!" This time I was running, and he was still running next to me.

"What are you so scared of?" he laughed.

I stopped short. "Ugh! Definitely *not* you! Fine! Will you drop it if I go to a club with you?" I was utterly annoyed that he would not leave me alone.

He smiled, pleased with himself.

"Maybe. I'll be by your dorm at 10:30PM to pick you up." He turned and began to walk calmly in the other direction.

"Ugh, whatever stalker!"

"I'm not a stalker," I heard him yell back while continuing to walk away.

Could have fooled me, I thought. Then panic filled my mind at what I had just agreed to do. I felt the need to clarify instantly.

"This isn't a date though! We are just two people going to the same place at the same time! We're basically carpooling together *only*!" I yelled back at him.

He didn't bother to turn back, but I thought I heard him chuckle.

"If that's what you want to tell yourself!" he yelled back finally.

My mouth hung open for a response, but closed when nothing came out. He had some *nerve*, I'd give him that, but he had another thing coming if he thought this was a date. I'd make sure I was the most unpleasant person to be around, too, just to prove it. Then this stalker would want nothing to do with me and I could go about my merry way. Hey, he might even try to get out of training me. *Take that!* I thought childishly.

I sighed and entered my building and began to climb the stairs to my dorm room. Inside, I tossed my duffel bag by the desk and sprawled out on the bed checking my cell phone for any messages. I was in the middle of responding to one of Kate's texts when a knock sounded at my door. I rolled my eyes in aggravation wondering how else this Jared guy could possibly irritate me any further.

"I said yes already, what do you...?" My words faltered as I opened the door and found Trey on the other side.

"Who did you say yes to?" he asked smiling, his voice brimming with curiosity and his eyebrows furrowing slightly.

I let a sigh out, thankful it was only Trey.

"Sorry, I thought you were someone else." I welcomed him inside and flopped myself down on my bed again.

He took a seat in my desk chair and motioned for someone else to come inside.

"Who?" he asked.

"A stalker," I replied annoyed at the thought of Jared.

A petite angel girl stepped into the doorway then, grabbing my attention. I put my phone down and sat up anxiously. This was the first angel who had approached me besides Jared, and I wasn't sure what to expect. Trey motioned to the girl who looked to be around our age and introduced her.

"This is Sophie, Sophie this is Alex," he said, explaining how they met touring the campus. Sophie took a few more steps into the room and waved at me. She had short cropped light pink hair that outlined her face and brown eyes with a paler complexion. She looked extremely dainty, although I knew better, and she was gorgeous. I was a little shocked, but I did not feel threatened by her. I waved back and smiled.

"It's nice to meet you, Alex," she said, still standing.

Trey began to explain how my parents had sent me to Crest as well. Sophie and I listened and exchanged a few glances. It was clear we both knew that Trey's story was...a little off, however, we remained quiet throughout Trey's introduction, only nodding when he finished. I was a little relieved when she hadn't ratted out who I truly was to Trey. I mean, not that she would, since it seemed like Trey didn't know she was an angel either, but it made me have some respect for her right off the bat. Almost like, *you keep my secret, and I'll keep yours* kind of a thing.

"So back to my original question, you said yes to a stalker, like, you're going out with him?" Trey asked wondering if I had lost my mind.

I frowned at him.

"I'm *not* going out with anyone. I'm just going to a club and carpooling with someone." I was uncomfortable and trying to phrase it properly so they would know *exactly* what it really was.

"But he's a stalker? What's his room and building number so we can go kick his..." Trey delved deeper, but Sophie cut him off quickly.

"Who is it?" Sophie asked curiously.

"Jared. I'm not sure of his last name."

Her eyes widened, and she giggled, smiling.

"Jared, the guy who's your new personal trainer? He's not a stalker; he's actually a pretty sweet guy." I was surprised to know she knew he was training me, but I then realized word must travel pretty fast here.

I looked at her as if she had just said something atrocious.

"You're kidding, right?" I begged to differ.

She smiled and nodded adamantly. "Seriously, he's not a stalker, but he must be really taken with you to have asked you out."

"That's one way to word it," I replied.

"We should all go," Trey began. "For one, I like clubs, and two, I would be doing your brother and parents a horrible disservice if I let you go to a club alone on your first day here with some stranger, especially some stranger who you said may be a stalker," he stated definitively.

He had a point, and after a moment of thought, this actually worked well in my favor. With Trey and Sophie there, I really wouldn't have to even talk to Jared, it would be like he wasn't even there.

"I like clubs," Sophie insisted, smiling at Trey and me. "What time?"

"Deal! Meet here at 10:30PM." I replied smiling, secretly wondering how this night would go. *Ha!*

"Sounds good. I've gotta run to my class, but I'll see you guys later, k." He smiled and left the dorm.

Sophie walked back to the doorway, and I got up and followed her. Before leaving, she turned towards me.

"I've just got to say, you're not what I expected," she said remaining cautious, but polite.

"Neither are you. You're the first angel I've met with pink hair," I countered, smiling and trying to break the ice a little.

She smiled back and twirled a strand of her hair in her finger.

"I like the color. Listen, I understand if you don't want to, but, it's got to be pretty rough with everything that you've been through, and then coming here, too. If you just want to hang out sometime let me know. I'm in the next building over on the first floor; number A-12." Her words felt genuine, and I was a little surprised to hear them coming from her. I hadn't been approached by any other angel besides Jared since I got here, so it was a little refreshing to know I had someone else to talk to, even if we didn't really know each other yet.

"Thanks," I said smiling. "Hey, you haven't told…"

She seemed to know exactly what I was going to ask and finished answering my question before I could say all of the words myself.

"No, Trey doesn't know yet, about either of us, that is. But this campus doesn't seem to hold in secrets forever."

With that, she smiled and waltzed off down the hallway towards the stairs. My suspicions about Trey not knowing the truth yet had been accurate, to my relief, but I wasn't sure what she meant by the campus not holding in secrets forever. Just how fast was the grapevine here? The thought of his reaction sent a shiver up my spine. I couldn't worry about that; it would only torment my insides.

I decided to call both of my parents and let them know I was settling in nicely. *Sort of.* Afterwards, I would head to the main office building again and pick up my schedule for classes. Trey had been assigned classes already, so that meant I had to have some too and I desperately wanted to clean up my grades. It wasn't like me to fall behind academically, and it made me uneasy to know I had. And it would give me some semblance of normality, too. That, and perhaps I could talk with Madam Eloa about a new trainer.

I made my way to the Atrium building and found the same receptionist from yesterday. She remembered me instantly and shifted her glasses towards the bridge of her nose when she addressed me.

"Can we help you with something, Alexandria?" she questioned, sounding impatient and short.

"Yes, I was wondering if my class schedule was ready for me to pick up yet," I replied expectantly, surprised she remembered my name. She seemed to tilt her head some in confusion.

"Ms. Constance, you don't have a class schedule. You're in training, with Mr. Jared Macomb, but other than that I don't have you down for anything." She looked back at me wondering where I had gotten the crazy notion that I had classes to take.

I tilted my head back at her, confused.

"What do you mean? I'm not taking any classes? I thought I'd be

76

training and going to classes?" I questioned, wondering how I was going to get my grades up and prove to my parents I was doing better here.

The receptionist removed her glasses and laid them on the desk, trying to get her point across to me more clearly and sternly.

"I'm sorry Ms. Constance, but we don't have you added to any of the classes here. For now, you are only in training with Mr. Macomb. If you have any concerns, I'd advise you to bring them up with Madame Eloa. She should be available in the next ten minutes." She nodded her head toward a bank of chairs against the wall, implying for me to take a seat and wait and stop bothering her.

I did as I was told.

Ten minutes later, Madame Eloa welcomed me into her office through the tall double glass doors, her champagne hair bouncing delicately as she walked.

"So, Ms. Constance, my receptionist explained to me that you are concerned about not having any classes scheduled with us yet, and are only training with Mr. Macomb." She sat in her office chair, her posture straight and proper.

Her office consisted of a glass desk with plush furniture. I nodded, glancing around the room.

"Yes, I was under the impression... that is Luther had said I would mainly be taking classes here, and that Crest would help me with some training as well. And I'm not sure Mr. Macomb is the right trainer for me either."

Madam Eloa smiled for a moment, but I couldn't be sure if it was at the mention of Luther's name, or if it was pertaining to my question.

"Now Alexandria, you must understand. It is simply *not* in your benefit *or* anyone else's if we simply throw you into a class or classes. At this point, you are scheduled to train with Jared only so that you can identify and learn to control your new abilities."

Her words sent a flow of frustration through my body, and I couldn't help but feel like everyone didn't trust me.

"What about my grades for the rest of the semester? How can I do better if I'm not taking any classes?" I questioned uneasily.

"We've already taken care of your grades for this year, you can take a look if you like." She said, handing me an official transcript.

I took the sheet of paper and glanced at the classes I used to take and the grades next to them. All A's. Although the paper should have made me jump for joy and smile, I couldn't help but feel like it was *cheating*. And I was *not* a cheater.

"I don't understand. These are fabricated."

She smiled again.

"Listen Alexandria, we are here to help you succeed. In order to do that there is a certain order that things must go. You will probably be cleared to attend classes on campus here soon. For now, though, learn what you can from Mr. Macomb, whom I can assure you is well fitted for this type of situation. His pedigree alone speaks volumes, and don't worry about the rest. We will take care of you, you just need to trust us," she stated finally.

I attempted a smile, but it was forced. I guess it was nice I didn't have to take classes and that things were already *'taken care of'*, but a part of me felt like this wasn't right and that I was just skating by without actually learning anything. I felt like it was the easy way out, and I felt grimy about it. It also was irritating to find out that I wouldn't be getting re-assigned to a new trainer. I'd be stuck with Jared. Reluctantly, I nodded and exited her office. I guess learning to be a hybrid angel was going to be at the top of my 'to-do' list. They say you can't let a new life in until you vacate the old life. So this is me getting ready to inhabit my new life. I wasn't shocked that nobody trusted me to attend any classes with their students here yet, but I knew there was more to the story. There were hundreds of loose ends, and I was determined to get through this and find out what was behind them.

Apollyon, it's good to see you. Although the visit seemed more of an intrusion, Uvall smacked the man's shoulders roughly and led him through his foyer towards his office. Apollyon tossed his coat on a chair, lighting a cigar and breathing in its scent as Uvall unveiled a crystal decanter nearby, pouring each of them a drink.

"It's unnatural for your home to be this quiet Uvall."

Uvall huffed. "Afraid it's been that way since the eclipse."

"Ahh, our glorious failed attempt at getting into heaven. How could I forget? Our hybrid didn't exactly pan out as we all suspected. To think how easy it could have been if she had. We could've overridden the Council, taken heaven, and everything for that matter. The balance could have shifted back into our hands for once. Even still. I'm beginning to think we were looking at things entirely from the wrong perspective. She can still be of use to us, just in other ways," Apollyon explained as he took the offered liquor.

"You sound positive."

"Delightfully. And you? How are you faring after things?" Apollyon's eyes glistened as he looked Uvall over, studying him for weakness.

"My house is in order. Not to worry," Uvall replied, plopping his tumbler onto the table and changing the subject rapidly. "How's the family?"

Apollyon stretched out as if aggravated by the question.

"Hmmm, Corson, Corson, Corson." The words came out as if he were testing how they sounded, uncertain, and far from warm and fuzzy for being his own kin.

"He's feeling his oats."

"Kids will do that."

"Mmmm." Apollyon puffed his cigar, studying it.

"Your brother seems to be taking charge where he's at as well."

"How is he?"

"Stubborn, unpredictable, ill-tempered, and miserable just like you were when you turned." Apollyon smiled devilishly.

Uvall took a swig of his scotch, letting the invasive taste of leathery caramel seep into his gums before swallowing.

"And Alex? Where is she now?"

"They've taken her to Crest. To train and turn her against us no doubt. I reckon they won't get very far."

"What makes you so sure?"

"Something tells me she's going to have an extreme undeniable pull to her fallen side. Courtesy of your brother," he said, raising his tumbler and taking a generous sip."

They sipped their drinks in silence, declining to divulge further what lay on each of their minds.

"She's also got a pull to angels. Which makes her dangerous. So, what now? We can't just sit and wait; we should act. It's what they wouldn't expect so soon after..."

"No. That's exactly what we're going to do. For now."

Chapter 8

I headed for the barn to visit Ajax and do some thinking. I could always clear my head around him. Afterwards, I went back to my dorm room to get ready, ignoring the other angels that walked a little faster past me, or the ones that gasped, appalled by my presence on campus.

Inside my room, I scanned my closet for something to wear. I hadn't been to a club before and after much deliberation and searching my closet for something I thought would be club worthy; I finally settled on a pair of dark blue skinny jeans, black closed toe wedges, a plain white t-shirt and a black leather jacket. I looked back at my reflection in the mirror hanging on the wall. I decided to skip any makeup and tousled my hair more to give it a messy beach look. I didn't want Jared to get the idea this was anything more than carpooling, and I definitely was not getting ready for him. It would make him grin that stupid grin, and I wasn't about to give him the satisfaction. I applied some lip balm and called it good.

Before I knew it, I felt the presence of Trey and Sophie at the door and heard a knock follow. I opened the door and let them in, catching the sight of Jared coming up the stairs. He smiled once he saw me and caught the door before I could shut it on him.

"You look good," he said, approving of my outfit.

I ignored his compliment and decided to tell him about Trey and Sophie.

"A couple of friends are coming with us tonight since we're all *carpooling* together," I said, reaffirming this was not a date and merely the same car everyone was riding in to get to the same destination.

"Sophie and Trey? Yea, I spoke with them earlier; sounds good." He said with a grin, brushing past me and greeting Sophie and Trey.

I just looked at him, surprised. How was it that he seemed to know about everything?

"Oh. How did you and Trey meet?" I asked curiously after he greeted everyone.

"He found me after lunch earlier and told me that if I got with you and broke your heart or if I was a stalker, he'd break my legs."

Trey rolled his eyes.

"Well someone's got to look out for this one," he said motioning towards me as he and Sophie left the room to meet us in the hallway.

Jared leaned down to my ear then. I could feel his warm breath on the nape of my neck, and I froze at his closeness.

"I didn't tell him that he'd have a hard time doing that, just said I was getting to know you."

A part of me felt a warm tremor trickle down my spine with his words, or maybe it was his closeness that caused the tremors. I could smell his cologne. Sweet and salty. A hint of jasmine and rosemary softening its musky trail... I snapped myself out of it. Get a hold of yourself Alex! I inwardly cursed myself along with my new heightened senses, and resecured the imaginary barricade around myself once more.

We left my dorm and headed towards the club, driving for about an hour and a half until we reached a bustling little city filled with restaurants and shops and people walking and dining. We went a couple more blocks until we reached the end of the street where a large three-story building sat. Blacked out windows made it impossible to tell if it was even open, but the throngs of people in line out the door, flashing lights, and steady 'boom boom' from the bass inside told me this was it.

Jared parked the car, and we crossed the street towards the club. I panicked on the inside for a moment realizing I had not checked to see if this was an 18 and up club so all of us could get inside. Everyone else was 18, but my birthday was another week or so away, and I felt embarrassed I had not asked about it before. Miraculously, none of us were carded as we entered. I wondered if it was just how we dressed, but then I noticed a nod exchanged between the guy at the door and Jared. It was quick and hardly noticeable, but nevertheless, it was there. I wondered how many times Jared had to have come here to get the 'You're good to go' nod. Catching the name on the side of the building before we were shuffled inside, I planted it in my brain. '*Echo.*'

Jared led the way as we weaved through masses of people. Bodies gyrated all over, and my attention turned from the rhythm of the music to the vibrations in the air. A lot of humans, some angels, and some fallen angels. I was surprised to feel the vibrations of fallen angels inside.

I heard Sophie yell that she and Trey were going to go dance. I watched their bodies disappear in the crowd before my attention turned back to Jared. He seemed to pick up on what I was sensing and answered my question before I could ask it.

"This is a hot-spot for everyone. Sort of a middle ground for angels and fallen angels; there are tons of places like this scattered everywhere."

I didn't respond. I couldn't help but feel a little nervous.

"Don't worry." He said dragging a bar stool next to him for me to sit on.

"No business is conducted in the club. Only outside. There would be too many witnesses otherwise."

I nodded, pretending the information soothed me a little, when in reality, I wasn't sure it did.

"How many of them can you sense?" He asked curiously. He whisked a bottle of beer from a passing cocktail waitress as he spoke, then took a swig.

I closed my eyes and focused on the vibrations throughout the room. I felt really uncomfortable. The number of people around me had my focus dizzied. This was the first time I experienced so many vibrations of all types all at once. I started to feel my palms sweat. What was I thinking coming to a place like this? Panic settled in and my heart rate increased.

I felt Jared's hand grab my wrist and I turned to look at him. It was obvious I was silently panicking.

"Look at me," he said when I tried to avert his gaze and touch.

"Just breathe. Think of the vibrations like music around you. Don't let it be overwhelming." I closed my eyes trying to quiet my nerves and did as he said. I pictured the wave of vibrations gyrating to the beat of the bass. My breathing became deeper, and slowly I felt the pounding of the vibrations turn more into a rhythm around me. They weren't dangerous. They were just there. I was OK. I felt my body calm and opened my eyes to find Jared's sea green eyes boring into mine and a pleased look on his face.

"See? You're just fine. You just need to relax." He motioned towards the beer on the table. I hadn't ever been drunk, now that I thought about it. The bottle seemed foreign to me. Maybe just a little swig couldn't hurt. I gripped the bottle and took a gulp, letting the brown foreign liquid fill my mouth, then I swallowed. I grimaced at the taste; it was more dry and bitter than what I had expected. Jared's laugh brought my attention back to him.

"You've never drank?" He shook his head smiling.

"So how many can you sense now?" he asked distracting me from the unpleasant taste in my mouth.

"Close your eyes and focus on their vibrations. Tell me how many you count," he said.

I closed my eyes, breathing deeply to ignore the massive waves of vibrations that fought to distract and disorientate me. I could see the dark blue vibrations ringing back to me in the blackness, almost like beacons signaling their locations.

"There are two on this level... three in the basement, and two more out the back," I said opening my eyes a few moments later.

He laughed a little under his breath, but his expression was one of surprise and bewilderment, causing me to second guess myself.

"Is that right?" I asked him, feeling like I had miscounted somehow.

He smiled back at me and tipped his beer back taking a few gulps.

"I only counted the two in here and the two outside." He continued to smile as he observed my shock.

When I didn't respond, he continued.

"It means this is one of the clubs fallen angels conduct their meetings at. This floor," he said stomping his foot, "is about six inches thick and below us is a hidden basement area reinforced with steel walls. Normal angels can't feel their vibrations through all of that, but you seem to be able to."

I couldn't help but feel pleased with myself. I'd have to add that to my list of perks since my transformation, and happily I took another swig of beer to celebrate myself.

A few hours must have passed, talking and dancing, but I hardly seemed to notice. I focused on the beat of the music reverberating through me and just let go. I felt invigorated by the atmosphere and let my hips move with the music. I could feel a hand wrapped close around my waist, and I turned to meet Jared's sea green eyes glimmering down at me.

"We should get back to Crest soon, it's almost 3AM," he stated smiling as I continued to sway with the music.

I nodded. I didn't want to go; I wanted to stay and let my worries drift away like they had been since we'd been here, but he was right. We needed to go.

"I'll be back in a minute, and then we can go," I said as I moved his hand and made my way through the twirling and grinding bodies towards the blackened hallway where the bathrooms were.

I wasn't by any means drunk, hell, I had finished one beer since I'd been here, but something inside me felt free and euphoric as if I was drunk on the intoxicating atmosphere around me.

Just as I was about to push the bathroom door open, I heard my name whispered through the air. Soft and low, like a familiar tune pulling at me. I turned to see a shorter stalky and dark figure lingering in the hallway. I immediately knew the stranger was a fallen angel, but instead of feeling threatened I followed the stranger outside the back door of the club. I couldn't be sure why, but there was a need to, and my body obeyed.

Under the dim flickering light of the building, the figure stopped and lit a cigarette. He turned back towards me, and the orange glow of embers illuminated just enough of his features that I could make out deep slices across the man's face. The cuts had healed but left large rough scars that swept over the man's charcoal skin.

"Who are you and what do you want?" I questioned cautiously, suddenly realizing I may have made a mistake following the man outside.

He took a long drag of his cigarette before responding, and I could tell he was shaking.

"We don't have time for names, all you need to know is that I'm a friend of sorts. You're being lied to Alex. You need to be vigilant with who you trust." His voice was husky, and his eyes darted between me and the alleyway like he was terrified something might reach out and pull him into the darkness forever.

"And why should I trust you?" I asked warily wondering what had him so distraught.

His tone heightened with anxiety.

"Listen! I'm here to warn you. You're being fed lies. I've got to go now, and for both our safety, don't tell anyone you spoke with me." His words were cold, but the fear in his eyes told me that he was truly afraid.

But afraid of what? Or whom? I was about to ask when I heard the sound of the door opening behind me and I saw Jared emerge. I turned back, and the figure I had spoken with had vanished; only a cigarette on the ground remained.

"What are you doing out here?" Jared inquired, his eyes stemming with concern and caution.

He scanned the distance of the alleyway and, finding nothing, looked back at me for an answer.

"I just...needed some air. You ready to go?"

He nodded and held the door open for me. I ducked back inside under his arm as he scanned the distance once more before following me back inside.

We drove the winding canyon road back to Crest and pulled into a parking spot, but I couldn't shake the words the stranger had spoken to me. *'I'm here to warn you; you're being fed lies.'* The words filled me with dread. Who was lying to me? And why was everyone insisting that I was in danger? A drunken Trey in the backseat of Jared's car snapped me out of my thoughts.

"This was a gr-great gr-great night guys! I mean woohoo!" He stammered clumsily, falling from the vehicle.

86

Jared laughed as Sophie and I went to help Trey. I hauled him up off the ground and balanced him. Jared came around the car and took over. Trey wasn't heavy for any of us, Sophie or me included. I could have easily hauled him up the steps to his dorm room, but I guess it seemed like the gentlemanly thing for Jared to do. I followed behind with Trey's wallet. Jared flopped Trey down on his mattress as I set his wallet down on the nightstand. Sophie bounded across the room kissing him on his cheek and waving to both of us before skipping down the hall and downstairs to her dorm room. I shook my head a little, smiling back at Jared as we walked out of Trey's room and out of the building.

"She likes him," he said, referring to Sophie and Trey.

I nodded and smiled.

"I'm glad. They seem like a good fit for one another," I said as our feet crunched along the pathway in the snow.

"You did really well tonight, too, by the way. I think you've got a lot of potential. If it's OK with you, I'd like to recommend you for some field work coming up." He kicked a bit of snow before turning to see my reaction.

I looked back at him confused and surprised.

"Thanks, but you do realize you just met me, right? And now all of the sudden after one day of training I'm qualified enough for the field?" I raised my eyebrows in suspicion. His certainty made me uneasy.

I wasn't even that certain about myself yet; hell I just figured out how to drown out vibrations tonight, and now he thought I was ready for the *field*? What did he mean by the field anyhow?

He smiled. "The *field* work I'm speaking of is in a month and trust me when I say you'll be more than ready by then."

I nodded. "Whatever you say Yoda." He smirked at my response.

"You know, if I didn't know any better I'd say you actually had fun tonight," he said as we made our way to my building and to my dorm room.

"Now don't go getting any..." Before I could finish my sentence, Jared's mouth met mine fervently. It took me a minute to register what was actually happening; I felt a part of me reach out and kiss him back. It was a different feeling than I had had with Nathaniel, I could feel a tingling hum flow through my body as if little electric sparks were being set off. As one part of me wanted to respond instantly to him, another part of me wriggled to understand why I was kissing an angel.

The sweet and salty scent of him filled my lungs completely. That's when the warning signals went off in my brain. The palm of my hand pressed against Jared's firm chest and shoved him back. His mouth parted from mine, but he stepped towards me again. My hand remained outstretched as my thoughts scrambled to come back to earth for a minute. I fought the urge to kiss him again or punch him in the nose. *What was wrong with me?!*

Jared remained silent, but a small smile crept across his face as he appraised my reaction.

"You should go," I managed to stammer out. He needed to go – now. He nodded, turning and leaving.

I braced my back against my dorm room door for a moment before I went inside and slapped my palm against my forehead. *I did not just do that. No, that did not just happen.* I tried convincing myself, but the little electric shocks were a reminder that it did just happen. I had kissed Jared. Jared! My trainer! What the hell was I thinking! I scolded myself inwardly. I've only known the guy for one day! Oh, hell. It was the beer. Alcohol made people do stupid, regrettable things and I had just done one of them. I was never drinking again.

I locked the door and kicked off my shoes, bracing my hands on the counter, still replaying the last few minutes in my head, bewildered. *Way to complicate things, even more, Alex.* I was sarcastically scolding myself when a familiar presence caught my attention.

"Tell me you haven't been here for longer than 30 seconds," I said as I turned towards Luther who, as usual, had cloaked himself in the darkest corner of the room.

My embarrassment had boiled to the rim, and I thought I could just die. Right there. He chuckled.

"That depends, do you like that guy or do I need to teach him something about manners?" he questioned, coming forward from the dark.

The scent of cigar clung to his clothes like a cologne. I rolled my eyes, embarrassed.

"The manners part might be a good place to start, but how about we just *never* bring it up again," I said slumping down in my desk chair.

He nodded, seeming to understand. It was obvious that both sides, the fallen angel side, and the angel side, were battling with each other inside me. It was the first time I began to realize the pull each one had on me, and it frightened me. I felt like the three of us were arguing inwardly, me, the fallen angel part and the angel part. I would have to learn to control each somehow, but I had no idea where to start.

"What's up?" I asked changing the subject to why he was here. He nodded, looking torn between wanting to tell me something and keeping it a secret.

"Nathaniel was spotted yesterday. He's back in the U.S. now." He watched my reaction.

I twitched reflexively with the news and hearing his name.

"Good for him," I said coldly as I twiddled a pen on the desk.

"I just thought you should know; other than that, it has been relatively quiet everywhere. No one has been mentioning you on any level to be worried about," he said finally.

I nodded. The sound of Nathaniel's name made a part of me stir inside; it was hope, or at least it felt like it, and it made me cringe. How could I be so stupid? I didn't like the hold he still had over me. Nathaniel was gone. Whatever it was that we had was history. Perhaps coming here was exactly what I needed to make all of that perfectly clear to me. Well, that and the recording Luther had me listen to. I was determined not to let Nathaniel affect me anymore. In the end, he would only hurt me.

"I'm sorry," I said, apologizing for my tone earlier. "I'm just a little on edge still you know?"

He smiled for a moment.

"All I ask is don't kill the messenger." He put his hands up in his defense, and I laughed.

"Thanks for the update Luther, and by the way, I would never dream of killing my favorite messenger," I said grinning. "I do have a question though. Why didn't you tell me about my assigned trainer, Jared Macomb?"

Luther sighed. "To be honest, I was afraid you wouldn't come because of him. Especially after Nathaniel, I just wanted you to give this place a chance. There aren't many safe places available for a hybrid, but I think you're safer here than anywhere else right now."

"And if it changes from being the safest place? What do we do?"

"Simple. I come get you and move you somewhere else that is safer. Don't worry, I'm keeping a watchful eye on you and everything else. Just try to learn as much as you can here while you can. As far as Jared goes, I've never met the kid; seen him, watched him, know his parents, and I think they couldn't have picked a better trainer for you here. He's a good kid, someone you can trust."

"Who happens to be incessantly annoying," I said.

"Weren't you two just..."

"Not one more word Luther. It didn't happen. I've already blocked it from my memory banks."

He held his hands up smiling.

We talked for a bit longer and then parted ways. I enjoyed Luther's company; he was the one person who knew my recent history, whom I felt comfortable divulging my private life with, well most of it anyways. Turning off my nightstand lamp I crawled under my sheets and stared out the window at the stars until hours had passed and sleep overtook me.

Chapter 9

I walked with my wings fully outstretched listening to the birds chirp in the woods around me. Glistening streams of light cast down through the trees creating pools of brightness and shadow. I stood smiling under one of the pools of light with my eyes closed. The light began to dim, and I opened my eyes to view a red eclipse burning down at me. Chillingly, all the light that had poured through the treetops became dark red pools. I began to run through the forest, my wings helping float me over rocks and fallen trees. A red light burst through the woods and when I opened my eyes again, I was tied to an operating table. I noticed the same syringe from before in the hands of the doctors, as dark cloaked figures watched in the background, urging the doctors to move forward. I began to shout and yell trying to break free of the chains. 'No! No! Not again!' I screamed. As the needle pierced my skin, everything turned black.

I woke with such force it flung me out of bed, and across the room. My wings and I shook uncontrollably as I watched a blue flame flicker and dissipate between my fingers and palms.

Was that...fire? My brain was scrambled as it tried to discern what had happened and whether my eyes were deceiving me. The door flung open, drawing my attention, and Jared rushed inside to my aide.

"What happened? I was coming to get you for training, and I heard a scream and a giant thud." His face was etched in concern as he knelt beside me and looked around the room for answers to the cause or an intruder.

My trembling did not subside as he helped me to my desk chair and ordered me to breathe deeply. Something caught his attention. He strode over and picked my comforter up off the floor, or what was left of it. He held it up and examined it. Giant burnt holes covered it. It looked more like Swiss cheese than a comforter. He turned to me with wide eyes and a raised brow.

"Alex, what happened?" His voice was dripping with alarm and turned more serious.

A flash of the eclipse passed across my vision again, and I squeezed my eyes shut, trembling and blinking it away again. *What was happening to me?*

I shook my head, unable to respond as the horrid memories of that day crept back into my thoughts. I could feel the needle prick my skin and the feeling of the hot liquid filling my veins. And then came the pain, that horrid bone-crunching, skin burning pain that enveloped all of me ruthlessly. I couldn't help but shake uncontrollably as a few tears escaped my eyes. I was reliving it all over again.

"Come on. Let's get you something to eat," he said helping me up.

I didn't fight him, I just helplessly clutched his arm in a steel grip and let him lead me out of the room. The angels in the building had gathered in the hallways wondering what all of the commotion was about and staring me down as I passed.

"Move! Clear out!" Jared's voice boomed as angels backed away, still keeping their eyes on me as we exited the building.

Over the next hours, Jared had tossed my comforter in the trash and taken me to get breakfast. I hadn't spoken one word to him the entire time. The trembles and shakes had slowly subsided over breakfast, but the deep-set fears lingered behind my eyes. I felt distraught and vulnerable, and him kissing me last night only added to those feelings. I didn't know what to say. He hadn't said a word either the entire breakfast to my relief, letting me eat and get changed without pressuring me for answers, but his eyes flickered at my every movement in apprehension and anticipation. I buried the dream next to my broken heart and tried to forget about everything as we made our way to the gym.

We entered the secret training room, and he tossed his bag across the floor then stopped in front of me.

"Alex, I need to know what happened." His voice was stern yet kind much in the same way Luther often spoke to me. But Jared's was almost a whisper.

I shook my head. I didn't know if I could go through it again, describing the terror I felt, but I needed to know if what I went through was what all angels, or more likely fallen angels, go through. But the terror silenced me, and I couldn't put a voice to it.

"I don't know what happened," I said flatly.

It was partially true, but deep down I knew what I had witnessed. The brilliant blue flames coming from my hands had clearly been real, what little remained of my comforter was proof of that. Jared approached me again.

"Alex, I can tell you're lying. I can help you with this, but I need to know what happened." He stepped closer and the smell of freshly fallen rain, and warm vanilla washed around me.

But I wasn't ready to let anyone get close to me. I tried to focus and stepped back from him.

"No. You don't know me well enough to know when I'm lying. I just need to focus, and I'll be OK," I said putting a little more distance between us.

He knew nothing about me, and I was offended by his arrogance. He grinned, but I could tell he wasn't going to drop the subject.

"Are you uncomfortable around me, because of last night..?" he questioned.

I glared at him. He *would* bring up last night, I thought repulsively. His arrogance and stupidity was taking me beyond agitated to furious that he'd bring up last night after this morning's events.

"No. And I don't need you complicating things for me right now," I declared.

He huffed.

I suddenly wished I could return to the moment he had kissed me last night and punch him in the face. I knew he was attempting to get under my skin hoping for a reaction, and he was definitely succeeding.

"You're not very bright, antagonizing a hybrid, are you?" I questioned sarcastically, but my tone hinted a warning. I was not in any mood to play his stupid games.

He smiled and stepped closer, mocking me.

"You're about as scary as a kitten." He pressed the subject, crossing his arms. "But if you're that desperate to kiss me again, I guess I'll allow it," he chided.

Yep, I was going to kill him.

"You kissed me remember?"

He smirked and uncrossed his arms.

"What was I supposed to do? You were practically begging for it." By the time he finished his sentence, I had already launched myself at him.

We hit the wall, and Jared laughed. *That. Was. It.* I was beyond livid now. He tossed me off of him and a fire within me boiled and bubbled to the surface. My head hung low like a bull preparing to fight, and my arms were at my sides awaiting the next attack. Jared's face turned from one of amusement to one of astonishment. And fear?

"Fire," he whispered, more to himself than out loud.

I tilted my head in confusion and followed his gaze to my hands. The same brilliant blue flame had encased both of my hands and was steadily making its way up my wrists. I held my hands up to my eyes in disbelief.

I felt panicky, and I looked back to Jared wide-eyed.

I wasn't being burned, but my mind was automatically trying to comprehend what was happening and how to be rid of the blue flames. I thought about stopping, dropping and rolling. Wasn't that what the fire department always said to do? But, when I returned my gaze back to my hands, it was just in time to watch the terrifyingly violent blue flames subside and disappear back into my body.

Jared smiled and raised his eyebrows as he walked towards me shaking his head in disbelief.

"You are special. I wasn't expecting that," he stated, keeping an arm's distance from me

My hands were not burnt, and the boiling feeling felt like it had seeped deep inside. It was as though I could still sense that feeling, and all the others, but from a distance. What took over next was rage mixed with panic. Had he seriously just been joking with me over that kiss? I looked back at him and punched him as hard as I could square in the face. He sprawled out on the gym mats and looked back at me in shock.

"What was that for!?" He yelled cupping his face as I watched the ruby red liquid stream from his nose, steadily increasing in speed.

A dizzy feeling came over me, and I fought my eyelids to stay open. I couldn't stand straight, and I couldn't comprehend why.

"For...provoking me...idiot," was all my brain managed to say before the dizziness won out. My pulse slowed, and I succumbed to the blackness.

The vibrations were the first that I felt when I came around again. The nurse left, and I could feel three other bodies outside the door. Angels. Groggily I tried to make out the whispers between them as I strained to open my eyes. I noticed a needle in my arm and immediately felt adrenaline rush through my body. I ripped out the needle and tossed it across the room, sitting up in bed and rubbing my arm as a slight lightheadedness rushed to my brain. I groaned and held my head with one hand, steadying myself with the other.

A short nurse came in and was instantly furious with me. She began yelling at me for pulling out the needle, stating that 'It was there to help me.' I turned to argue with her and dared her to try to put it back in again when Jared walked in and urged the nurse to leave. She smiled at him, glared at me, and left.

He eyed the needle on the floor, picked it up and noticed my eyes locking on it. Putting it down on a nearby tray, he stood in front of me, arms crossed as I dangled my feet off the edge of the bed, holding myself up and feeling some strength return to my body.

At first, I didn't meet his gaze; I was still upset. He had pushed me to my breaking point, and I felt a sense of betrayal. How could I trust someone like that?

"OK, OK so maybe I took it too far, but now we know another one of what I assume to be your many talents," he stated, grinning slightly, trying to make light of the situation.

"That was your plan? To figure out what I'd do when I snapped?" I looked at him disgusted, trying to mask my hurt.

I understood he had wanted me to snap so we could figure out what really happened to my comforter earlier this morning, but what he had said to make me 'lose it' was wrong. And I wasn't going to let him think any different. He'd hurt me, just like every other guy. He'd used me to get what he wanted, and all he wanted was a reaction.

He unfolded his arms as it dawned on him that I was truly distraught.

"Hey, listen, I didn't mean to…"

"To what? Hurt me? To do what everyone else has? Save it." I said putting my hand up as I got the courage to stand on my two feet, feeling myself return to normal with every breath.

"Alex, I was just trying to help you. A reaction was the only way I'd be able to figure out what happened and help."

"Well you got your reaction, and I don't need *your* help." I said as I grabbed my jacket off the hook and stalked out of the room.

Jared didn't follow me, and I was glad. I hadn't meant to open up to Jared that I had been hurt before, but he had cut me deeply and he needed to know I wasn't some science experiment.

I couldn't stay on campus. I just wanted to be anywhere but here. Without knowing the destination, I jumped in my car and started driving. I'd been lucky that Luther had brought it with him last night, so I could leave campus if I wanted to. I felt stupid and used, and worst of all I had let it happen. I had bit the bait hard, and now I was aware that not only was I a hybrid, but a fire invoking freak as well. It wasn't until some hours later when the gauge on my dashboard flashed its warning letting me know that I was dangerously low on gas that I decided to pull over at all. Ironically, I recognized an exit and took it; it was the same little town from the night before where we had gone to club Echo. I cursed under my breath, pulling into a gas station and got out of the vehicle to fill my tank.

My body sunk into the side of the SUV and I let my head fall back against the cold aluminum.

I thought I heard my name being shouted, but I ignored it and chalked it up to my emotions being all over the place.

"Alex! Hellloooo!" I snapped out of my stupor.

The short pink hair is what ended up catching my attention on the other side of the street as I watched the girl bounce towards me giddily.

"Sophie?"

My face must have looked dumbfounded to find her here, and she seemed to pick up on my distress immediately.

"Are you OK? I just sensed you were nearby and..." she said, her giddiness subsiding.

I guessed she was noticing the dried tear streaks down my face.

"I don't really know anymore," I said as I hung the pump up and closed my gas cap tightly, slamming the cover closed.

"Come on. You can tell me all about it," she said, taking my hand and shoving me in the car then getting in the driver's seat.

She parked the car in a parking lot down the street and hauled me into Echo. It looked different in the daytime, the dark blacked out windows and exterior seemed out of place in the daylight, even if it did sit by itself on the end of the street. I began to protest but realized how empty the club was, there were a few people here and there, but otherwise, the rhythmic hum of the music still played through the speakers.

"Why are we going in here?" I asked. It was definitely more private than talking anywhere else since no one would be able to hear what we were talking about above the music, but I wasn't sure it was going to help me forget about everything I wanted to. Nor was I sure I even wanted to talk about anything.

Sophie ignored my displeased tone and kept a hold of my hand till we reached a small booth tucked away in the corner, and after fetching several glasses of water from the bar, she slid in the seat across from me.

"What happened?" She didn't skip a beat with her interrogation.

"I don't think it's a good idea for me to talk about it. I'll only get upset." I took a drink of my water and tried to relax.

"So you're just going to bottle it up till you explode?" She was frowning.

I huffed at the word explode.

"Well, seeing as how I apparently actually *can* explode at any time now, I don't really know what else to do." I stated. I was frustrated as I slumped back in the booth.

She tilted her head.

"Did something happen with Jared?"

I scowled at the name for a moment.

"I'm just realizing that everyone's got some sort of an agenda, you know? I'm just the science experiment everyone's enjoying poking and prodding to get a reaction."

"You might want to ease up on him; he seems to really like you. He's just trying to help you figure out what your abilities are," she said taking a drink.

"Well, he's got a pretty stupid way of helping me. I'm going to end up really hurting him or someone else at this rate, or worse...and let's be real, he's only trying to further his agenda at Crest so he can graduate and become a guardian." I said as I swallowed the lump in my throat, remembering the feeling of the fire taking over.

I had completely lost control. Scratch that, I no longer had control of anything in my life and it was utterly terrifying.

"Alex. What happened?"

"I...I don't even know. I just lost control, of all of it... and then there was fire, I passed out after punching Jared, and that's all I know." The words came out scattered as I tried to remember how the fire manifested itself in my hands. The scary thing was that a part of me actually liked it. It felt strangely intoxicating having that much power.

I looked around making sure no one was near us again. The low and steady vibrations of two fallen angels beat near the back of the club, and I couldn't help but focus on them.

She cocked her head.

"You mean you can manifest fire!?" She squealed with excitement on the other side of the booth.

"Shhh!" I yelled back trying to silence her along with my secret.

"I don't know. I think so?"

"Sorry, sorry. But you do realize no one else can do that right? I mean, it's never been heard of.

I frowned back at her.

"Yeah, I'm beginning to get that. Wait, don't you even care that I punched Jared?" I asked with some amusement.

She waved her hand at me.

"He probably said something he shouldn't have. But you manipulating fire is way more important. It's incredible! You've got a gift girl, you should embrace it."

A gift? The words sounded foreign and preposterous.

"Yeah, well..." I said holding my hands up not knowing what else to say. Her comment had just hit me. *No one else can do that.*

I'd be lucky if I didn't kill anyone with this new *gift*. My thoughts drifted away as my ears pricked at the voices of the two fallen angels who had moved closer to where Sophie and I sat. Their voices were fuzzy and I struggled to make out what they were saying. Several words stuck out. *Deal,* and *Apollyon.* I shuddered at the name. Sophie's voice snapped me out of my concentration.

"Listen, Jared may not be the most eloquent with his words, but trust me when I say he can help you get control of this. Just try to ignore his methods and focus on the outcome. Imagine what you could do if you learned to control this," she said, staring intently before taking a sip of her water.

I stared back at her, silence overcoming both of us. Her words weighed on me.

"What's the deal with this place?" I asked changing the subject and feeling curiosity get the better of me, especially after overhearing the fallen angels.

"What do you mean?"

"I mean, you're telling me everyone always follows the rules around here? I don't buy it."

She shrugged.

"Those are the rules. I've always felt something was going on behind the scenes sometimes, at least at this particular club because it's so close to Crest, but rules are rules, and we don't have proof."

"What's with the 'rule' thing anyhow?"

"The Council implemented it a long time ago, things used to get pretty messy before that, and they say it helps us blend."

"And this *Council* makes all of the rules?"

She nodded.

"They basically try to keep some kind of order between us, fallen angels and humans, consider them judge, jury and executioner."

I nodded and chewed the inside of my lower lip, and decided to let it go, for now anyway.

"Thanks for making me talk," I said with a small smile.

I might not have wanted to talk about it, but Sophie was right, eventually, it would cause me to implode. It felt good being able to talk with someone, especially about what I was going through. There weren't too many people I could just talk to openly these days and although I didn't know Sophie very well, it was difficult *not to* open up around her. She seemed to have an extremely attentive, happy and genuine way about her that made her the perfect person to talk to.

She smiled.

"That's what friends do."

Sophie and I finished our waters at Echo and headed back to Crest. I closed the door to my dorm and locked it. It was a few seconds later as I downed a glass of water in the kitchen that a knock sounded on my door. It was an angel, and a twitch of my nerves told me it was someone I was expecting and not entirely ready to see yet. I strutted over to the door, and opened it with slightly more force than needed, not saying a word.

Jared straightened as I opened the door.

"Ehem. Hey. I just wanted to check in on you," he said shoving his hands deep in his pockets.

Sophie's words had reverberated in my head the entire ride home. As much as I was furious at Jared's methods, maybe he could help me control this. Sophie seemed to have a great deal of faith in him, as did Luther and Madam Eloa. We had to set some major ground rules, but I had to give him a shot as I was not going to make any headway on my own. I turned, leaving the door open and motioned for him to come inside. He was quiet for a moment while he shut the door, then he began to apologize.

"I'm sorry if I crossed the line, I was honestly just trying to help identify what you're capable of. That's why I was charged as being your trainer and honestly, I really want to help you with this. I realize now it may not have been the best way to do things, but I never meant to hurt you, I promise. I was just trying to help, Alex." His words felt sincere, and the glum look on his face told me he was genuinely sorry.

I shifted slightly, not expecting such an upfront apology, even if it was what I'd wanted.

"Do you really think you can help me control this?"

His sea green eyes bored straight into me, and he answered firmly.

"Yes, I can."

I chewed the inside of my lip.

"How?" I needed a straight up answer.

"Well...?" Jared scratched at the back of his head indicating the obvious.

I shook my head and stood, making it clear that we were not going down that road again.

"No. You don't provoke me, like ever. It's not safe...and I really don't need that on my conscious right now. That's the deal."

"Deal. You just need to do all of the work then."

I glanced back at him and away, nodding.

"Meet me, same time tomorrow morning at the gym, and we'll get started."

I nodded and stood by the door motioning for him to leave.

He walked out the door and turned around again.

"Does this mean we're...?"

Before he could finish, I slammed the door closed.

"Nope!"

I huffed, feeling Jared's vibration leave the building and turned to my little kitchen for a late-night snack. I settled on some crackers when I couldn't find anything else, remembering that I hadn't exactly stocked the kitchen with food yet. Sitting on the counter, I looked out the large bay window in the living room and wondered just what I was in for.

Chapter 10

It was a brisk, frosty morning and the glass inside the warm gym had fogged. I sat cross-legged on a rubber mat facing Jared as he instructed me on how to begin.

"Now, let's go over this again. Close your eyes. What do you feel right before the fire comes?" he asked, scooting himself closer in front of me. "You need to be clear so you can call that feeling forth anytime you want to use it."

I opened an eye warily keeping tabs on what he was doing.

"Close your eyes. Hands on your knees, palms up."

I shut them again and breathed out slowly.

"Right. Ummm... anger? I guess?" I said, crinkling my face.

"You need to be more specific. Describe it. What does it feel like?" he implored, stressing the word *feel*.

I quieted my mind and focused on the feelings I had been relentlessly fighting to keep at bay ever since my transformation took place.

"I can feel this boiling inside of me. It starts slowly at first... burning and scratching its way to the surface. And then, I don't know... it just takes over. It's almost unbearable. I'm not sure how else to describe it," I said, struggling to identify the feeling clearly and nervous I'd wake the sleeping beast inside of me by speaking of it.

He nodded and scratched his chin.

"Keep your eyes closed and focus on that feeling only. Let it come."

I huffed out a breath and closed my eyes, peeking once more before closing them completely. I tried to let go of all my other thoughts and any other emotions. They were like water slipping through my cupped hands. Everything completely cleared from my mind.

I focused on the heat in the pit of my stomach. I could feel it beckoning me to call it forth, similar to how my wings begged to be unfurled, but more violent and demanding. I granted it permission and was surprised when a blast of heat and fire shot from my hands towards Jared. He swiftly ducked out of the way just in time. I covered my mouth in horror.

"Sorry! I'm sorry! Maybe we shouldn't do this," I said, appalled at how quickly the heat inside me had boiled over and simmered back down again.

He laughed and shook it off, but I could tell he was a little nervous and more cautious. This time, sitting more to my left and with slightly more distance between us, he instructed me to repeat what I'd done.

"No, I'm fine. Now let it out again, but this time, try to focus on controlling it as you feel the energy. Make it do what you want. You're in control." He encouraged me to continue, remaining vigilant as I began another attempt.

I nodded and closed my eyes. *You're in control Alex; you can do this,* I said inwardly, giving myself a little pep talk before beginning. Once more I called forth the heat from within, and this time instead of just releasing it, I held it. When it wanted to burst through me and outward, I steadied it. My breathing was jagged as I felt it slide its way through my veins to my fingertips. It wanted to be in control, but it became surprisingly obedient when I fought back.

"You're doing great Alex, keep that feeling and control and when you're ready open your eyes slowly."

The heat swirled and spread through me quickly and more than once I fought against its need to explode forth. I began to control where it spread through my body, slowly directing its path from the center of my chest to my arms – from my arms to my wrists – and from my wrists to my hands. It was beyond difficult and took all of my focus, but I already sensed it would become easier as time went on and with more practice.

Continuing to focus on my hands intently, I opened my eyes and was startled to see them blazing a light blue and dark sapphire. I was dazed, mesmerized by the brilliant blue blaze, but it wasn't a vicious blaze. The blue glow which seemed to be part of me – not an external thing – kissed the tops of my fingertips and palms delicately. Just as smoothly as it came, I beckoned it to return within me again. I watched as the blue hues simmered beneath my cool skin once more, back through my arms and deep into my chest cavity where it lay dormant. Cool skin. Now that was something I didn't understand. I could not burn. The flame itself was harmless to me. When my eyes met Jared's again, his sea-green eyes gazed at me in wonder, and he smiled.

The next several weeks were spent focusing on my new talent. Fire. I could create it and manipulate it, and after throwing around discussions with Jared and Luther, the answer to why I had this ability when no one else did remained elusive.

We sat on the cool rubber gym mats, my mind wondering what this new talent meant for me. Jared seemed much more enthralled than I was with my unique ability and he had a hard time keeping a smirk off his face after he realized I wasn't going to accidentally incinerate him during our first 'fire training' session. I wasn't quite sure what to make of my new fire talent. I could see the perks, and I tried focusing on those more than anything, but I was worried about controlling it. It was yet another item that I would need to learn to work with, so I wouldn't hurt anyone. I was still just trying to deal with the pulls between the fallen angel side of me and angel side of me. Now we were about to add a blaze of fire to the mix too. There wasn't any turning back though. I would have to figure out how to control everything and move forward.

Days mashed together and turned into weeks and I had frequently spoken with Derek and Kate as well as my parents, giving them updates on my 'school work' and life at Crest, but, otherwise, I had stayed utterly focused on my training. Jared had helped me get this far, and I wasn't about to let any of my progress go. I was thrilled I was somehow learning to control this new part of me with more and more ease with each train-ing session we had. Ultimately, I was just thrilled I wouldn't be hiding in bathrooms anymore. I had even learned to create burning balls of fire and throw them, but after an incident where I had turned some of the mats into raging infernos, Jared decided to keep a fire extinguisher handy. Just in case. He had also tried to get me to train outside, but I enjoyed the privacy of our secret gym area; that and at least I couldn't create a forest fire if I accidentally made an error.

"Nervous today?" I asked playfully.

He snorted and smiled. "Let's see... I've got my fire extinguisher, fire blanket, water, and sage. Nope, I'm good."

I rolled my eyes and pushed him playfully at the mention of the sage. He laughed.

"I just can't believe you're not intimidated by me at least a little bit," I said truly surprised.

He shook his head. "Even if I was nervous, you're a good person, you've just been dealt a crappy hand of cards. Or at least that may be the way it seems right now. If there was any time I was nervous with you it was the night when I kissed you." he said looking back at me, his sea-green eyes searching for something.

"But, you kissed me back," he finished after a moment.

I half smiled at him, unsure of how to respond and looked down at my hands. We hadn't spoken about that night. Part of me was certain of how I felt around Jared. I felt OK to be myself, not only my semi-unstable hybrid self but the real Alex Constance. The other part of me knew I was not ready for anything serious. I was still trying to figure out how to for-get the first man I had ever fallen in love with – a man who had torn my heart apart ruthlessly. And over the past several weeks I had randomly been tormented with the face of that man, his touch and his captivating deadly eyes in my dreams.

I wasn't sure what triggered the dreams, but I had had more than a handful of them and was desperate to make them stop. Throwing myself at training seemed to be the best way to forget about it all. I had done my best to mask everything from Jared and everyone, but deep down I knew he knew. When he caught me staring off randomly into space, he seemed to instinctively know I was thinking of someone, but he could only guess who that someone was. Either way, I had grown more comfortable around Jared and even boldly fond of him. And although I wasn't willing to reveal my past, he seemed content with letting me be Alex Constance, part fallen angel, part angel, and he wasn't running from any part of me.

One day during our usual training, he said suddenly, "We should petition you for the field soon. Madam Eloa and Abraxos will be excited to hear of your improvements."

I smiled. "I hope."

Over the last few weeks, Jared had kicked up our training a notch. Well, quite a few notches maybe. My wings would furl and unfurl on command, I could fairly easily call forward fire and use it in defense if needed, and I had also honed my senses regarding the presence of other angels - fallen or otherwise. It was only very seldom that I 'lost control.'

Besides the enormous increase in my ability to handle my new skills, along with some grueling training, I had been able to tag along on several assignments, under Jared's watchful supervision of course. I sighed slightly as I thought back on those assignments. I had broken down a door so Jared and several other angels could restrain and interrogate a fallen angel. I hadn't participated too much in the interrogation itself, more or less watched and acted as back up, but I had been given great reviews from Jared and Abraxos after each assignment. That's what was so confusing. I had done everything they'd asked and somehow still did not make the cut to play key roles on field missions; even Jared had said it was impressive how quickly I had picked things up after we started training. I couldn't figure it out. I pushed the thought from my mind and silenced my phone after writing a quick message to Kate.

It was my birthday today. I officially was turning 18 years old, and I couldn't have wanted to avoid it more. It was just now six in the morning, and I knew calls were going to be steadily streaming in from my parents, and from Kate and Trey. In fact, Kate had already called me last night and was now feverishly texting me to know when we could hang out, and that I was absolutely celebrating today whether I liked it or not.

Kate: *'Happy Happy Birthday! Now get up. We r planning ur bday since u keep trying to avoid it'*

Me: *'In class. Call you in a few k.'*
Kate: *'It's your birthday! What on earth are you going to class for?!!!'*
Me: *'Lol call you later promise :)'*
Kate: *'Fine! But get your party pants on. Xoxo'*

I grinned and shook my head, tossing the phone down and looking back at Jared while stretching my arms out.

"So what's on the agenda today?"

He smirked at me.

"Wrestling."

"Like, WWE?" I asked, tilting my head.

He laughed. "No, like grappling."

"Whatever you say, Yoda, just watch those hands," I said rolling my eyes as a mischievous grin flashed across his face that made my pulse quicken.

Within the first 15 minutes, I learned that I had very poor grappling skills. Jared seemed to be enjoying himself as he restrained me in a full nelson, nearly lifting my feet off the mats as he drug me backward.

"You should really start trying to fight back or something," he said. "This is simply way too easy."

"Ugh! Gee thanks, trainer!" I yelled back at him as I wriggled and tried to squirm out of his grasp, only finding that each time I did, it became more futile as his grip tightened.

Then it hit me. He hadn't said anything about not using fire. I closed my eyes and beckoned the heat forward, but focused the energy on my head, arms, back, and legs. Just as quickly as I called it forward the heat radiated from my skin and Jared let out a yelp and cursed, releasing me completely. Triumphant, I turned to face him, showcasing a proud smile with my hand on my hips. He glared back at me.

"You're going to singe my eyebrows off one of these days, I swear."

I shrugged.

"Maybe you shouldn't play with fire then. Didn't your parents ever teach you that?" I taunted, delighted with myself.

He rolled his eyes and smiled.

"OK, so you're fine with grappling now, we'll check that off the list."

"Hmmm... did that, did that...rope climbing, sprints, and knife throwing then for today."

I groaned slightly. I hated running. It was funny really, not even my becoming a hybrid had changed that, even with having more stamina. I. Still. Hated. Running.

Freshman year I had decided to try out for the track team. That same day I realized I just was not meant to be a runner. The grace of the long-legged beauties that glided past me proved my awkwardness, and I decided to leave it at that.

Unenthusiastically, I followed Jared out of the gym. We ran along the giant perimeter of Crest over five times. Even being a hybrid, that was arduous. The sweat streaked down my arms leaving behind a wet shiny residue. My lungs burned with every rise and fall of my chest as I inhaled and exhaled, and my legs struggled to meet the demands of my brain, asking them to push forward again and again. By the time we ran back to the gym, all I could do was collapse on the mats inside our training room. I felt the cold metal of my water bottle which Jared had placed in my hand, and I greedily drank the entire thing. Sitting up, I gulped the icy liquid down and felt it travel through my throat to my stomach, leaving a refreshing cooling effect throughout my body wherever it went. He smiled at me.

"Ropes now. Come on."

I huffed my body up and went to the ropes. Starting with a jump off the mat I climbed up, one hand following the other, the bottoms of my feet pressed tightly together as I extended my legs. Up and up I went until I touched the ceiling, then back down, only to do this repeatedly for another ten times.

The muscles in my arms and legs seared and I wondered when the scorching feeling would stop. When we finally finished knife throwing, I was exhausted. Strangely, I relished the ache of my muscles and body after each training. It hurt, but it felt rewarding, and I felt stronger each time. If I couldn't earn my own grades, I could at least earn all of my training while I was here.

We gathered our things and pushed open the gym doors. I felt the refreshing cool air kiss my skin, causing my nerves to tighten and relax reflexively. That was when I stopped in my tracks.

"Kate?" I said surprised.

"Ahhh! There you are! Oh my God! They told me you were here so I...

so *this*... is your class? Now I understand," she said eying Jared up and down with approval.

Jared let out a chuckle, and my cheeks flushed.

"Um, what are you doing here?" I asked politely, surprised to see her.

She put her hands on her hips and looked at me hotly, bewildered at my question.

"Do you really think your best friend would let you spend your birthday all alone and in classes for that matter?"

"It's your birthday?" Jared said looking from her to me.

"Uh..."

"Yes! It's her birthday! This 18-year-old is going out tonight! I already talked to Trey and Sophie, who's super cute by the way. I dig the hair. Anyways, they're going with us – you're invited too..." she nodded toward Jared, "along with any friends you may have."

"You never mentioned anything." Jared turned to face me, still hung up on the fact that it was my birthday.

I scrunched my face and relaxed it again.

"Yeah, I was kind of hoping to forget it.

Kate took my hand and began to lead me away from Jared. He didn't say anything as we walked away, but when I looked back at him briefly, his brows were furrowed, which usually meant he didn't like what he had heard or was in deep thought.

"Oh my God! You didn't tell me you had class with Super McHottie Hot Pants!" she whispered, rolling her eyeballs back towards Jared as we rounded the corner on the concrete pathway.

"Please do *not* call him that, and yes, we are just friends. That is all," I said definitively.

She laughed.

"So, what's his name then, because I want to call him McHottie Hot Pants."

"Jared."

"That's hot."

"Kate! Focus here!"

"Right, sorry. I'm just saying. *That's* who you've been hanging out with! And you didn't say a word nor snatch it up?"

"No, there was definitely no snatching."

"Well, you're giving me all of the details about this little *friendship* over lunch. I'm parked over there," she said pointing towards the parking lot.

"I should really shower first..."

"No. I'm starving. Come on... oh God. Yep, you're showering first." She covered her nose as she fanned my arm away from her face.

I laughed.

"Thank you."

After getting ready, Kate and I decided to meet my mom for lunch and made our way towards the city.

We pulled into a familiar Chinese restaurant my parents had been taking me to since I was just a girl. I loved the memories it brought back with my family every time we went there. My grandma fishing out the tiny corn bits from her egg drop soup and slipping them into mine because she knew they were my favorite. Derek and I having chopstick wars; Mom and Dad together; the happy, stress-free times of my life where I was utterly naive and ignorant of the curveball life would throw my way one day.

My mom waved to us from a corner booth and we slid in across from her after embracing.

"Of all the places you want to eat on your birthday," Mom said smiling and shaking her head slightly.

"I like it here." I smiled back at her.

"So, who's this new boyfriend I'm hearing so much about?" she asked, grinning and nonchalantly taking a sip of her water.

"What boyfriend? Kate!" I said giving her a slight shove and rolling my eyes at the ridiculous statement.

"What?!" Kate yelled back grinning with my mom.

"OK, so I may have texted your mom when you were in the shower, but it's just because we care," she said innocently.

"So?" Kate pressed after the waiter took our order and I hadn't responded.

"There's not much to say. We have class together, and he happens to be male."

Kate rolled her eyes in disbelief.

111

"A Super McHottie Hot Pants male."

My mom laughed.

"Do you like him?" My mom looked back at me.

"He's... annoying, sure." I replied.

"Denial," Kate chirped.

"Just make sure you give yourself some time to... heal... from things. Listen to your gut," Mom said, trying to delicately touch on what had happened with Nathaniel and me without bringing it up.

I had never told anyone what had really happened between Nathaniel and me. Especially the recording Luther had had me listen to. I would take it to my grave. But the way everyone tentatively brought certain topics up indicated that I was not as crafty as I thought and no matter how hard I tried to hide it, they knew I was sad since he'd gone.

Once again, I tried to change the subject from Nathaniel. It seemed to be the only way I've ever been able to keep moving forward since hearing that recording.

"My gut tells me to eat this sesame chicken and to have no regrets," I said as the waiter placed three steaming plates on our table. They were always inhumanly quick with orders here.

They both chuckled.

"What are your plans for your birthday?"

"Trey, his new girlfriend, McHottie Hot Pants and all of us are going to a club up by Crest later, but getting this girl, a dress is first on the agenda," Kate said, giddy with the thought of the activities to follow.

"I figured you'd need something like that. This is from your dad and me," Mom said smiling and handing me a shirt sized, rectangular box.

I gave her that 'you know you didn't have to' look and opened it.

Inside, I moved the fragile folds of white tissue paper to reveal a little black dress. My fingers pulled the dress delicately out of the box to reveal it completely. It had a halter neckline, fitted waist that made the bottom of the dress flare out slightly, with an open back and a bow that would daintily rest above my lower back when it was on. It was simple, elegant and perfect. I gleamed back at my mom.

"I love it. Thank you!" I exclaimed, exiting the booth to hug her.

"Now you've got a little black dress for any occasion," she said, smiling at my happiness.

"That's perfect! Now you just have to help me find a dress, and we're set!" Kate squeaked in excitement.

After stopping by my dad's work and visiting for a while, we made our way to the mall, and the search began. Three hours later, after the dressing room resembled more of a hamper than an actual dressing room, Kate finally found a bright teal A-line dress that came to the knees and had just enough bling for her on the waist. Darkness had already blanketed everything around us as we curved our way through the canyons back to Crest to get ready. I felt anxious, and I wasn't sure why. Trying to let loose a little, Kate and I rolled all the windows down and blared some tunes. I blocked all of my emotions out. I had to remember I wasn't in the company of Jared now and if my wings exploded in the car on the way back, well, let's just say 'all hell would break loose.' Humming along with song after song, we finally made it back to Crest; some of my anxiety had dissipated, but much of it continued to linger.

I slipped into the soft little black dress and found it hugged my body perfectly. Leave it to my mother to know the exact dress that would make me feel *pretty* on my birthday. I smiled, grateful that I was able to see her today and feeling slightly guilty. I felt how alone she was each time I saw her. It wasn't something she consciously made me feel, but nevertheless I picked up on it. Like a desperate boat in a storm searching for a lighthouse to lead it safely home. I wished there was something I could say to comfort her, but I knew there was nothing that could be said to make it better or easier.

It may have been easy to try and pick sides between my parents at who I thought was justified, or to just be mad at my dad because he had begun dating another woman, but deep down I knew it was somehow never going to work between my parents. The thought had been burrowing inside me for quite some time, and only now was I beginning to feel its ruthless truthfulness. But hope made me shy from the thought once more and push it from my mind. I would hope until that hope had fully disintegrated.

I ruffled my hair slightly giving it some volume, but aside from that, I let it be. Dabbing a smidge of blush on my cheeks, and putting on some mascara, I finished off my makeup with some striking dark matte red lipstick. Kate had also finished getting ready and we couldn't help but smile at one another.

A knock sounded on the door followed by some voices and Kate bounded towards it, quickly opening it for everyone.

"Is the birthday girl ready yet?" Trey asked, smiling on the other side of the door.

"Oh, she's ready," Kate said, smiling.

Chapter 11

I was laughing so hard I could hardly stand straight. Jared led me past the throngs of bodies back towards our booth where Trey sat. Sophie and Kate continued to dance. He watched them from a distance and smiled as we sat down.

"It's so good to see you smile," Trey said as Jared helped me into the booth and then went to refill everyone's drinks.

"I smile... don't I?" I asked, a bit taken aback by his comment and slightly offended as the giggles subsided.

"You haven't in a while, but I'm glad you are now." He looked back towards Sophie and Kate.

"How are you doing at Crest? Do you like it?" I asked suddenly, wondering if there was something that was bothering him.

He shrugged his shoulders before looking back at me.

"My parents think it's good for me so far. Hey, you'd tell me if something was ever wrong, right? Like you know you can always tell me anything." He changed the subject suddenly and leaned forward across the table, startling me with his strange behavior.

Something in his eyes seemed wrong like he was afraid.

"Yeah... Trey are you OK? Is something wrong?" I asked leaning in towards him.

He exaggerated his nod and took a giant swig of beer.

"Just some things I heard; anyways, parents are really on my case." He blew off my question as Jared returned with a tray holding an assortment of waters and drinks.

My mind swirled for a moment. I tried to understand what could be bothering him. And considering he was not of the angel variety, I assumed it had nothing to do with that. I had had a few beers and found myself quite... buzzed to say the least. Apparently, my distaste for beer dissipated quickly after several of them. We had been there for at least three or four hours at this point. Kate and everyone had made it a point to make me have 'a good time.' Well, they accomplished their mission all right; I was definitely buzzed.

A surge of emotions was building inside me. Sophie and Kate boogied their way back to the booth.

"Come dance with us!" they screeched.

"I'll go!" I exclaimed, never hesitating and desperately wanting to get out of my own head somehow.

They grabbed my hands helping me out of the booth, and we jostled our way into the crowd of shifting bodies.

I danced along with the beat, swaying my hips and closing my eyes, feeling the rhythm when I felt a hand wrap around my waist and draw me closer. The vibration the stranger gave off was low, and something in my state of mind enticed me to move along with it. It was only when the song changed that I opened them and found a dark pair of eyes staring back.

I stopped dancing and pushed his hand away. The man grinned and reached for me again, but as I pulled away the stranger's face darkened. I backed into a rigid body and realized it was Jared's. His face was emotionless, but his fists belied his thoughts. They clenched and unclenched as the stranger laughed and disappeared into the crowd.

"You shouldn't dance with *them*. It's dangerous," he said, calming down, but trying to instill the severity of what I had done.

I could feel the room spin slightly and felt sick, and confused. It was just one dance right? And wasn't I technically one of *them*? I thought referring back to the fallen angel.

"I don't know what happened. I just..." But I couldn't finish my sentence. I knew why it had felt good to dance with that stranger. I'd felt Nathaniel the entire time I'd danced, and the fallen angel side of me relished in it. I felt like screaming at myself; I still loved him. The guy who had ripped my heart out! How pathetic was I?

"I want to go home," I said, turning back to Jared who seemed somewhat sympathetic.

He nodded and we gathered everyone, but not before I chugged the rest of Kate, Trey and Jared's beers. My goal? To forget about Nathaniel. This was my day, and he would not have the satisfaction of ruining it. I was going to have 'a good time.'

"Easy. I gotcha," Jared said, steadying me as we crossed the parking lot.

"I can get drunk! Me!" I yelled excitedly, pointing at myself.

He shook his head smiling, and everyone laughed.

"Sophie knows!" I yelled over my shoulder to her as she giggled.

"Of course she can, she practically guzzled an entire keg to herself five minutes before leaving," said Trey.

A hybrid could get drunk; I could mark that off on my list of things learned about this new me. Jared locked me into my seat and got in the driver's side as the others packed into the back. I blasted the music and sang and danced in my seat with the girls. Trey and Jared just laughed. My buzz slowly rose into an overly drunk state over the ride home, and I felt myself slip off into a dreamless state. Exactly what I was hoping for.

A click sounded, and I felt someone's hands slide underneath me and lift me out of the leather seat. My eyes rolled opened slowly as my head rested on the stranger's shoulder. I struggled to give my body orders and even more so for my body to obey those orders.

"Where's everyone?" I stammered trying to configure my surroundings.

"In their dorms, don't worry they're fine. I don't think you should be left alone though, you're a little drunk" he said, and I could tell a grin was on his lips as he said it.

I grunted as my eyes forced themselves closed without my permission.

"Don't you get any ideals...," I said suddenly as my brain finally registered what he had said to me.

He chuckled.

"I think you mean ideas. But, yes, I won't," he replied, but his tone was serious as I felt us ascend the stairs.

"Mmm, you smell like...vanilla...and rain..." Blackness took me, and I welcomed the deep sleep.

It wasn't a sound that woke me, but a smell. Warm vanilla and rain. I stretched out, gathering a pillow and smashing it under my face. My body felt hot, and I began to kick the covers away from my legs beckoning the cool air in the room to kiss the tops of them.

"Whoa, don't kick too much, you're still in a dress...or do." The male voice rocketed me out of my slumber. My eyes shot open, and I sat up quickly.

Jared sat in a desk chair on the other side of the room drinking what I presumed to be coffee, and waved at me, grinning slightly at my bewildered expression. My palm met my forehead as a giant head rush and pounding headache overwhelmed me. Once the head rush had passed, I looked down at myself and realized I was definitely still wearing the same little black dress from the night before, but it had scantily ridden up in my vigorous sleep. Embarrassed, my cheeks flushed bright red as I snatched the comforter and drew it to my chest quickly.

"You slept well," he chuckled, taking another sip of his coffee. "I made a pot. Figured you could use some."

My mind raced wildly. I ignored his words and struggled to reclaim what had happened the night before. Had I...? No! No! No! No! I wouldn't have...would I? Panic shot through my body as he grabbed and filled a new cup for me and brought it back. I took the outstretched coffee, my hands shaking slightly. I couldn't ask anymore.

"What...um...happened last night, Jared?" I said locking eyes with his sea-green orbs.

"You mean, why are you in my bed? You don't remember do you?" He leaned towards me in the desk chair, but something shined with amusement behind his eyes.

My heartbeat raced.

"Yeah, that crossed my mind, and uh, no...no, not really." I had honestly no clue what had happened. "The last thing I remember is leaving the club. I don't even remember getting back into the car." A giant black hole had stolen the rest of my memory. This is why people don't drink. And it sure as hell is going to be why I'll never drink again.

He smiled then.

"You can calm down, nothing happened. I let you sleep in my bed since I couldn't trust that you'd be OK by yourself last night. I took the chair." He smiled and took a sip of his coffee.

"Right. Um...thanks?" I said feeling my cheeks flush even more red at the fact that I had presumed he and I... yep, I would also take that to my grave. What was wrong with me!? I couldn't help but feel extremely vulnerable and exposed in his bed, so I desperately tried to just wrap my head around what else had happened last night.

"Does this mean my birthday was a 'good time' then?" I asked half-heartedly, trying to focus on anything but my current embarrassment.

He smiled. "I think everyone had fun, you especially. You're quite the singer. Now *that* wasn't in your file, and neither was your birthday surprisingly. I found out quite a few things about you last night." He chuckled.

Oh. My. God. My mouth hung open as my embarrassment skyrocketed.

"You gave Beyoncé a run for her money I think." He refilled his cup of coffee and hummed the tune I had apparently sang last night.

I fell back in the bed and pulled the sheets over my head.

"I think I could just die."

He laughed so hard I could picture his back arching.

"It's a catchy tune at least," he said leaning against the counter and looking back at me.

I sat up again and tossed my legs over the side of the bed. My wild hair fell to one side of my face.

"OK then! I'm going to go now," I said, searching for my shoes unsuccessfully, trying to flee.

He continued to watch me for several minutes as I desperately searched, his eyes burning hot into my back with amusement.

"Ehem." The shoes daintily dangled from his finger as he held them outstretched towards me, a permanent smirk plastered to his face.

I grabbed the shoes from his hands and avoided all eye contact. I literally was the most embarrassed I had ever been. I couldn't suppress my trai-torous cheeks where I could feel blood compacting and burning two red hot holes in my face, nor could I hide the clamminess of my hands and general frantic awkwardness.

"Yep! OK then!" I said as I snatched the shoes from his fingers and fled for the door.

"OK then." He chuckled as I left.

I rushed inside my dorm and slammed the door shut, dead-bolting it. Bracing my body against the door for a moment, I closed my eyes and caught my breath.

"Alex? Geez, could you be any louder?" Kate said rolling out of bed and stumbling to the kitchen to turn on the coffee pot.

She dumped a few things out of the cabinets until she found a bottle of ibuprofen, then popped the top and downed a few tablets like they were skittles as she pulled up a chair and sat.

"You're still in your dress...?" I could tell an idea crept into her brain, and I stopped her from even speaking the embarrassing words out loud.

"No! We didn't. Nothing like that... he slept in the chair and gave me his bed."

She giggled a little.

"Quite chivalrous. I have to say I'm a little-shocked *nothing* happened," she said smiling.

The coffee maker clicked indicating it was ready to consume and I hopped up to pour us each a cup.

"Was I singing Beyoncé last night?" I asked wide-eyed, handing her a cup.

Kate nearly spit it at me, before swallowing her first sip and bursting out laughing.

"Yes! I almost forgot about that!"

"Oh my God," I said gulping down some coffee as I tried to hide my shame.

We giggled for some time, exchanging stories of the night until Kate announced she had to go home and get some chores done before her parents got home.

I walked her out and headed for the barn to take Ajax out for a ride.

The gravel outside the barn crunched under my boots as I slid the wide steel doors open. I hadn't bothered to put a saddle on him today, only a bridle. I easily jumped up and swung my leg over Ajax's bare back and headed for the outskirts of the school grounds.

The padding of Ajax's hooves on the grass matched with the silent atmosphere around me was relaxing, and I couldn't help but let my thoughts trail. I felt my wings roughly push against the skin on my shoulder blades, begging to be let out. I breathed in deeply and released them.

"You should be more wary about letting your wings unfurl." Luther's voice made Ajax rear and I scolded myself for not feeling his vibrations sooner.

"Luther. Holy crap, you scared me." Ajax snorted loudly, and I patted his neck.

Luther stepped out of the shadows on the other side of the iron fence that bordered the perimeter of Crest's property. His face was one of deep thought, as it always was, but concern seemed to be etched in the creases now. He looked as if he hadn't slept in a while.

"What news do you have for me today?" I asked him.

"You should be more careful about your wings; they draw... attention." His expression had not softened yet, and I felt a slight shiver grip its way up my spine. Something was wrong.

"Yeah, sorry... I guess I just wasn't thinking. Is everything OK?" I was concerned. His appearance out here made me think there was more than just my wings on his mind.

It was unlike Luther to be this serious. Usually, he pretended everything was fine so as not to upset or stress anyone out. This was unusual for his character. I watched as he shifted slightly and looked down at his feet then returned to meet my gaze. His posture had softened, but his gaze still held something darker that I couldn't understand.

"Been a long week. I'm sorry I missed your birthday." He sounded genuinely regretful. "I just came to check in on you. And to tell you to be careful. There's been a lot of activity around lately, on both sides."

"It's OK. What sort of activity? I thought you said things were quiet?"

"It's unclear right now, but there's suddenly been lots of talk about you."

I nodded. "Like what?"

"Just keep an eye out. Nothing's clear yet. It was good to see you, Alex," he said and turned to leave.

"Yeah, you too..." My voice trailed off. "I'll see you soon?" I shouted to him. He nodded and disappeared into the woods.

I couldn't help but feel slightly shaken from my encounter with Luther. Something was definitely bugging him, and if I had to guess, it was more than everyone merely talking about me. A chill sent goosebumps across my arms. I turned Ajax back towards the barn and retracted my wings. I remembered the figure in the ally. *You're being lied to.*

Outside of Ajax's stall, I was surprised to see Jared sitting on a bench across from us. He jumped up at my presence and smiled. A plain white box was cradled between his hands.

"You ran off so quickly this morning I didn't have a chance to give you your present. You OK?" he said, handing me the box and noticing my shakiness.

"No, I'm fine. You got me a present?" I asked letting the leather reins slip from my fingertips as I took the outstretched present and stared at it for a moment.

He nodded.

"Had I known it was your birthday I would have had a little more time to plan, but..." He trailed off slightly and watched me open it.

I peeled the small strip of tape off the front of the box and lifted the lid. Inside lay a silver necklace with folded wings, and in the center of the wings was a small purple crystal.

I was thrown by the beauty of the necklace and even more thrown by the fact that Jared had bought the necklace for me.

"A friend of mine hand-makes jewelry here... thought it was fitting," he said when I didn't respond.

"It's gorgeous... I... uh... thank you." I looked back at him and then at the necklace. I was floored he had thought of me to this extent, and I was at a loss for words.

"Help me put it on?" I said, pulling my hair to one side.

He moved towards me without hesitating and clasped the necklace around my neck. I was surprised to find the metal folded wings felt warm as they delicately rested on the top of my chest bone. Instinctively, I touched the pendant.

"You OK? You like it?" he asked, sensing something else was on my mind. I put Ajax in his stall.

"I love it; it's not that... just... I think last night is catching up with me is all." I was attempting to brush off his question. I was unsure about how much I should reveal about anyone – any other angel – in my new circle of 'friends.' I trusted Jared and the whole school thing. The people there. So far, at least. I just didn't think it was time to talk about Luther's visit.

"I know you're not tired; look, if it's about '*that guy*,' I get it. I just hope I was able to give you something he couldn't," he said, making sure to put his hand up and finish before I could object to what he was saying.

His assumption wasn't far off, but another part of me felt the gift was too... intimate. How much did he really know about me? How much information was he given and by whom? I didn't know how to define our relationship. I felt somehow screwed up from my first real '*fake*' relationship, and I wasn't the only one who knew that. I felt guilty that I couldn't just accept his gift, but it was difficult to accept.

My feelings for Nathaniel continued to dissolve whatever happiness I encountered. Somehow, they continued to pry their way into my mind through dreams, feelings, urges, and whatever else they could grab a hold of. And they all revolved around Nathaniel.

A moment of silence filled the air as I looked back at Jared. He seemed undeterred, and instead of being angry, he seemed worried. As if he were trying to decipher just what I was thinking and feeling.

"Thank you for the gift," I said, smiling slightly and looking into his sea-green eyes as my hand hovered over the wings.

He smiled.

"It looks good on you."

And with that, he turned and left the barn.

Chapter 12

"Where are you at with the hybrid?" the man cloaked in darkness asked, irritated by their meeting.

"Things are progressing. She's close to being under our control. It takes time though," the man in the silver suit replied brushing his hands over his pants.

"We don't have time! We need things to progress now!" The man slammed his fist on the desk, showing his face in the glimmer of light from the nearby lamp. "You know who we made a deal with, either we deliver, or..."

The silver-suited man put his hand up.

"You don't need to tell me something I already know. It'll be done," he said before exiting.

"Good. *Partner*."

Although nothing had yet come of Luther's warning regarding the flurry of new 'activity,' his visits had become slightly more sparse over the next few weeks I gathered whatever was going on was taking up much of his time.

He was good at monitoring things. It was necessary. More necessary than I realized at the time, but he knew *constant vigilance was the only way to survive*. Had he said that? Or was this profound thought something that came to me through one of my new powers? Nevertheless, it had me watching my back a little more wherever I went, and these days, usually Jared accompanied me almost everywhere.

He and I had gotten much closer in that time as well. I felt more relaxed around him now, and I didn't feel so strange or conflicted wearing the necklace he'd given me for my birthday.

The fallen angel side of me still fought the day to day life surrounded by angels. Some days the pull to be off campus was so powerful I couldn't fight it. I had to get away, whether it was for a few hours or all day. I'd visit my parents or Kate or simply just be alone for a while. Other days, I felt safer and more at home on campus than out in the streets. Strange that I should consider the regular world – what used to be my 'normal' – as some sinister place and not the other way around.

No other angel on campus other than Sophie had gotten used to me up to this point. It always seemed as though they sort of tolerated my presence, but wouldn't interact with me more than glances here and there. Had they been briefed to not interact with me? I wondered. I didn't know if they were able to pick up my vibe correctly. I wasn't sure how it all worked yet, but surely they knew I was a half-breed and a hybrid. I guess in angel world, this wasn't exactly a 'winning' hand. These were questions I was surely going to find answers to, but for now, I was apparently 'off limits,' and they were wary.

I was proficient at blowing it off, however, trying not to notice it, but some days were more difficult than others. *Why?* I wondered.

Maybe it was just typical – expected – teenage behavior. I just wasn't used to this rigorous and confining lifestyle. And all the possible stress and emotional distress that goes along with being a teen coupled with... whatever I am.

Soon the rumors about my new abilities began to spread like a wildfire. Before I knew it, pretty much every angel and fallen angel on – and off – campus had found out. It seemed though, for the moment at least, that I had nothing to worry about.

The one thing that had changed lately was that I hadn't seen very much of Trey. When I first arrived over four weeks ago, he'd been his usual self, but now he seemed more and more distant each time I saw him. I don't even know if he's been around the campus much. When I did run into him, it seemed there was always an excuse for why he couldn't talk or hang out, and it always had to do with his family's business. I had to admit it irked me a little bit. It seemed like an obvious excuse to use if he didn't want to hang out anymore, but it all had happened so quickly since that night on my birthday, just a few weeks ago, that I knew something wasn't right.

He seemed to be avoiding me, and I was bound and determined to corner him one of these days and find out why, when he was on campus that is.

When I heard from anyone it was generally Sophie; she told me he'd been on and off campus quite frequently with his parents; she suggested I call his parents – or my own – to see what I could find out.

Mom, Dad, and Kate had come to visit me as well and I was planning on returning home for a while soon. I missed everyone deeply and only wished there was a way for me to explain to them what was happening with me. Unfortunately, it went against everything I'd been told to do by angels and fallen angels. I could not, under any circumstances, let on what I was to anyone.

My back hit the gym mat, and before Jared could follow up with a strike, I gripped his arm and flung him onto the mat with me. He grunted causing me to smile. We tangled into a mass on the floor, each of us attempting to get the better of the other through grappling. Back and forth we went, I'd had him in the beginning of a choke hold, but before I could lock my arm and seal the deal, he turned and unfurled his wings throwing my body back from his. I regained my awareness and was about to counter, but he already had me trapped in his death grip. My arms were pinned to my sides as his wings wrapped around us holding me firmly. I looked up at him shaking my head.

"I could easily get out of this you know." I said letting a grin slide its way onto my lips.

"Hey..." he began warily. "We agreed, no fire. You need to learn without it just as much as with it."

I rolled my eyes.

My body was pressed so tightly against his I thought I might suffocate if he squeezed any tighter.

"OK fine, you win this one," I said giving up after wriggling didn't seem to be working.

He smiled triumphantly at his success and released me.

Grabbing a drink of my water, I zoned off for a moment before Jared snapped me out of my thoughts.

"You gave up pretty easy today. I'm surprised."

I shrugged. "You win some you lose some, right?" I said, not really phased by it.

He nodded throwing his jeans in his gym bag.

I pulled my hair tie out, letting my hair fall and rubbed the side of my neck.

"Hey, you want to go off campus for a bit? I'm supposed to go meet with someone to ask them a few questions. Want to come?"

His bag was draped over his right shoulder as he waited for my response.

Today was one of those days I didn't want to be on campus, the fallen angel part of me practically screamed internally when he asked.

"Yeah sure. Wait, are you on assignment?"

He smiled.

I slapped his shoulder as a smile crept over my face.

"Am I allowed to go on this one, I mean, have I been cleared?" I asked excitedly.

I'd been asking Madam Eloa and Abraxos as well as having Jared ask if I could attend assignments now. Jared had recommended me for an assignment awhile back but I hadn't heard anything at this point and I was beginning to grow bored.

"Already cleared it with Abraxos, He asked for me to take you."

"Yes! Who are we meeting? Where?"

"Easy there turbo, go shower and I'll fill you in on the way."

I bolted for the locker room, desperate to actually be of some use and see some action, if there was any action that is.

I felt Jared enter the locker room and sit on a bench around the corner from the showers after I had stripped down and gotten in.

"Who are you meeting with?" I yelled filling my hand with shampoo and lathering my hair.

"He's a fallen angel that we've been trying to catch up with for quite a while now; we're just supposed to ask him some questions is all."

I heard a locker door close and felt him moving closer towards me. I stiffened slightly.

"What are you doing?" I asked getting uncomfortable as his vibration rounded the corner.

"Relax, Alex, I need to shower, too," he said and I could feel the smile on his face knowing he'd made me uncomfortable.

The shower next to me turned on and I went back to conditioning my hair, but my pulse had quickened.

His shower turned off before mine and I heard him step out and rifle through his gym bag.

Wrapping the towel around me tightly I made my way around the corner to my locker, past Jared who had already thrown his jeans on and was drying his hair with his towel. I ignored his perfectly toned body and kept walking.

"Is there anything I should know beforehand? Any tips?" I asked throwing a black V-neck long sleeve on with a jacket and jeans.

"You dressed?"

"Yep," I said, glancing up at him rounding the corner as I put my shoes on.

"Nothing too much really, just follow my lead, I'll ask him some questions and we can let him go. Otherwise, that's about it. You'll do fine rookie, don't worry," he said winking, appraising my outfit.

We drove to a tiny town I hadn't ever heard of some hours from Crest and made small talk on the way there to pass the time. He seemed to be ever curious about my past though and kept trying to sneak in personal questions in hopes of getting an answer. Specifically, about Nathaniel and what had happened to make me turn into what I was. I deflected them like a shield or gave vague answers, not wanting to delve into my past, particularly my past with Nathaniel. It was over and I was doing better without the mention of him. Or at least that's what I kept telling myself. Nevertheless, it seemed to be working for the time being. Jared dropped it, but I could tell he still wanted the full story.

We reached our destination and pulled into a parking spot that over-looked a shanty bar with a flickering neon sign out front that read, 'OPEN - BUD LIGHT SPECIALS'.

Jared's face scrunched in concern.

"What is it?" I asked, scanning for vibrations, and feeling several extremely faint vibrations inside the bar, but otherwise nothing.

"I don't know, something doesn't feel right. Seems really quiet."

"Isn't that a good thing?"

He didn't respond and we got out of the car and made our way across the gravel street to the bar.

The entryway was dark as the door swung shut behind us. Music from a jukebox sounded but skipped and kept restarting over and over again, only reaching the first verse of the song each time.

Jared pushed me behind him and the hairs on my neck stood on end when I smelled it. A coppery sweet smell filled my nostrils, overwhelming my senses. Blood. Rounding the corner we stood frozen, witnessing the silent massacre of bodies that lay strewn about the bar. Humans, the bar tender, a waitress - everyone that had been in the bar was dead. The majority of them had been shot. The two low vibrations I'd felt outside had dwindled to one and I walked around the bodies towards it, my hand to my nose trying my best to keep my composure and keep the smell of the dead out.

Strewn out in a booth was a charcoal colored man. His hands shook as they tried their best to cover the huge cavern that had been made in his chest from shotgun rounds. The marks on his face shook my memory. It was the same man from the club that night who had warned me. I rushed to the man and grabbed a nearby towel trying to apply pressure to the wounds.

"Jared! Here!" Jared bolted to me and appraised the man, touching my wrists after a moment.

"Alex..." he began, but didn't continue.

I looked back at him for help, knowing what he was getting at. He just shook his head.

"He's right." The man coughed, causing a mouthful of blood to spill onto his chin.

130

"It's too late for me, but you..." He choked.

"Who did this?!" I yelled, turning back to Jared for answers and realizing from his face that he had none.

"Watch...yourself A-Alex." His breathing was barely there and I pressed the wound more trying to stop the continuous flow of blood.

"Watch myself? Watch myself from what? From who?!" I desperately questioned trying to make out who had done this to him and what he was trying to say.

"There... there are traitors." His last words barely came out a whisper and I wasn't sure if I had heard him correctly.

We were silent for a moment as I stared at the man and the blood-soaked towels and my blood covered hands.

Jared eventually pulled me away and back to the car. Explaining that we needed to leave in case whoever had done this came back. My mouth hung open in shock and when I didn't start moving, Jared wrapped an arm around me and quickly escorted me back to the car. He peeled back out onto the highway and began dialing someone.

I couldn't get the man's face out of my head, nor could I forget the gory images replaying in my mind. The dreadful cavern that had torn through his gut leaving him and the booth in which he lay saturated in crimson. I had never even known the strangers name, but he had given me two warnings now. The first, that I was being lied to, and that there were traitors, but what and who was he referring to? And how did he know me by name?

I couldn't ease my tension or slow my pulse as my mind raced through all the possible suspects. Who was he talking about? Who was lying to me? Was it Apollyon still? Uvall? Were they somehow still involved in all of this and after me? What traitors was he talking about? I didn't even know which *side* he was referring to.

Jared interrupted my thoughts as he snapped his phone shut.

"The man in the booth is who I was sent to speak with. He had information on some recent fallen angels. I don't know what happened, but clearly someone got to him before he could tell us anything."

"Did he say which fallen angels?" I asked hopeful we might have something to go on.

"No."

It was silent on our way back to Crest, but I couldn't shake the eerie feeling that was causing my stomach to churn in discomfort. I wasn't sure why either, but I neglected to tell Jared that the man had shown up at the club before and warned me. Something just told me to wait and I heeded it. Besides, it wouldn't do any good if I couldn't figure out what it all meant and who was behind everything.

Chapter 13

The rain hit the ground around me creating a rhythmic 'shhhhshhhhh' sound. I walked quickly along the familiar path I had taken since I had first come to Crest, tucking myself further inside my jacket. I liked the rain and wouldn't have minded getting wet so much had it not been for an unexpected call I received from Jared this morning asking me to meet him in the Atrium.

My pulse raced and I wondered if my training was over yet. Was I ready for the actual field? I sure felt ready mentally and physically and I was honestly in need of a challenge. Six days had passed since the bar massacre and I needed to get off campus so I could further investigate what I only imagined certain fallen angels were up to.

Abraxos had apparently ordered Jared to be hawk-like after we told him what the man in the booth had said, and although I enjoyed his company, I couldn't go anywhere without him knowing. I kept my fingers crossed as I reached for the Atrium building doors and stepped inside. The receptionist waved me through and pointed towards Madam Eloa's glass doors.

I knocked once before entering and found Eloa, Abraxos and Jared already seated inside. The room got quiet as I entered and sat beside Jared. He smiled noticing the necklace hanging from my neck.

"You wanted to see me?"

Eloa smiled politely and motioned towards Jared.

"Jared's been telling us good things about your progression lately. He seems to think that you're ready for the field now, especially since you've proved yourself on the test assignments," she stated.

Abraxos eyed me, waiting for my response.

"I'd have to agree with him. I need to be challenged and no offense, but I can only be challenged so much in a gym and on test assignments," I stated confidently.

It was true. I needed this and wanted it more than anything. I wanted to prove to myself and to everyone that I was ready for bigger things. That, and I was nowhere nearer piecing together the bar massacre that had recently occurred. I'd been able to tag along on several small assignments to try to collect more information or witnesses, anything really that could give us a clue as to who murdered those poor people and which fallen angels might be involved, but our trail was as dry as a desert. No leads, no witnesses, almost like the whole thing never even happened.

Abraxos wanted us to chalk it up to a random, unfortunate event, but whoever killed those people had a reason, and my instincts told me it wasn't a coincidence that we didn't have any witnesses or leads to go off. The only thing we did have to go on was the words the fallen angel had spoken to me. Why would someone like that lie when they knew they weren't going to live? I didn't think they would which gave us our only clue.

On top of the recent events, I personally still wanted to move past everything that had happened – with Nathaniel, my transformation, all of it. I wanted to finally put everything behind me for good and move on.

Eloa nodded and Abraxos stepped forward.

"We've assigned you to accompany Jared on the next field mission. You'll leave tomorrow," he said as he slid a folder across the glass desk towards me.

"I suggest you read up on the assignment. You're an ally to us Alex. A great one at that. If you think you're ready, we'd like for you to complete your oath. We could have big things in store for you." He watched me carefully awaiting my response and all eyes landed on me.

"My oath?" I repeated wondering what he was talking about and feeling a lump rise in the back of my throat.

He exchanged a look with Jared, who shifted in his seat, before responding to me again.

"It seems this was not brought to your attention before; I apologize. The oath is simple. It states that you will vow to uphold acts this Council deems necessary. What angels deem necessary to do. You will be welcomed as one of us forever, protected and considered family," he said keeping his eyes on me.

I hesitated before responding. The need to belong felt overwhelming, almost unbearable. I had felt that Crest was, in a way, my new home, but to have every angel see me as family was something I had not yet experienced, and it almost sounded too good to be true. They wanted me. I was an ally to them and I would finally not be such an outcast. I thought for a moment then Jared piped in.

"We *can* keep you protected. From *anyone*, that is. They just ask you do the same in return." His words sounded hopeful.

"How does the oath work?" I asked. I didn't like the sound of being held to a vow.

Abraxos cut in before Jared could respond.

"All you need to say is, 'I, Alexandria Constance, solemnly swear to adhere to the Council of Angels. I give myself freely and I vow to ensure peace and order using force as necessary, and to protect my angel brethren.'

My thoughts went rampant for a moment on whether to say the oath or not. And although 'fallen' angels were assumed to be bad, I was still part fallen angel and I didn't know enough about that to make any kind of logical, rational or informed decision. Still, I was an outcast and would always be an outcast unless I made the oath.

The fire churned inside the pit of my stomach, warning me, while another side made me realize this had been what I was asking for all along. Was I being lied to right now? Before I knew it, I was saying the words out loud. Whatever fears I had no longer mattered, I had made the oath. I was one of them now.

"Welcome to the family Alexandria," Abraxos said as a wide smile spread across his face and he exited the room.

Madam Eloa smiled and shook my hand before also leaving the room. I breathed out and felt a weird warm feeling wash over me. It vanished as quickly as it had come, leaving me wondering if I had truly felt anything at all or if I had just imagined it. Jared and I left the building not saying a word, but I couldn't help but notice him sneaking glances my way, and the slightly shocked look on his face. I hugged him as soon as we reached the overhang outside the Atrium, unable to contain my excitement any longer.

"Thank you!" I screeched.

He laughed and hugged me back.

"I don't know why you're thanking me. You're the one who put the work in. Congratulations Alex, you're one of us now," he said, smiling down at me.

I nodded.

"True, but without your mad expertise and training I would still be accidentally lighting things on fire." I laughed, remembering the time I had tried using my fire techniques to heat up a microwavable pizza. I ended up evacuating my entire floor. And I was pretty sure most of the angels on level U in my building were still salty about the whole thing.

It had started to pelt rain and Jared and I ran, but this time he led us towards another building, different from the direction of my dorm room.

"Where are we going?" I asked as I jogged alongside him, jumping through puddles on the path and splashing cold water up my pant leg.

"To my dorm. I've got all of the items that we'll need there, and I want to go over the assignment with you as well."

I hadn't been back to Jared's dorm since I'd rushed out the morning after my birthday. My cheeks flushed slightly in the rain as I thought back to that morning. We walked through building C's doors and rounded the corner, then up the stairs a few flights till we reached C-10. Like mine, his room was situated on the far end of the floor where it was the quietest. He slid his key into the lock and it clicked open. He held the door open for me to enter first.

"Welcome to my domain... again, and excuse the mess," he said, scratching the back of his head and motioning me inside. The room was darker than expected. I flipped the light on as I stepped inside. Files were strewn about on a desk along with hand written notes, and an assortment of clothes, some weapons and other gadgets lay scattered across the bed. It looked vastly different from when I had been there the first time, but I'd gathered he'd been trying to decipher the bar incident as well through reports.

I strode over to the side of the bed to view the artillery we'd be taking with us. I was surprised to find more cameras than actual weapons. Thanks to the extra weapons training Jared had given me, I was able to identify what I was seeing. Several short barrel Mp5 rifles and knives lay next to a duffel bag.

"What are the cameras for?" I asked, picking up the tiny lenses and examining them.

"This assignment is off the books. We are to observe and gather intel only. Absolutely no one from the other side can know we were there." He opened the closet and pulled out a few clothing items, then turned back to me.

"These were made for you." He handed me black skinny pants and a long-sleeved matching top, a black tactical belt, black boots complete with knife sheaths, a small zip-up tactical mesh vest, and a thigh knife holder. In total, it looked as if I would be suited up to the nine's ready for battle. I felt the smooth fabric of the clothes between my fingers and it felt lightweight. I also noticed the size seemed to be exact.

"I take it you gave the tailor my sizing," I said looking back at Jared, picturing him rooting through my clothes back before our first training session.

He smirked at me and began to give me the details of the assignment.

"As I mentioned, this assignment is only for us to gain information. We want to know who is there and get pictures of as many of them as possible," he said, motioning to one of the tiny lenses, "and gather any other related information. We'll use these to set up areas around the bunker where the fallen angels are meeting. They'll automatically snap pictures of anything that moves in the area while we're there. We'll have our rifles, but will only use them if needed. They're mainly for the wild-life, just in case."

"What do you mean? Where are we going?"

He smiled. "Louisiana swamps, and they're filled with alligators so you'll need to be on the lookout. We don't want anyone to become aware of our presence because of a gator." His tone lowered a bit, keying in on the importance of applying vigilance and stealth.

After giving me the rundown of the items we would be bringing, we went over the file together. I pulled the first picture from the file attached to several other documents and froze. My body tensed as I instantly recognized Apollyon's face. Sifting through the file quickly, I found more pictures with documents attached to them. Corson's, Cassius's and lastly a blank file. I could feel my body go rigid as a board as I examined the photos of the men who had kidnapped me, threatened me, and forever changed my life. Although they were missing other key members who participated in ruining my life, they had managed to identify some of the key people. Jared's hand touched my shoulder and I twitched instinctively before looking up at him.

"These three were there that night you were changed, weren't they?" He gathered more than asked.

I nodded slowly.

"They're going to wish they hadn't been." I said tossing the photos on the bed in front of me and gazing at them once more.

"We've been tracking these three for a while now, but there are others we need you to help identify and learn the whereabouts of. Now that you're one of us, you can help us watch these guys. If they break any of the rules, you better believe you'll be there when the time comes. You're an Angel Interceder now, like other Angel Interceders," he said, attempting to comfort me.

I tilted my head to the side.

"An Angel Interceder?" I said the words out loud like I was trying on a pair of shoes and getting used to them.

Jared nodded at me before my questions came flying.

"Wait, what do you mean watch them? I thought we'd be going after them, after all they did try and take over heaven, right?" I was puzzled and perturbed at why we wouldn't be acting on the offensive towards someone like Apollyon.

He tossed his shirt on the floor and kicked his boots off as I strained to keep eye contact with him.

"But they didn't. They used a human which is usually against the rules, however, you weren't really human to begin with, and you never opened the door for them. Technically speaking, they didn't do anything."

My wide-eyed, shocked, facial expression demanded Jared get his head examined and explain himself.

"The rules state that no angel or fallen angel is allowed to hurt humans for their own species' gain. Unfortunately, there aren't any rules about the treatment of half-humans, especially since all of them were supposedly wiped out aside from you. Each species is supposed to go about their own lives peacefully. If either one is seen as becoming too powerful or trying to take over anything, they're stopped. Basically, any threats are eliminated to keep the peace between everyone and keep our identities secret from humans," he said flatly.

"The Angel Council decides who has overstepped their boundaries and who hasn't and decides what to do with them from there. Abraxos is one of those on that Council."

I nodded, trying to understand what this 'Council' actually does, trying my best not to be cynical while another part of me burned deeply.

"Why don't you take this file with you tonight as well as your equipment and look it over again. I'm going to shower, but I'll be by to get you at 2AM so we can leave." He headed for the bathroom.

When I didn't move, he stopped and turned back to me with a broad smirk plastered on his face.

"Unless you want to watch me shower or something," he said, winking.

I rolled my eyes.

"Definitely leaving immediately!" I called back as my cheeks flushed.

I sat on the bed looking at the pictures for another moment before hearing the shower turn on. I filled the duffel bag with my equipment and clothes and headed for my dorm.

I tried to relax that evening. I officially had a supernatural family now. I had even noticed the other students attempt a smile at me on my way back from Jared's dorm. That was something that I had not encountered since I had come to Crest. It was also surprising to know how quickly the news had spread. Was I somehow different now? I surely didn't feel any different, only I was beginning to feel... slightly welcome now that I had a duty to everyone. I was an Angel Interceder. I felt my pulse race as I said the words out loud again. The fire within me churned at the name and I quieted it. This was exactly what I needed and wanted, right? To belong, and this was my first step in that direction. The other part of me would just need to get used to it.

I dialed Trey. The ringing noise went to voicemail and I left another message, this time slightly more irritated. He hadn't returned any of my calls lately. It just wasn't like him. I left him a voicemail to call me back and brushed it off, figuring he was busy with Sophie or something and then closed my eyes and tuned out my thoughts so I could get a few hours of sleep.

It was dark for a minute and when I opened my eyes I found I was in Jared's dorm room again. Puzzled, I looked around and saw Jared lying on his back on his bed with his eyes closed. Wondering how I had gotten there in the first place and desperately not wanting to wake Jared and make things even more awkward, I began to slowly creep towards the door to leave.

"You feel OK after taking the oath?" I heard him say suddenly, causing me to almost trip on some of his clothes.

I turned back towards him to see he was sitting up watching me.

"Um yes?" I replied, appalled that he had caught me. But, my answer sounded more like a question.

He shook his head, moving from the bed, and walked towards me. My heart fluttered as his sea-green eyes flashed while he approached.

"I called you here, in my dream, if that's what you're wondering." He seemed amused at my embarrassment and confusion.

"You can do that? I mean, we can do that?"

He nodded, and a burning in my chest churned at the memory of my latest dreams with Nathaniel. Were those real? I dismissed the notion before giving it any credibility. Those were just dreams, different from... this sort of live dream. They had to be.

"So if this is a dream... you can't feel this right?" I asked as I shoved him playfully.

He laughed.

"Nope, I can actually feel that because you wanted me to."

"Oh." I felt a little foolish and I couldn't help but notice his bare-chested perfection.

Apparently, I still needed some lessons on how the whole dreams thing worked.

"Just like you can feel this," he said pulling me in for a kiss.

The smell of warm vanilla and fresh rain filled my nostrils as the spark from before began to tingle its way up my spine. I kissed him back, ignoring whatever fears or doubts I had. Following his lead, the kiss deepened, but remained delicate and soft. Kissing Jared felt different, it was smooth and gentle. Sparks shot up my spine as our lips met, sending goosebumps down my arms. My guard went away. He pulled back catching his breath for a minute and smiled down at me.

"And you felt that because I wanted you to," he said, satisfied.

I regained control of my breathing, and my hands lingered over his bare chest, feeling his heart beat. I slid my hands away slowly.

"I should... go," I murmured before I pushed back from him and the dream blurred and faded out.

I woke in my own bed and could feel the heat radiating from my body. I took a deep breath in and checked the clock. 1:30AM. I threw off the covers and headed for the shower. The hot water doused my skin as the smell of warm vanilla lingered in my nose.

That was twice now that I had kissed Jared. So much for trying to be strong and not complicate things. I could feel a part of me beginning to like Jared. I knew I did, yet another part of me fought the idea like a sickness. My heart beat skipped as I replayed the kiss again in my head. Soft and inviting, almost pleading for me to never pull away from him. I had to shake the thoughts away though. I had just recently gotten my abilities under control and finally had managed to reign in most of my emotions, but I had not gotten over the fear of another heart break. I had built up too many walls to take them all down at once.

After my shower, I pulled on the outfit Jared had provided. My pulse quickened as I thought about our assignment. The danger and thrill beckoned me while I remained focused on the objective. I had to get this assignment right, otherwise there was no guarantee I'd ever be allowed on another field mission. That thought put me in a panic. What would I do with myself? Strictly observe and gather intel; that was all I needed to do and I would. I had to. I slid a knife in my boot and added a few more to my thigh sheath and vest when a knock sounded at my door.

"Come in," I called as I appraised my outfit in front of the mirror ensuring that I had all of my gear. Jared waltzed into the room with a smirk on his face, his eyes widening some as he took in the outfit that fit me like a glove.

"Ehem. You look good."

"Thanks. You do, too," I retorted, eyeing the all-black military style attire that hugged his well-trained muscles.

A tingle ran up my spine as I thought of our dream-kiss again and I battled to retain my composure. I needed to focus on our assignment, not guys, not kisses and not feelings.

"So how are we getting to Louisiana?" I asked, trying to break the awkward silence between us and get free of his gaze.

I filled my front vest with the tiny cameras.

"We are flying to Houston and taking a boat through the bayou, then we'll have to walk the rest of the way. It's too remote of an area to get to any other way, especially undetected," he said glancing at my outfit once more.

"And by flying you mean...?" I inquired wondering if he meant taking a plane or actually flying.

He chuckled. "We are actually going to fly there."

I had noticed when dressing that my shirt and vest were fitted with openings at the back so any wing action wouldn't destroy the garments. Upon closer inspection, they seemed expandable, but when closed, were cleverly concealed by the design of the garment – an extra fold of fabric pleated into the pattern.

"Abraxos has fitted our outfits with these." He stepped towards me and placed his hand on the small round piece of metal attached to my vest.

I looked closer and realized the pendant had a symbol on it, a crest similar to the one Nathaniel had worn around his neck, but it depicted a thick black dash across it.

"It's a cloaking device. No one, including humans, will be able to detect us as we fly. Angels use these to get around quickly while remaining undetected, and since you're an Interceder now, you're going to need this."

I smiled at the thought of actually being able to fly without any fear of revealing myself to anyone, and I could feel my wings shift inside my back anxiously. We strapped the rifles onto our backs along with any remaining equipment before I locked my dorm room and followed Jared out of the building.

It was quiet on campus as the dew from the evening rain cast a low fog that clung to the ground around us.

"You ready?" Jared beamed with anticipation.

"Ready." Our wings unfurled. My pulse quickened and I just knew... I just knew how to fly! I had practiced only a few times with Jared...

He nodded and winked before kneeling and propelling himself into the air. I knelt slightly and closed my eyes, launching myself in one swift movement, upward, letting my wings propel me skyward with ease. This would be my first long flight.

The wind breezed through my feathers and I felt the jet streams in the air. I opened my eyes to watch the campus grow smaller as we soared higher.

The landscape was dark, but my eyesight sharpened to illuminate the blackness below. I was awe-struck by the beauty this new perspective brought of everything around me.

I turned to Jared whose bright white wings beat steady and strong. He nodded and beckoned for me to follow, and without hesitating, my wings embraced the order. We flew for an hour, but the time flew by quickly to my dismay. I dove up and down through the clouds and felt my wings fully stretch out as they never had before. I relished the freedom and joy flight brought me and I suddenly wondered if I was worthy of such a gift.

Jared grabbed my attention, pulling me from my thoughts as he signaled for us to land.

My watch read 3AM as my feet delicately touched the dirt just outside of Houston. My wings stretched out once more, as if remembering their euphoric flight, before folding away into my shoulder blades. I peered around at our surroundings.

I could see the glittering lights of the city through the trees nearby as Jared readied a small, dingy, metal boat on the edge of the bayou. He pulled on the cord and the motor gurgled for a moment, sputtering to life and spewing gray smoke into the air. He waved me over and I hopped aboard.

It was eerily quiet on the bayou, except for the constant whine of the motor as we surged toward Louisiana. Another hour passed as I listened to the bayou gradually come to life around us. I could hear splashes in the water from disrupted alligators and shrills from birds alerting everyone that dawn was almost near.

Jared and I had remained silent most of the ride, taking in the different senses around us and the moist humidity that soaked into our skin, each of us diligently going over our assignment in our heads.

"We're almost there," he announced, looking down at his watch as we approached the shoreline. He shut the motor off and let the boat drift to the edge. He hopped out and pulled the boat in, tying it to a low hanging tree over the water's edge before helping me out.

Jared began to reiterate our assignment details once more.

"The compound is located 20 minutes south east of our current location. We'll walk the first ten minutes together before splitting up. You'll be positioned on the south eastern point of the compound and I will be on the north western point, about 600 clicks away.

You'll need to position the cameras on the trees facing the compound without being seen and stay in position for approximately one hour. We should be there just in time to catch the identities of the fallen angels leaving the compound. We'll give the cameras time to take photographs of them, and then we'll reconvene back here at 7AM. If you're not back by 7:10AM I'm coming to look for you. Understood?" His eyes searched mine for confirmation before he set my watch and let my wrist fall back to my side.

I nodded and unstrapped the rifle from my back placing the sling over my neck and threading my right arm through it. The strap rested comfortably atop my right shoulder and I held the butt of the gun loosely in the crease. We headed up the bank of the river towards the dense tree line. Stepping through the trees, a thick fog rose from the black water and clung to the heavy foliage around it, unable to escape. My boots submerged below the filthy murk almost to my knees. We pressed forward, diligently placing one foot in front of the other so as not to draw attention to our presence.

"So, about that dream last night..." Jared began innocently.

Neither of us had managed to bring it up until now.

"What about it?"

"Well I mean I liked it, kissing you that is. Did you like kissing me?"

I shook my head in disbelief that he could be thinking about that right now.

I tried to focus on my footing again and on the surroundings.

He shrugged. "I'm a guy. So...is that a yes then?"

A hiss and the snapping of jaws brought us instantly alert and we shouldered our rifles. My heartbeat raced as I eyed the surface of the bayou and we stayed motionless for more than several minutes before deciding to continue. Knowing Jared was not going to drop the subject, I obliged him with an answer.

"I may have liked it, but I'm not someone you should get involved with. You've got a lot going for you and I just don't want to mess that up," I replied trying to find the right words to how I felt.

I liked Jared to be honest, but I wasn't sure having feelings for me would be the best thing for him or me. Given that I am a hybrid and a complete and utter emotional, unpredictable mess. Suddenly, he stopped.

"This is the end of the line; you'll go that way from here." He pointed southeast.

"You know one-word answers work best right? You're allowed to just admit that you liked my kiss without adding some excuse with it." He was making it known he was irritated by my comment.

I rolled my eyes and laughed a little.

"I'm complicated remember?"

"Sure, sure." But his face had turned serious. "I'll meet you back at the boat at 7AM. And Alex... please don't be late." He hesitated before giving me a reassuring and nervous smile that I would be OK.

"Be careful."

"You too," I replied with a small smile.

With that, I headed towards the south-eastern portion of the compound, alone.

Chapter 14

E very sound had me on high alert. I remained focused; aware of my surroundings as I waded through the water. It was almost 5:15 AM now
with the time change and a thin slice of light began to cut through the
darkness causing the top of the murky brown water to shine. The fog had not
dissipated since we began our journey on the bayou and I had to continually
check my compass to ensure I was heading in the right direction.

I moved a slimy piece of moss hanging low from a branch and sank
lower into the muddy water as a wooden cabin on stilts appeared in the
distance out of the fog. A large wooden wrap around porch and dock
surrounded the eerie bayou home and I gathered this had to be the compound Jared was describing, although it resembled nothing of the
compound or bunker I as I had expected.

I remained silent as I observed the home from behind a cluster of
thick trees growing every which way out of the swamp. There were three
fan boats tied to the dock.

Removing the small cameras one at a time from my vest pocket, I
placed a few of them on select trees overlooking the compound before
shouldering my rifle and settling in. Some time had passed and I had
almost mistaken two drifting logs for alligators. I breathed out slowly
again and focused on the vibrations inside the home.

Six fallen angels remained inside the compound. I leaned against the tree and rechecked my watch. The creak of a door drew my attention back to the cabin and I crouched in the water against the tree and watched as five fallen angels stepped onto the porch.

I perched my rifle silently through the opening of the trees and peered through the scope to identify the men. Cassius's face came into focus and I pulled my face from the scope for a moment before peering back through the lens. The fire within me rumbled. I moved to the male figure next to Cassius and my finger instinctively flipped the safety off and moved onto the trigger. I watched Apollyon as he shook hands with a male I did not recognize. My finger twitched to pull the trigger, but I refrained as the assignment objectives flashed across my mind again.

The other two fallen angels looked similar to the henchmen Uvall had lingering at his mansion and I finally recognized Azza as one of them. I snapped a few photos with a camera, watching the men load themselves into the three fan boats and take off. The water rippled around me in their wake as I remained crouched in the water.

Where did the sixth man go? There had been a sixth, right?

I wondered if I had felt the correct number of vibrations inside the compound. I had to have, there were six fallen angels and I was sure of it. Uneasy and cautious, I checked my watch again, 7AM. I had to get back to the boat and Jared or he'd come looking for me. Not having much of a choice I grabbed the cameras, and began to slowly creep away from the compound.

The fog had consumed the cabin behind me and dense swamp lay ahead as I began to make my way back to the boat. The snap of a branch sounded behind me and I shouldered my rifle quickly as my senses spiked. I sensed a fallen angel and the hairs on the back of my neck stood up in alarm. It had to be the sixth man from the compound.

How had I missed him following me?

A splash sounded and I positioned myself next to a thick tree for cover. The water rippled in front of me and I turned in time to dodge an alligator lunging for my mid-section. Without thinking, I grabbed my vest knife and hurled it into a space just back of the eyes, where a bullet or knife would penetrate the tough anima's hide straight to the brain; a generous tip Jared had given me on our way over. The alligator struggled for a few seconds before its body went limp. I pushed the frightening animal farther away from me with my boot and stepped back from it, with my breath caught in my throat; then I felt the edge of a serrated sharp blade rest firmly against my neck. The fallen angel had taken my rifle in the process – leaving me weaponless except for the thigh and boot knife. My hands instinctively rose slightly to show I did not plan to fight back, but my right hand itched to grab my thigh knife. Not loosening the pressure of the blade on my throat, the fallen angel spoke.

"Give me one good reason I shouldn't kill you." His voice was menacing, but something seemed darkly familiar about its deep velvety timber. My voice shook as I responded.

"N-Na-Nathaniel?" I stammered in disbelief, wondering if my mind was playing tricks on me or if it was truly him.

I felt the blade leave my throat after a moment of hesitation and the man stepped back. My hand instinctively touched my throat and I turned to see if my ears had in fact been lying to me. My eyes met a pair of deep navy blue orbs. He was almost the same as I remembered him; short, dark black hair and a tall muscular build, but his muscles seemed more defined now, if that was possible. It looked as if he hadn't shaved in several days. But his eyes were what scared me the most. They were different, somehow more animalistic and wild.

His hand holding the blade dropped to his side and he seemed just as startled to see me standing before him. We stood just gazing at one another for a moment, almost trying to figure out if this was real. It felt like forever since I had last seen or spoken to this stranger, and the last time I had heard his voice was from Luther's recording.

"Alex? What are you doing here?" His voice was smooth and velvety, but his tone had a sharper unknown edge to it.

A lump caught in my throat and I struggled to respond at all. Curses filled my head and I wished I could just yell at him right there for everything he'd said. It was only after the longest moment staring at one another that I responded.

"I could ask you the same thing." My voice was cool and nonchalant, but an inferno lit inside of me.

I could feel the rush of emotions hit me like a tidal wave all at once; disbelief, anger and adrenaline. He didn't reply for a moment but took a step towards me. I stepped back, uncertain of how to react to him and remembering the blade at my throat minutes earlier. He stopped and eyed me, his brows furrowing, but a splash of water close by broke the standoff between us. I could feel Jared's presence nearby and knew Nathaniel could sense him, too. I glanced at my watch whilst never taking my attention off of Nathaniel; 7:10AM. Jared was absolutely looking for me.

"I have to go," was all I could say before I began to step back and wade away from him.

I did not turn around until I had put some distance between us and until I was comfortable he wasn't going to come near me. I looked back at Nathaniel one last time before the fog closed in around him, and I heard my name whispered under his breath.

"Alex."

I followed the direction of Jared's vibrations feeling like I had just seen a ghost. Jared's voice called from beyond the fog, serious and concerned.

"Alex! Are you OK? What happened?" he said as he appeared through the mist ready for battle.

He gripped my shoulders to confirm that I was OK, checking for any wounds.

"I'm fine. It was just a... an alligator." I breathed as he tried to make out my blank bewildered expression.

He took this in for a moment, his eyebrows furrowing in question.

"Where's your rifle?"

I pointed towards the fog behind me.

"With the alligator," I said, not wanting to divulge my encounter with Nathaniel.

He nodded and escorted me to walk in front of him as he scanned the fog once more before following behind me back to the boat. We climbed into the boat with my thoughts still spinning. *Nathaniel was back.* Not only was Nathaniel back, but he was involved in something the angels were more than just interested in. A part of me wished I had asked

Nathaniel what brought him back, and what he knew about this meeting of fallen angels. He could have been a good source of information if I were able to keep my wits about me, but he seemed unbalanced and...dangerous. If only I'd had more time with him. Time to ask questions. Time to find out what he'd been through and why he betrayed me...

Could I still trust Nathaniel? Was he the same? He didn't slit my throat, but then again that wasn't saying much. He was different. That was undeniably true. I didn't know what to trust anymore; my mind told me I was an idiot if I thought he was trust worthy, but deep down my heart desperately wished he was. I still wanted to believe that his love for me had been real. Had been. Maybe his transformation or initiation or whatever it was they did to him had changed all that.

We flew the remaining distance back to Crest and Jared and I each headed for our dorms. We hadn't talked on the return trip and I wondered if Jared had picked up on the fact that the alligator was not the only thing that had appeared before he found me. I tossed my duffel bag into the room letting my back slide down the door, closing it, and held my head in my hands. I let out a deep breath and was taken out of my thoughts quickly when a knock sounded at my back. I hesitated for a moment before I got up and opened it to find Jared on the other side. His hand rested on the door frame and his face was serious.

"Abraxos wants to see us for debriefing, bring the cameras with you," he said flatly.

I reached inside my vest and grabbed the tiny lenses, then followed Jared to the Atrium. I could feel the other students' eyes on us as we made our way into the atrium and past Madam Eloa's office. So much for being able to clear my thoughts for a bit. Jared led the way down the hall towards a heavy steel door. He scanned his finger print on the front of the pad and the door buzzed us through.

Continuing down another hallway, we passed several offices before entering one with blacked out windows. Jared escorted me inside.

The room was empty except for an oval dark cherry table surrounded by chairs and one giant black TV that hung at the front of the room. We sat silently for a moment before Abraxos entered holding a stack of files.

Several other men followed behind him closing the door. He tossed the files on the table and smiled, kicking back in a chair. One of the men retrieved the cameras from us and began uploading them into the TV before taking a seat near Abraxos. A lump caught in my throat, wondering if I had accidentally caught Nathaniel on camera. They began scrolling through the pictures in a slide-show, skipping any that didn't show anything of even remote importance to them.

"So, Alex, how many fallen angels were present at the meeting? And which of those can you identify for us?" he asked, passing me the remote to scroll through the images.

I cleared my throat.

"Five men sir; the first identified was Cassius, then Apollyon along with two of his henchmen and this man whom I do not know," I said scrolling through the pictures to the individual I had seen shake hands with Apollyon.

I couldn't understand what had possessed me to lie and I scolded myself as the words left my mouth.

Abraxos smiled and took a few notes before turning to Jared.

"And you? How many did you see and identify?" His tone was more ominous.

Jared shifted in his chair uncomfortably for a moment avoiding Abraxos's gaze and sneaking a glance at me before answering.

"There were six men sir. I saw six," he said, tossing a file onto the table.

"The man shaking Apollyon's hand was photographed a while ago in New York. He's been seen working with New Creation Investment Group before, but I can't tell you why he was there today. His name is Melcom." My ears pricked up at the sound of the company name and I looked back at Jared questioningly.

He gave me a look as if telling me to not bring it up at the moment and he refrained from saying anything on the subject.

Jared clicked the remote. "This is the sixth man I can't identify."

The screen filled with a picture of Nathaniel looking back over his shoulder as he left the compound and my heart dropped in my stomach. I held my breath. Jared glanced back at me. He has to know I lied, and if he knew, so did the others.

Abraxos shifted some in his seat but wouldn't take his eyes away from the screen for a few minutes. He huffed before responding to Jared.

"That would be Nathaniel Archais Corvix." He got up from his chair and glanced between us.

"Take them to complete the rest of their debriefing. I want a full report by the end of the day," he said looking back at the picture. That's all for now. I'll be checking in with you in a few days." His glance lingered on me longer than I was comfortable with and I watched as he and the other men left the room, leaving Jared and I disturbingly silent. I turned towards Jared who collected the file he had tossed on the table. Ignoring me, he grabbed the file and we followed the men out, Jared being escorted in the opposite direction from me. We looked back at one another before we were no longer in sight and I felt my hands go clammy. I'd lied about seeing Nathaniel there, and Jared and Abraxos knew it.

The man suddenly stopped at a doorway and ushered me inside. The room couldn't have been much larger than a closet with a computer, a sizeable scanner-like machine and a notepad. For the next four hours, my 'debriefing' comprised of retracing Jared's and my exact steps during the mission, right down to the minute, where we were positioned relative to the compound, who we encountered/observed, logging the weapons that were taken and returned, and the list went on. The only good portion of my debriefing was compiling an idea on what the fallen angels were up to with the previous spy operations they allowed me to be privy to now.

It looked like they were gathering forces again, but I wasn't sure why. They'd failed in trying to use me to open the portal to heaven, so what was their next move? It seemed improbable that they would attack angels right now after such a loss. I sat rigid and disgruntled while the man hooked me up to a machine. I was becoming frustrated that I couldn't fit the pieces together and that I'd been confined to this stupid room for long enough.

"This is the final portion of your debriefing.

It verifies if your story is as accurate as you claim. The man said snidely as it dawned on me he was hooking me up to a Polygraph test.

"My written account of everything and the recording aren't sufficient enough?" I asked cautiously.

The sweaty heat of fear licked at the nape of my neck. I wasn't about to confirm anything about Nathaniel and my encounter. I'd already lied, and I wasn't going to confirm the reality that he was back. He was a liar and a stranger.

The man finished hooking up the machine

and I seized my opportunity. A small ball of fire shot out and annihilated the polygraph machine sending it smashing into the wall in a ball of fire and debris.

"What the hell!?" He bellowed jumping up.

I fought to keep from laughing and shrugged innocently.

"I'm still learning how to control it. I take it we're done now?"

"Get out of here!" The man waved his arms at me stomping out the fire. I smiled and gladly removed myself from the room, making my way back through the hallway and out of the atrium.

Returning to my dorm room, I tossed my key on the desk and shut the door, Jared catching it before it could close entirely. Before I could open my mouth, he put his finger to his lips to shush me and motioned for me to follow him. His strange behavior caught my attention quickly and I followed him out of my dorm and out of the building, noticing the files clutched in one of his hands. It wasn't until we reached the far edge of the campus behind the barn that he cornered me and began his interrogation.

"It was *him* wasn't it? That's why you didn't tell them. Isn't it?"

"Who? Jared, what's this about? I just spent over four hours being interrogated, get to the point," I said hotly.

"Nathaniel. He was your guardian angel before, wasn't he? That's how this whole thing started." The mention of his name sent a spear-like feeling through my gut.

"His name is all over this freaking file, Alex. You can't lie to me about it, I was just made aware of your history together."

My eyes narrowed at him and I tried to remain calm.

"I don't know what you're talking about." I crossed my arms as the pit of my stomach burned at his tone. It was *none* of his business.

He rolled his eyes at me.

"Take a look if you like, but I know, Abraxos, knows, every top angel pretty much knows!"

I grabbed the file he flapped at me and flipped through it. They had the account of what had happened at Uvall's mansion with the transformation and the massacre afterwards that Nathaniel had created, but it also had several more intimate photos captured of Nathaniel and me. Pictures of us embracing outside after the car accident when Corson had attempted his kidnapping, and one photo of him and me sharing a kiss." I held the picture, feeling my gut wrench and my eyes moisten. The images had evidently been taken by an angel sent to spy on us. Damn them. The burning in my heart heightened and I let the flames from my fingertips lick at the edges of the photograph until it was fully engulfed. Watching the pieces crumble and fall as ash.

"So it is true. He's the one that you've been hung up on, isn't he?" I barely heard Jared's words as I contained the whirlwind of fire in my chest.

"Alex, you need to understand something, he's not who he was. He's a killer."

"What's that supposed to mean?" I demanded.

"He's one of them! What do you *think* I mean by that?" he said, spitting the words out with disgust.

I shook my head, wanting to forget all of it, but as Jared rattled on I couldn't take it anymore.

"Yeah, well he wasn't always! He's only one of them because of me!" The words spewed out quickly and I wished I hadn't said them. I began to pace back and forth for a minute as the guilt hit me like a freight train.

Jared's eyes narrowed but his face softened a touch when he looked back at me.

"He was the angel who was supposed to kill you, but he didn't." Jared spoke matter-of-factly.

A tear streamed down my face as Jared said the words and I brushed it away harshly.

"No.... he didn't. Listen Jared, I don't know why he was at that compound, but I *am* going to find out."

"I think it's obvious why he was there, given his background. He's their attack dog."

"Why does everyone keep saying that?" I asked irritated. "And what is with his background?"

155

Jared ignored my question and continued. You need to listen to me Alex, you *cannot* lie to the Council like you just did. There are consequences to breaking your oath. Things *I* don't even know about." He took a step closer to me, his voice lowering in tone.

"What do you mean? What kinds of things?"

He hesitated.

"Angels have disappeared before. You just need to be careful OK?" His tone dripped with fear.

A shudder ran through my body and I rubbed my temple attempting to relieve the stress.

I needed to put everything about Nathaniel on a back burner. And I needed to try to understand the fallen angels and their movements. What were the connections? What are they after?

"I need to know what you know about Trey's family business, New Creation Investment Group. I'm going to need your help if I am going to figure out what the fallen angels are after," I said stopping and giving him the file back.

He turned towards me and scratched the side of his jaw. He was trying to put the pieces together about what had happened between Nathaniel and me, and his eyes flashed with something I couldn't recognize.

"This is nuts."

"Ok, I'll help you, but trust me when I say it's for the better if you *don't* see Nathaniel anymore."

"No problem there," I said, knowing Nathaniel and my relationship had been fake all along. Relief filled my body and I couldn't help but smile appreciatively. Jared seemed confused by my comment, but nodded.

"Got any coffee back at your dorm?"

"Promise to not lie to the Council anymore?" he pressed.

My eyes rolled sarcastically. "Would it make you feel better if I pinky promised?"

"No."

"Then tell me about New Creation."

I had already investigated every file on the company that Jared had access to. Unfortunately, he didn't have access to much. The majority of what we had was through public records. It seems even the angels didn't know all of what New Creation was involved with, but without proper evidence, they hadn't been given authority to take it much further than an overview of the company. That, and the Council had apparently ruled that delving into human lives without proper evidence or reason was 'frowned upon'. Perhaps that was one of the reasons why Trey was accepted into Crest; were they spying on him? I wondered. A few hours of re-energizing with some coffee and reading through the public records and tax information on New Creation had made me cross-eyed; that and the image of Nathaniel and me kissing continued to pick at my subconscious. I finally called it, taking some of the files with me, leaving Jared and returning to my own dorm.

Chapter 15

In an effort to forget my little escapade with Nathaniel in the swamp, I had torn through the file of Melcom, the man Jared had described to me after our debriefing as working with New Creation Investment Group and had come up empty thus far. Frustrated, and slightly annoyed, I shut the file again and slid it away from me while leaning back in my chair. I had nothing. Literally no leads whatsoever on where to even begin with why Trey's parents would be in bed with fallen angels. The angels seemed just as curious about it as I was, and I needed an answer.

I rocked the chair back on its two legs with my arms crossed behind my neck. And then it was as if a light bulb went off in my head. I frantically stripped the file open again, searching desperately for a document I had overlooked. My fingers thumbed over the paper quickly and I snatched it up to read. It wasn't the name that had stood out, but the address that had caught my attention. I plugged the address into my laptop and just as I had expected, the club Jared, Trey, Sophie and I had gone to for my birthday popped up. *Echo.*

I smiled at my first clue. Jared had said no business was conducted at the club, but what if he was wrong? *What if everything was just happening beneath that steel floor, right under our feet?* Luke Banoff seemed to be the signer on the investment deal and his wife Sarah Banoff was the agent according to the documents. I closed the file and took it with me as I headed for Jared's dorm.

I could hear music blaring from the hallway as I approached. I knocked loudly and when I got no answer I burst inside impatiently. I was stunned to find Jared in the kitchen baking, or attempting to bake. The smoke alarm sounded and I shook my head and tossed the file on his bed as I went to his aide.

"What are you doing?!" I shouted over the music as I watched him burn his hand taking something out of the oven.

He tried responding at first and then ran to shut off the music. He tossed the oven mitts on the table and let his head drop back in defeat.

"I was making a birthday cake for my sister. She's turning 14 in a few days and she's always wanted a home-made cake on her birthday," he said slumping against the counter.

I chuckled.

"And who gave *you* the idea to become Mr. Betty Crocker?" I asked playfully. The smoke alarm stopped beeping and I looked at his creation. It resembled more of a chocolatey mud pie than an actual cake.

"Apparently that's *all* she wanted from me this year as a birthday gift."

I nodded still amused, trying to refrain from laughing.

"Well, first of all, you're doing it all wrong. You don't have enough flour at this elevation and your oven temperature is off," I said looking back at him and motioning towards the sad brown catastrophe on the counter.

He shook his head.

"I should have known to ask for a woman's help than try and tackle this one on my own."

"I tell you what, I'll teach you how to properly bake a cake if you come on a teeny tiny assignment with me," I said, hoping my bribe would work.

His eyes narrowed some as he crossed his arms skeptically.

"What assignment? Don't tell me you've just been given some authority here and you're already abusing that," he stated in a friendly but ominous tone.

"No. As a matter of fact, I am doing an Interceder's job and investigating a possible breach of rules." I grabbed the folder from his bed and handed it to him.

This took him by surprise as he sifted through the file coming up empty and looking back at me.

"It's one of New Creation's investment deals. So what?"

"Look at the address. It's club Echo. I don't recognize the owner of the club's name, but what if it's a fake name? I searched and there isn't much to go off of for the owner. What if this was a deal made between Trey's parents and fallen angels without them being aware of who they were dealing with? It's also where I suspect secret meetings are being held." I proudly plopped myself down on his bed.

He scratched his head for a second before answering.

"Maybe. It could also be neutral ground. Even if you're right, we can't just storm a fallen angel club. You have no proof," he said flatly, handing the file back to me.

"We have to go check it out! It's the only clue we have at finding out who else is involved in New Creation and what they're up to," I retorted, trying to convince him of our position.

He shook his head. He wasn't buying it.

"We have no backup, we don't even know how many fallen angels are there if we do start snooping around. I don't like it."

"Jared, come on. There's no rule stating we can't just go check it out. If it's really nothing, we'll leave. No harm no foul, but if I'm right, we could have the exact information the Council and angels have been searching for themselves. Besides, if you don't come with me I'm still going to go, but I'll be by myself."

He studied me for a moment in thought.

"It would take time to get permission or the authority to engage with fallen angels if you are right. We'd need to report to Abraxos immediately, he's the only Council member on campus who we can divulge everything to. He could give us the authority to assess things from there. If the club is a secret meeting place for fallen angels, the rest of the Council members will want to know about it. This could be something big." He finished his ramble and continued to ponder silently.

"So? Is that a yes then? I asked hopefully.

"Fine, but we do not engage until we gather enough evidence so that Abraxos gives us the authority to do so, and there is *no way* I'm letting you go by yourself," he said coolly as he threw on a plain gray t-shirt.

He motioned back towards me, eying the same outfit I had worn from the swamp earlier.

"Is that what you're wearing?"

I looked down and realized I hadn't changed or showered since we had returned. *Whoops.* The smell wafting from my clothes was far less than pleasant. I chalked it up to being high strung after our debriefing with Abraxos.

"Too much?" I asked turning my head in amusement.

Not only did it smell like a swamp, but I resembled a cross between tomb raider and someone in the military, not exactly the best 'club-outfit'.

He laughed.

"I like it, but too much for this venue, doll. Go change and I'll be by to pick you up in a half hour."

I nodded and headed back to my dorm. Almost two hours later we were just outside of the small town where Echo was situated. I had showered and changed into skinny jeans, boots and a black V-neck t-shirt with a leather jacket.

I peered through the foggy windshield and my heart rate spiked as the club lights appeared in the distance. I could hear the faint thumping of music invade the beat of the raindrops relentlessly pounding the hood of the blue Yukon. We pulled around the corner of the parking lot and Jared shut the engine off. I reached for the handle of the door and he stopped me abruptly.

"I really don't like this." he said watching the outside of the club.

"Ten minutes, that's all I'm asking for." I hoped he wasn't going to back out on me now.

Reluctantly, he nodded slowly and we exited the Yukon, crossed the street quickly and entered the small line of people waiting to get into the club.

Minutes later we were inside Club Echo. It smelled like sweat and dampness from the outside. Strobe lights flickered over the gyrating bodies on the dance floor. Jared and I squeezed through the crowd until we finally found some space by the wall opposite the bar. We scanned the crowd searching for the vibrations of angels or fallen angels. There seemed to be fewer fallen angels here than when we had come previously.

I could sense no angels and only three fallen angels, all located beneath our feet in the hidden steel basement.

"Three fallen in the basement," I half whispered, half yelled into Jared's ear so he could hear me over the giant speaker behind us.

He nodded, but I could tell he was uneasy that he couldn't feel their vibrations through the steel tomb below us. The buzzing vibration hit me again like a wave crashing into me, alerting me that a fallen angel was moving. I concentrated and could feel the fallen angel moving closer to us. Someone was coming up the stairs from the basement, and now could be our only chance to act. Without hesitating, I pushed my way through the grinding bodies with Jared in tow.

The all-black, steel basement door opened and slammed shut as a fallen angel headed down the hallway by the bathrooms and out the back door of the club, lighting a cigarette on his way out. Jared nodded at me and a split second later we burst through the back door after the man. A few seconds of shuffling feet and Jared had him kneeling on the ground in a choke hold. The man gurgled some and then snorted and spewed angrily at us.

"You filth are going to regret this!" he spat between breaths as he struggled to get free of Jared's iron-tight hold.

Pulling his hood back, he looked to be no older than 15 with shaggy brown hair sticking to his cheeks as the rain wet his head. We dragged the kid closer towards the dumpsters in the alleyway so we were out of site and under the cover of the club's roof from the rain.

"Don't know how when we're not breaking any rules. We're not conducting business inside the club unlike you, are we?"

The kid didn't respond so we pressed for more answers hoping to get him to slip on one of them.

"Why are fallen angels working with New Creation Investment Group? Who's involved?" Jared questioned him, applying a little more pressure to the kid's neck before letting him speak.

"I'm not tellin' you nothin'!" the boy retorted angrily, a nervous smile touching his lips.

I tilted my head, bending down slightly so we were more at eye level.

"Then why don't you take us to those who will." I glanced at Jared who didn't like what I was getting at.

Jared huffed before releasing the kid's neck and immediately grabbed and twisted his arms behind him, pushing him forward so he could lead us back in. The kid hadn't expected us to want to go into the basement, but knowing he had backup there, the kid's eyes narrowed and a deceitful smile slid across his lips.

"Your funeral," he said and winced at Jared's grip.

A pair of belligerent girls stumbled out past us laughing and hiccupping, utterly oblivious to our presence as we slipped past them and headed towards the basement door. Jared's grip loosened allowing the kid to input a three-digit code into the door knob. A quick blow to the back of the head and the kid relaxed and fell limp in Jared's arms as I opened the steel door. No one seemed to notice as Jared let the boy slowly sink to the ground by the bathrooms. To anyone who might walk by, he looked like he had passed out from drinking too much.

Jared followed me through the door, shutting it behind us tightly. It was almost pitch black on the stairs with only a dim light illuminating the bottom step. The silence that filled the air was unsettling and we remained still for a moment before slowly descending the cold concrete steps into the steel basement.

At the bottom, there was a bar and several tables, all empty. A flicker of light caught our attention across from the bar and lounge area. Shadows danced under the crack of a door as several voices along with laughter and music filtered through. My nerves quivered with anticipation as Jared and I exchanged a look. We had come this far, but it wouldn't be long before someone would recognize the familiar vibrations radiating from us. We would have to use the advantage of surprise to our benefit.

The sound of the doorknob snapped me from my thoughts and I reacted instinctively. I spun and kicked the door in with a force that impressed even me. A scurry of people and shouts sounded from inside as Jared and I bombarded the room.

Inside, three black, stretched leather lounge sofas surrounded a short, sparkling, blue, glass table. A separate poker table sat in the corner from the lounge chairs as the overhead lighting created a dramatic red glow that contrasted with the glossy black floors and the purple lit walls. Two men drew guns causing the scantily clad women at their sides to shriek in fear. Jared and I remained still for a moment taking in the gunmen and the room.

"We just came to ask you a few questions, not here to break any rules," I said keeping my voice even and raising my hands slightly in front of me.

"You might want to ask *them* to leave," I stated, nodding to the four human women who were now shaking.

Not needing a second invitation to leave, the women rushed for the door, grabbing their purses on their way out, desperately wanting to remove themselves from the situation.

They kept their guns pointed at us. The older of the two men had silvery black hair and was dressed in an expensive suit. He was the first to speak.

"You two have a lot of nerve coming here. What the hell do you want?" he demanded heatedly as he looked from Jared to me.

"We want to know about New Creation Investment Group, and why they'd be dealing with you lot." Jared's tone was condescending.

The younger man wore a purple silk shirt and tie and sneered at us. He slinked back comfortably in the leather sofa and snorted.

"How about we kill you instead? That seems better."

"I don't think you understand; we're not leaving here until we get some answers," I replied monotonously, my hands still raised.

"And let's be real, you don't want angels coming in here investigating the shooting of one of their own, not to mention an Interceder. Why don't you just answer some questions instead?"

"I like my odds," the man said.

The heat in the pit of my stomach yearned to be released and I granted it wholly. In an instant the bright blue flame licked at my fingertips and hands and shot towards the two men in a fiery bolt of blue flames, burning the guns from their hands. They frantically flailed for a moment trying to put out the fire that had hit them. Jared collected the guns and I took a seat opposite the two men. Jared moved towards the corner of the room to observe my interrogation and keep watch.

The men's eyes widened as they watched the blue flame dissipate in my hands until it was no longer visible. I definitely had their attentions now. I smiled. Secretly enjoying this new power and control I had, it was almost euphoric.

"Now, what do you know about New Creation?" I quietly leaned forward on the sofa.

The younger man snorted, but did not comment. The older of the two men clapped his hands with a sarcastic smile strewn across his face.

"Well it appears the hybrid's already chosen sides." He drew a pack of cigarettes from his jacket pocket and pulled one out.

"You want to know about New Creation Investments?" He paused and lit his cigarette. Well, there isn't much to tell." He received a death glare from the younger man next to him, but continued anyway.

"The Banoff's owe us a debt for helping them in the past. They're working that debt off, but until it's paid off, that debt will transfer to each successive generation." He finished taking a long drag of his cigarette, smiling as he savored the burning gray smoke hovering in the air around him.

My eyes furrowed.

"What sort of debt do they owe you?"

"The type that can only be paid in blood or sweat. We're their puppet masters, we pull the strings and they dance. If they don't, we take payment in other, more deliberate ways. Their payment for us handling any of their dirty business in life."

Why did they seek your help? What do they owe you for?" I questioned.

The man shrugged nonchalantly.

"Why does anyone? They wanted status, power and more money of course. The only way for their debt to be paid is to fulfill their oath." he stated firmly. "It cannot be undone. The debt must be repaid."

"When will their debt be paid?"

He shrugged, bored with the conversation.

"If they help fallen angels move ahead like we did them, the debt should be paid."

I nodded, sitting back in the sofa as I took in the information. My thoughts swarmed over the word he had used, 'oath', and a slight chill rose up my spine as my sworn statement re-played in my head again. Jared spoke up then, taking me from my thoughts and back to the present moment.

"What about business being conducted in the club?" he said as his arms remained crossed in front of him.

The man blew a puff of gray smoke into the air and it clung to the ceiling.

"Not sure I can help you there."

Jared was about to interject when the vibrations of several fallen angels entering the club above us flooded my senses.

"We should be going." I stood up quickly, directing my comment to Jared.

He nodded in understanding and headed for the door, taking the guns with him. I moved swiftly behind him towards the exit.

"Sure you're on the right side hybrid?" the older man called out. His voice trailed sarcastically behind me.

I paused and looked back, but any words I wanted to say caught in my throat. His gaze was scrutinizing and concerned. Jared's voice caused our gaze to break and I exited the room looking back at the older man once more before shutting the door behind me.

We bolted up the stairs and pushed the door open, making our way to the back of the club. The fallen angels' vibrations were nearly on top of us as we slipped out the back door. We sprinted down the alley and Jared dumped the guns in the dumpster. Our footsteps splashed through the puddles as we ran through the rain, rounded the corner, and made our way across the street to the parked Yukon.

Slamming the doors behind, Jared fired up the engine and peeled out of the parking lot heading back to Crest before anyone could know what we had done.

My adrenaline began to slow and I thought about what the man had told us. Was that why Trey had been sent to Crest? To get ready for the family business and to help repay the debt they owed to fallen angels? I wondered if Trey had known all along about angels and fallen angels and had become distant because of it. Since the night of my birthday, I'd tried to contact him, but he hadn't returned any of my calls and always seemed to be off campus. I've known Trey most of my life and that went completely against his character. Did he know about me? I was going to confront him as soon as I could and find out.

Chapter 16

We drove back to Crest, silently at first. My mind muddled with thoughts of the oath Trey's parents had sworn. If this 'debt' was bound to fall into the hands of each successive generation until it was 'paid', that could only mean one of my best friends was in trouble. Judging by the way he had been avoiding me lately, I had to assume he knew about angels. There was simply no other explanation.

And the question the fallen angel had asked me still hung in the air.

'Sure you're on the right side hybrid?'

I felt more than confused. I felt helpless and frustrated all at once. I had finally just started to feel like I belonged somewhere and now I felt like I was right back to where I had started, uncertain about where I belonged and what I was doing.

"That was *not* how I pictured that going," Jared said in a low voice as he focused on the road ahead.

"At least we got *something*, and that's what we came for."

Jared met my gaze.

"I'm sorry about your friend, nothing will happen to him though as long as he abides by his oath."

"That's what I'm afraid of. What if he doesn't?"

We exchanged glances once more before becoming silent, wrestling with our own thoughts for the rest of the car ride back to Crest.

Jared pulled his Yukon in front of my building and kept the engine running.

"I wouldn't mention tonight to anyone, I'm pretty sure we broke a ton of rules back there."

I nodded in return.

"Yeah, I feel like I'm a bad influence. Thanks for going with me though. See you tomorrow?" I asked, raising an eyebrow.

"See you tomorrow Alex."

The halls were quiet inside as I walked up the stairs and down the hall-way to my dorm. The sound of the rain on the roof echoed through the still building. Fiddling with my keys, I unlocked the door and sensed a fallen angel inside. Luther was probably checking in on me again, likely due to our last encounter. My senses told me he was nervous, his energy seemed... spooked and it made me more than uneasy. Luther had always been able to comfort me and I needed to hear that things would be OK right now.

I shut the door behind me, locked it and strode towards the kitchen to turn on the light.

"OK Luther, hit me with the latest and greatest," I asked as I tossed my shoes off in the closet and filled a glass of water.

A male figure shifted in the dark letting the light bounce off him. I took a sip of my water and nearly spit it out when I saw Nathaniel's icy blue orbs piercing me.

"What are you doing here?" I stammered, unable to keep my voice from shaking.

The feeling of the cold blade on my throat resurfaced in my mind and I set the glass down, backing away slowly. He held his hands up slightly and continued to move towards me. A counter was all that separated us now.

"Visiting night clubs lately are we?" His velvety voice cooed softly as an almost indistinguishable grin came over his mouth.

Was he following me? How else could he have known I was at Echo?

"Maybe. A girl is allowed to go out you know." My breathing was short and quick and my heart throbbed wildly.

He nodded his head, seeming to ignore my defensive response, and leaned on the counter.

"I know you were at Club Echo earlier tonight with another angel. You should be careful is all I am saying." His brilliant eyes met mine with something that struck me as odd, and it angered me: concern.

"Are you following me? And why do you care all of the sudden what I do or don't do?" The fire in the pit of my stomach sizzled as I fought to keep my emotions in check.

Was he really trying to tell me he was watching out for me now? After all this time, and after what he had admitted? Now he suddenly cares?

The thought burned as it hit me.

No. He couldn't care less about me, he'd admitted it and I'd heard it straight from his mouth.

He straightened.

"You know I've always cared for you Alex. I didn't... I didn't know that was you in the swamp. I didn't know you had come to Crest either. Now what were you doing at Club Echo earlier?" He sounded pained as he spoke and then concern put an edge to his voice.

"Well now you know. There weren't too many places for me to go after you left," I said, fighting back the gargantuan lump building in my throat and the swell of tears and anger wanting to push their way forward.

I felt him move closer and my senses spiked as the smell of pine and mint hit my nose. I had waited and yearned to smell that combination of scents – his scent – again. Apparently, that recording wasn't clear enough for me. I breathed and focused on refusing what I wanted most. To embrace him, to tell him how much I missed him and how being with him was the only thing that had made sense to me. But I couldn't. And even if I did, it wouldn't be reciprocated. I would remain reserved and guarded. Hiding my feelings would be easier than getting hurt a second time.

"I'm sorry I left you. It was the only thing I could do at the time to make sure you were safe. Whether you believe me or not is up to you." He spoke softly, watching me.

I couldn't take any more lies, so I changed the subject.

"Don't. Just... don't," I said with my hand up. I wasn't about to hear his fake apology. "Why are you back?" I questioned nonchalantly, pushing all my emotions back again.

I could feel the intensity of his gaze making my hands clam up and I had difficulty meeting his gaze. Those eyes had tormented my dreams ever since he'd left and I didn't trust that I wouldn't be hypnotized by them again into believing that he genuinely cared.

"You endangering yourself at night clubs could be one reason." He kept a straight face, his tone low and criticizing.

"I'm sure you know that I'm plenty capable of protecting myself now. Why don't you tell me what *really* made you come back?" I pressed, knowing there was something he was keeping from me. That's what he did, after all; he hid things. He was a *liar*.

He paused and huffed out a breath at my question, but something in his eyes flickered brightly as he watched me.

"I came back for several reasons, you're one of them." He said it so matter-of-factly, as if I shouldn't have expected anything different, that I fought the urge to shoot him with a bolt of fire right there.

"And the other reason?"

"To keep a watchful eye on the angels and be of use to fallen angels if needed."

I raised my eyebrows mockingly, wondering why I had even asked.

Of course.

"You're here to spy on everyone," I confirmed.

"Pretty much. Now are you going to tell me why you broke into a fallen angels' private meeting area?'

I hesitated for a moment, watching him carefully. If Nathaniel really wasn't on my side, this would be the way to find out. Besides, he probably already knew why I was there anyway. I contemplated a few seconds, then decided I'd see where this conversation would go.

"I wanted to find out why New Creation Investments is working with fallen angels. Apparently, the Banoff's swore an oath that's been passed down to Trey now. I won't let one of my best friends be forced into serving anyone, particularly supernatural bad guys." I let my gaze linger on his cool blue eyes and a part of me stirred restlessly.

Nathaniel nodded his head in understanding, but his reaction told me this wasn't new news to him. The rumbling of my cell phone on the kitchen counter broke my thoughts and made both of us stir uncomfortably. I checked the screen and saw a new text from Jared.

Fallen angel reported on campus.
Keep an eye out.

Yep, just a little late on the notice.
"You should go. They know you're on campus," I said hastily.

He hesitated and I couldn't help but wish he'd bolt towards the window as I tried to keep my distance from him.

He seemed slightly amused for some absurd reason as I pushed the window open, letting the damp air in and the smell of freshly fallen rain. I waved my hand sarcastically towards the window for him to get out.

"I want to see you again," he said in a velvety voice suddenly blocking the window.

"No." I hadn't meant for the word to come out as harsh as it had, but I couldn't help it. And part of me was relieved I had come off harsh. I was terrified that whatever was left of my heart this man would crush, because as much as I didn't want to admit it, he had the power to do it. Hurt flashed across his face and I fumbled my words.

"I just... I don't think that's a good idea. You've really got to go, someone could have already seen you by now."

"I'm not leaving again Alex." His tone was dangerously serious, and it made the hairs on the back of my neck stand on end.

I watched his body disappear out the window and fade into the blackness outside.

The rain pelted my face as I shut and locked the window tightly. I'd have to be better about feeling vibrations, or paying attention for that matter. I couldn't let myself have surprise encounters like that. And from Nathaniel no less. I let my body fall back onto the soft comforter as I stared up at the ceiling and thought about Nathaniel's request. It felt almost unfair the pull he had on me. I had tried ignoring it, forgetting it and pretending it didn't exist, but each time I was around him I could feel myself fall into those icy blue orbs again. My emotions ran rampant and I was exhausted. Soon my vision blurred and I drifted to sleep.

The sound of waves smashing against the base of a cliff drew my attention. It was dusk and a brilliant sunset painted the sky with bright yellow, blue, and pink. I stood at the cliff's edge peering down at the rocky drop-off below.

"Beautiful isn't it." A voice spoke gently above the crashing of the waves.

I turned, recognizing Ezekiel. It was the second time I'd met him where he wasn't wearing a shirt. As strange as this would have seemed with anyone else, with Ezekiel, somehow, this seemed to be his natural state. It never felt odd to see him this way. I wasn't sure how old he was, but I got the feeling he was much older than Nathaniel and the other angels and fallen angels I'd met. His wings were unfurled, but remained loose at his back, dragging against the ground tenderly. I peered back over the cliffs.

"Especially if you're into heights." I was mesmerized by the awesome space and the shift in the energy. A strong wind blew inland from the sea, carrying the piquant smell of sea salt with it.

He chuckled and looked back towards me.

"You're part angel Alex and you're still afraid of heights?" He was in a light-hearted mood.

He was right, it seemed ridiculous now, but the human part of me still lingered with that fear.

"I'm a lot of things now-a-days; funny... my fears always stay... different fears, but there's always something there."

He nodded.

"I brought you hear to warn you Alexandria. I've been watching you. I heard you swear the oath to become an Interceder for the angels and yet I believe that your feelings for certain... individuals remain. Even through your change." He tilted his head as he looked at me contemplatively, searching for validation of his words.

"Do you care for him?"

"He lied to me and betrayed my trust."

"That isn't a no..." I cut him off before he could finish.

"It doesn't matter anymore. Why is he back? What are the fallen angels after? Do you have any new information on what's going on lately? Anything at all that can help me understand?" My tone softened as I finished.

"Nathaniel is a fallen angel now Alex. He's following orders from what I can tell, although some of his movements suggest he's not following all their orders. Visiting you, for example, is not something they want him doing, ever. His tie to you is what they've been trying to sever ever since he turned. Seems they want to make him their own personal assassin, and assassins can't feel, otherwise they become liabilities.

"There have also been whispers about what the fallen might be up to, but each lead we track has been turning up empty or dead. Since your transformation, I believe certain angels have gone astray in their duties. I do not have the authority to act on these beliefs. I need proof to bring to the Council first. And I fear even they have become corrupted." He shook his head heavily.

"What does that mean? The Council is supposed to uphold the balance; if they're gone there's no one left to control either angels or fallen angels. And that means..." The thoughts of what anarchy would reign afterwards made my skin go cold and I shivered. Every human would be left without protection, rules would be null and void, and angels and fallen angels would be at each other's throats.

"Chaos. It would be the Dark Ages all over again, when there was no balance." His eyes went glassy, filling with what I could only assume to be memories from that time.

"What are you asking me to do?" I asked as the severity of the situation crept in.

"I need you to help me weed them out. Stay true to your oath. I fear I cannot help you if you don't, but try to help me uncover who among us has lost their way." He stepped closer to the edge of the cliff and looked below.

"But how would I know if an angel has lost their way?" My pleading that he had asked this of the wrong person went unheard.

"You still don't understand. You have been chosen for this life Alexandria. You are more than an angel or a fallen angel, you are a hybrid and you have the potential to bring peace to each of our species, to bring peace between us. Follow your instincts Alexandria, they will keep you safe," he said, his wings now fully outstretched.

His body drifted over the edge of the cliff effortlessly and he flew in the direction of the sunset. I called after him desperately.

"What if you're wrong?!" The sunset was beginning to wash away in the distance. I yelled and I could hear my voice fade under the sound of the crashing waves against the shingle.

Chapter 17

T he dream from the night before lingered on my mind as I finished getting ready and headed to the barn to see Ajax. I needed to clear my head and there seemed to be only one of two ways for me to do that. Train more or ride. I knew I'd probably run into Jared at the gym, but I wanted some quiet time to clear my head, so I opted for a ride with Ajax.

Ajax pranced excitedly in the cross ties as I saddled him. I pushed the solid steel doors open and jumped into the saddle, heading him towards some trails, opposite the one we had taken before, that lay scattered under the cover of the trees on campus. We walked and galloped for a while until a giant 12 foot iron fence blocked our path. The trail we had been following continued beyond the iron fence and I sighed in frustration as Ajax pawed the ground.

"You could go around it you know." An all too familiar voice sounded huskily in the woods just beyond the fence.

Alarmed, I turned towards the voice and found Nathaniel resting against the base of a large pine on the other side of the fence.

I was frustrated I hadn't felt his presence again until it was too late.

"You shouldn't be here. What if someone sees you again?"

Nathaniel ignored my comment and strode towards the fence nonchalantly.

"I wanted to see you. I knew you'd eventually take Ajax through here so I waited."

I opened and closed my mouth when the right words to say to him didn't come out. Sometimes I felt as if he knew me more than I knew myself. He braced his hands against the iron fence and he continued when I didn't respond.

"Meet me tonight." The tone of his voice caught me off guard. He sounded almost distressed, like he not only wanted to see me, but that he *needed* to see me.

"Please Alex. Meet me at 23 E. Drayton tonight."

Ajax became antsy and reared, causing my gaze to tear momentarily from Nathaniel. When I looked back, he was gone. I turned Ajax and galloped back towards the barn in a hurry, trying to ignore Nathaniel's request. So much had happened since he had left. The tape replayed in my mind again and I cursed. Was he playing me again? Or did Ezekiel's words contain a sliver of the truth; did he still have feelings for me? I'd fought so hard to be rid of his memory. It had only caused me so much heartache and I couldn't believe that he still cared for me. I needed to just move on. That meant forgetting everything. It was too late, and I wasn't the same girl I had once been. I couldn't meet him, and I couldn't bear to ask him if the tape was real or fake. I couldn't risk the possibility of a heartache all over again, and that was that. I unsaddled Ajax quietly and fed him some extra treats before I headed back to my dorm.

After showering, I headed across the courtyard to Trey's building. I had to speak with him about the danger he was in with the fallen angels and what that whole thing was about. And I had to forget about Nathaniel.

I knocked loudly on his door and waited for a minute as I heard someone shuffle inside. Being the only human on campus he was extremely easy to sense, and even though he had been avoiding me lately, I wasn't about to let him this time. I decided I wasn't going to wait any longer. I burst through the door and there were him and Sophie on the sofa, making out.

Stunned, shocked, embarrassed... ah, make that feeling extremely embarrassed.

"Oh my God, um sorry, I didn't realize you were, uh…" I trailed off as Sophie smiled, completely unaffected by the intrusion.

My attention turned to the pin on her jacket, the same one Jared had given me so no one would detect us as we flew. Sophie smiled as I put two and two together before she bounced out of the room, leaving Trey cursing and glowering at me.

"I was going to answer the door you know. You didn't have to practically break it down."

I shrugged and apologized and we both shifted uncomfortably for a moment.

"So… that's great about you and Sophie, huh?" I asked trying to lighten the mood.

"Yea, we've been dating for a while now." He was still avoiding eye contact as he leaned against his desk awkwardly.

"Oh. She's nice, I like her," I replied wondering how I had missed that news and if it had been that long since he and I had last spoken to one another.

He nodded.

"Is there a reason you just came barging in here or are you just here to approve of my relationship?" he questioned bitterly.

"Whoa, where is this coming from? And if you'd checked your phone you would have noticed I've left you a ton of messages that you never returned." The harshness in his voice took me off guard. I had never seen Trey like this and frankly, I wasn't sure how to handle it.

"OK, I get it, you've been a little busy, but I'm worried about you. Listen, I know about your parent's and the oath they swore…"

But I was not able to finish my sentence. Trey jumped up from his desk and approached me with loathing in his eyes.

"You have no idea what you're talking about. I think you should leave Alex." His eyes were cold.

"Well excuse me for caring! What I'm wondering is why it's not obvious to you that what was once a solid friendship between us has turned into… well, you avoiding me and now being hostile. Is it something I've said or done? Please, enlighten me."

There was a moment of silence as we stared each other down.

"Look, Trey, you have no idea what these people are capable of; they can hurt you and they will if you give them the opportunity," I spoke hastily, trying to make him understand the danger he was in.

He laughed sarcastically.

"YOU care! That's a joke if I haven't heard one before! You've been a ghost lately Alex. Going on missions for the angels and forgetting about everyone back home. What makes you care all of the sudden? You couldn't even tell me or your family what you *truly* are! Isn't that right hybrid?"

His words sank into me like hot knives piercing my skin. I gulped as the guilt washed over me. Trey threw up his hands and paced the room as I hung my head for a moment.

"When did you find out?" I asked quietly, feeling ashamed I had tried to hide it from him when I knew he would ultimately find out somehow.

"Just after your birthday. Talk gets around you know, even with a human on campus." His voice began to come back to its normal tone.

"I'm sorry Trey, I'm sorry for everything. I never meant to hurt anyone, I was just trying to protect you all. Not to mention I was being watched like a hawk. They said fallen angels would use you or my family against me if anyone else knew. The only way I could keep you all safe was by keeping what I am a secret. Looks like I couldn't even get that right." Tears flooded my eyes.

He had stopped pacing, but an angry intensity still protruded from his body.

"Maybe it's time for you to start paying attention to things closer to home Alex. Starting with your family. As for me, I can take care of myself," he said, pushing past me and leaving the room.

I stood motionless for a moment as the guilt swept through me. Trey was right, I needed to get back to my family or at least make the effort to visit them more regularly than I had been. Other than a few brief texts, it had been months since I last contacted anyone back home.

I turned to leave the dorm and found Jared standing there. He gave me a halfhearted smile as I wiped a tear off my cheek.

"How long have you been standing there?"

"Long enough," he said.

"So, what is it?" I wanted to turn the attention from me to why he was there.

"Abraxos wants to see both of us now. He has a new assignment."

I breathed out a sigh of annoyance.

"Is there any way we can re-schedule?"

Jared's uneasy look of remorse gave me the answer.

"Right." I moved passed him and we headed in the direction of the Atrium.

I was glad he didn't pry about Trey and my fight. To be frank, I wasn't sure if I could handle what else this day was about to throw at me. We passed the gym and the door with the keypad entry, down the hall, past the debriefing room, and down a set of concrete stairs.

We eventually came upon one lone room surrounded in concrete and what looked like steel. The steel door shut behind us and a small aluminum table with four matching chairs sat inside. It resembled an interrogation room similar to the ones I had only seen in movies.

Jared and I took our seats as I tried to focus on what new assignment Abraxos could have for us. But my thoughts kept turning back to my family and what Trey had said. Regardless of what Abraxos wanted, I needed to make sure my family and friends came first from now on. And I needed to talk more with Trey. This 'deal' was not going to go away and, if what Ezekiel had said was indeed true, about me being the savior of sorts, it was up to me to find a way to change things, even if Trey didn't want to 'talk about it'. He was definitely hurting, and I was beginning to realize that the onus was on me to help.

I couldn't imagine myself as any kind of a knight in shining armor, a protector who saves the world...

Abraxos entered the concrete room followed by a tall gangly man whose suit mirrored that of Abraxos's. Each sat across from Jared and me and thankfully didn't bother with exchanging pleasantries.

"I have only a few minutes to explain this to you both, so pay attention. We have been issued an order from beyond the Council. That means this is not a request or a suggestion, this is a command. As such, you as a guardian," he said, looking first at Jared then me, "and you as an Interceder for angels have a duty. You have the authority to take immediate action and you will be provided with only a few weapons; Gregory here will outfit you once we are done here. These are your targets." He slid two manila folders across the cold table towards us.

"These will not be easy targets, but you effectively have one week to eliminate all of them; if you don't, then each of you should reconsider your professions." He finished and left the room.

I tore open the manila folder and pulled out the five profiles; a file with Nathaniel's face on it jumped out at me and I immediately raced after Abraxos. Jared called my name and followed, but I ignored him.

"Wait! Abraxos!" I caught up with him as he was ascending the concrete stairs.

He turned to me with furrowed brows as Gregory followed behind Jared and me.

"What is it?" It was more of an aggravated statement than a question.

"Sir, are you asking us to eradicate all of these people? What if some of them aren't as bad as you think?" And what about a peace between the species?" I spoke hastily and tried to remain calm.

Abraxos's glare did not cease. He took an intimidating step down, closer to me. His face lurched over mine.

"There can be no such peace between the species. Our kinds will never mix," he sneered.

"Jared, I think Ms. Constance needs to be taught what a command is again. Why don't you fill her in?" he scoffed before nodding to Gregory and proceeding up the stairs and out of view.

I stood mouth agape as Gregory announced that we were to follow him. Silently, Jared and I complied. I couldn't believe this!

Gregory stopped at another steel door down a corridor. After punching in a code, the door whined open and revealed a small room with one wall of weapons. Taking a closer look, all of the weapons displayed the exact same hand engravings and carvings that I had seen previously. My eyes lingered over the twisted gold designs and my mind flashed back to the dagger I had plunged deep into my chest to stop the Fallen from accessing the portal to heaven. I remembered it like it was yesterday. A pain in my chest deepened and we inched closer to the wall. These were weapons used to destroy angels and fallen angels specifically. My breath caught in my throat as I noted there were two of each, two knives, and two handguns with two seven-round magazines each.

"You each may know how these work, but I'm going to go over it with you anyway. These are not your ordinary weapons and they do not kill the same way either." He pulled a knife off the wall and brought it towards us for closer review.

"You can use this weapon the same way as any other knife, only the enemy must be stabbed in the heart in order to do the final trick and eliminate them. It releases a massive pulse of energy and burns the entire heart within a split second, killing all hope of them healing themselves. The victim's chest will collapse and burst open revealing a fist-sized orb.

"Fallen angels have orange orbs, whereas, angels have blue ones. You *must* bring back the orb of every fallen angel that you have been ordered to eliminate. *No exceptions.*"

"No one said anything about collecting orbs." Jared's tone turned deadly as he spoke in a low voice.

Gregory stopped and eyed him.

"The Council has ordered the collection of all of the fallen angel leaders' orbs; it is non-negotiable." He spat defensively.

Jared's eyebrows remained furrowed and his glare steely as he shifted his weight and let Gregory continue.

"Back to what I was saying... after you have collected the orbs and given them to the Council, you'll have completed your assignment. The handguns can be used to kill the fallen angels as well, but can only be shot with the bullets contained in these clips. These bullets pack the same burst of energy the knives do and will burn the victim's heart the same way.

"Once you complete your task you will be relieved of these weapons once more. Any questions?" He demanded rather than asked.

We remained deathly silent. Gregory smiled, pleased with our response, and bagged up a set of weapons for each of us before leading us out to the main gym.

Jared and I didn't say a word as we exited the gym, but I could practically hear each of our hearts beating wildly. I followed Jared back to his dorm and didn't wait to begin demanding an explanation of what had just happened.

"What the hell were we just asked to do Jared?!" I half whispered half yelled as I tried to contain my emotions.

Truthfully, I was beyond freaked out, I was absolutely terrified.

"I never remember signing up for killing people and taking their souls!" My voice raised an octave.

I couldn't contain my fears any longer as the sloshing of fire churned and burned within me.

Jared tossed the bag of weapons on the bed and ran his hands over his head. He seemed just as freaked out and bewildered as I was.

"You swore an oath to uphold the Council's decisions Alex, as did I, even though I'm a guardian angel."

"Yes, but that doesn't mean I can just murder five people in cold blood! Tell me you're not seriously considering this Jared?"

"You don't understand Alex! We don't have a choice! As soon as we swore that oath, we lost all ability to say *no* to their commands. We have to go through with what they are asking or..." His voice faded as fear developed in his eyes.

It was the first time I had seen Jared this fearful and I felt more than uneasy seeing his reaction.

"What will they do to us if we don't?" I asked quietly feeling my stomach ache.

Jared turned to me then and shook my shoulders forcefully.

"Don't you *dare* think about not doing this Alex! No one has ever returned after an oath has been broken, especially one of this magnitude. They will do unimaginable things."

A lump caught in my throat and I paused before looking up at him sorrowfully.

"I can't do it Jared..." The words came out softly, but Jared cut me off before I could finish.

"He's been hunting angels Alex. Nathaniel has. Ever since he turned, they've been using his skills to their advantage; he's not an angel anymore. And after what the others did to you, how could you *not* want them dead?" he questioned harshly.

It was true, Apollyon and some of the other fallen angels in the folders we had been given had tried to use me, changed me, kidnapped me and had hurt Nathaniel, but what the Council was asking us to do was far worse than what had been done to me. This was murder.

"I need some air," I stated turning for the door with the bag of weapons still clinging to my shoulder.

"I *won't* let you break your oath Alex. Either you do it, or I will," he said flatly, his eyes pleading with me to be reasonable and understanding.

"I just need some time to think." I left the room and shut the door behind me.

I walked back to my dorm feeling the full weight of my choices. Inside my room, I dumped the knife and gun on the bed and stared at them blankly, my head filled with thoughts and fears. *Could I go through with it?* Perhaps for someone like Corson, I thought as memories of the horrible man re-entered my mind.

The question was, was I capable of killing a man that had professed he had only left me to protect me in the first place? A man that came into my life randomly and somehow from the beginning had had a pull on my heart? A man that I had loved, and even if he had never loved me or had fallen out of love with me, could I do that just to save my own skin, or to uphold a series of words spoken aloud?

Ezekiel's words poured back into my head. *'Obey your oath as I don't know if I can protect you if you don't.'*

The golden engraved knife stared back at me menacingly. Taunting me. Without thinking, I grabbed the knife and checked the time. Dusk had fallen and it was already 8:30; I changed into the clothes adorned with the pin concealing myself from other angels and fallen angels. Leaving the tactile vest off and replacing it with a black jacket, I concealed the knife in the small of my back.

I had no idea what I was doing, I just knew I had to go to 23 E. Drayton.

Chapter 18

At first it seemed Nathaniel had given me an address to nowhere, until the area began to become familiar. I had been flying for several hours over mostly forest when I set down quietly behind the familiar cabin Nathaniel had taken me to before I was turned. I had never seen an address on the cabin before, but with the help of a GPS I was able to cross reference the closest address. This was exactly where he had said to meet him.

The cabin had always looked somewhat abandoned, but the bullet holes in the nearby trees and on the cabin itself told a different story, causing my pulse to quicken as the images of the night Nathaniel and I had been taken re-entered my mind. Much of the snow around the cabin had melted, and mud had replaced it with the recent rains. I pushed the images of that night out of my head and scanned for Nathaniel from the tree line, finding his vibration coming from the other side of the cabin by the lake. I hesitated before moving out of the tree line. After a few minutes, my body seemed to override my mind and I slowly followed the dirt path towards the lake.

I couldn't help but think that all of this had started because of a broken oath, and now I found myself in the exact same position. The irony was almost unbearable. I rounded the corner of the cabin and stopped when I saw Nathaniel standing alone, facing the lake, with his back to me. The fire in the pit of my stomach churned and I froze, my breath catching in my throat.

"I was really hoping you'd come." Nathaniel's velvety voice called out softly.

He turned towards me when I didn't respond and our eyes glued to one another. I walked towards his deep frosty blue eyes, unable to tell my body no, but stopped some feet from him on the dock. He looked more like himself, or at least like the Nathaniel I had known before. A smile took over his face, the distance I kept between not seeming to bother him, though I knew he had noticed. He searched my face wonderingly. Uncomfortable under his gaze, I reverted my eyes to the lake.

"I thought this would be a good place for us to talk, just us. And for you to enjoy some peace and quiet for a bit." He did not shift his gaze from me.

"Peace and quiet." The words sounded foreign. I hadn't been able to find peace or quiet no matter how much I sought for them.

"That's a nice necklace, "he stated aloud, locking eyes with the pendant Jared had given me.

My hand instinctively reached for the winged pendant hanging delicately around my neck. I shifted and changed the subject.

"What did you want to talk about?" I questioned, trying to hide the slew of emotions overwhelming me.

"I wanted to talk about us, and everything that has happened. I want to try and fix things." He moved a few more feet towards me.

The flames churning inside me grew heavier and my mind became fuzzy. I couldn't go through with it, I didn't even know why I had come. *What was I thinking?* I cursed my stupidity.

"I can't do this. I shouldn't have come." Fear was now taking over.

I turned and began to run from him. As I went to round the corner of the cabin and fly, a gentle but firm grip on my wrist stopped me. My skin ignited with longing where he touched me causing me to gasp as he pulled me to him.

"Please hear me out. Stay. We can just talk." His voice was smooth and velvety, but his eyes begged desperately for me to reconsider.

The churning inside my stomach changed to a yearning. The smell of pine and mint filled my senses once more and I couldn't resist. The least I could do was hear him out and then leave. I nodded slowly.

Nathaniel led me inside the familiar cabin once again. It felt as if it had been another lifetime since we were there and since I was only human. We stood in the kitchen as I tried to distance the gap between us some. I couldn't think clearly with him near me, and it frightened me. Deep down I wondered if my connection to him was somehow stronger now since I became a hybrid. The pull he had on me was intense. I was drawn to him, like the proverbial moth to a flame, but this flame could kill me, or worse...

"Listen, Alex, I know I wasn't there when you needed me most, I thought I was protecting you by leaving and I realize now I just ended up doing more harm than good. I've done some things I'm not proud of, I've made some bad choices, but you were and still are the only right thing in my life. You've only ever been the right thing."

His words tore into me. I was so confused,

"What about what you said? The... the tape?" I stammered, trying to make sense of everything.

His eyes did not harden, but his body went more rigid after my question.

"So that's what they did. Alex, my feelings for you have never changed. Whatever you heard, whatever you've been told, *none of it* holds any sliver of truth."

I searched his eyes. He was telling me the truth. My body fell a little as I fought to keep a tear from escaping my eye. All this time I had believed he didn't love me. The realization that he *did* care hit me hard and caused everything to clear. I loved him too, but now things were reversed. I couldn't be with *him* for *his* own safety, we just couldn't be...

"Nathaniel, I can't..., we can't..." I stammered out trying to stop him as he moved towards me.

How could I tell him we couldn't be together? And about what I had been sent to do? He was pouring his heart out to me entirely.

I tried to keep him from saying anything further, but he persisted.

"I love you Alex. I'm not going anywhere, and if I have to wait for you to love me back, I'll wait. I don't care how long. You're the only thing that makes sense in this crazy world and I refuse to lose you," he said flatly.

Without warning, the tears I had been trying to keep concealed escaped. He smiled and moved closer. I couldn't stop the words that came out of my mouth and I no longer wanted to. I had to tell him everything. I had to.

"I swore an oath Nathaniel! You don't understand, I can't be with you even if I wanted to." The words came out unevenly as my composure broke.

His eyebrows furrowed as he took my hands in his.

"What do you mean? What did you swear?" he asked gently, but I thought I saw a glint of anxiety flash through his eyes.

"I'm an Interceder for the angels Nathaniel. I swore to uphold the Council's decisions and protect angels." He remained quiet allowing me to divulge more.

"I thought I had finally found a place where I could be myself and just try to be...normal for a bit..." I trailed off, pausing, and then continued.

"They want you dead Nathaniel. We got the news earlier. They want me to... to take your orb." I managed to finish my sentence, but the words felt dirty and bitter as they came out.

I could feel his body go rigid once more, but he didn't say a word.

"How were they planning on doing that without..." But he didn't have a chance to finish his sentence as I had already reached for the knife in the small of my back and flung it on the counter.

I turned and cried uncontrollably. I could not kill Nathaniel because deep down I knew that I still loved him too.

I heard Nathaniel pick up the blade and turned to see him study it for a moment in shock.

"*Defensor lucem*... they found them. We all thought they were lost forever, but somehow they found them again."

He set the knife down and began to approach me.

"I'm sorry," I muttered. "I can't do it. I won't."

His lips came crashing down on mine as our arms intertwined. His hands pulled me in closely to his body as my hands found their way to the back of his neck. I needed him just as much as he needed me and the intensity of our kiss skyrocketed. The fire within me came alive in that moment, and all the feelings that I buried for Nathaniel came rushing back in crushing waves of heat. I no longer cared about my oath or duty to anyone. His kiss was passionate and desperate, like he needed and missed me more than I could ever know, and our kiss deepened as I tried to meet that need. I couldn't hold back the fire that had grown inside me; I welcomed it. My kisses slowed as I heard Nathaniel whisper huskily.

"Whoa."

I soon realized much of my body was reverberating a bright sapphire glow. I was on fire. Quickly, I pulled away from him and began apologizing as I focused on sending the fire back below my skin. He didn't seem phased at all. I cocked my head in confusion as we both caught our breath.

"I didn't burn you?" I questioned in disbelief.

A smirk came over his face that made my heart flutter.

"If that's not a sign, I don't know what is," he said touching my hands once more and continuing when the shocked look on my face did not dissipate.

"You didn't burn me Alex. Your fire can't hurt me, it's almost like I'm immune to it because you want me to be." He tucked a strand of my hair behind my ears.

"Why couldn't you do it? Why couldn't you kill me?" he questioned softly, suddenly taking me off guard.

"I would rather have that then have you break your oath, you know that, love." His velvety voice was soft as he pressed to know what I was feeling and thinking.

"I just couldn't, I...I love you Nathaniel. I'd rather..." Cradling my cheek in his hand, he pressed his thumb to my lips before I could say anything further.

"I don't want to hear you say that. I've had to witness it once before, and I'll never let that happen again." His tone was heavy and he kissed me once more.

"Can we just stay here tonight?" I asked, closing my eyes and letting my body rest against his in an embrace.

"I'm not going anywhere," he said, and kissed the top of my forehead.

Chapter 19

The sound of birds chirping drew the attention of my ears as I slowly began to wake. A warm breath on my neck and arm across my waist brought back the memories of last night.

I had stayed with Nathaniel at the cabin and we had fallen asleep intertwined. A smile came over my face. I slipped out from under his arm and paused before closing the door to let him sleep. I hadn't planned to stay the night at the cabin with Nathaniel, I hadn't expected to hear him profess his love for me either, nor I for him. Not to mention I knew I was basically breaking my oath by being with him. It seemed I had already made my choice, staying with him last night only proved that.

I turned the coffee pot on and looked out the small wooden kitchen window as it brewed. It was warm outside and the sun's rays created a glasslike finish on the top of the lake revealing a perfect reflection of the sky and mountains.

I heard the kitchen door creak as I poured two cups of the coffee and doused mine with cream. Nathaniel sauntered into the kitchen with a grin plastered on his face and took the cup of coffee I offered. Each of us leaned back against the kitchen counter and eyed the other, unsure of what to say yet perfectly aware of what the other might be thinking. Nathaniel's grin didn't falter. My cheeks flushed and I tried to conceal it with the coffee cup.

"So..." I began nonchalantly.

"So," he replied, his icy blue eyes glistening, causing a heat wave to run through me.

"What are we going to do about my oath?" I asked quietly as I took a sip of my coffee.

"God you're beautiful," he said ignoring my question and gazing at me admiringly.

I shifted uncomfortably as my pulse quickened. The feeling of butter-flies in my stomach had me feeling giddy, but I couldn't help feeling something else – a cold shiver running up my spine: fear.

"I'm being serious Nathaniel. How are we supposed to make this work?" My smile faded. I shook my head.

He looked down at the ground for a moment before closing the dis-tance between us and taking my hands.

"We'll figure it out, we always have, right? Even if we have to lay low for a while. I'm not going anywhere Alex." Something in his eyes made me wonder if he truly believed we would be OK.

I gave him a half-hearted smile. It had seemed like forever since we had been together and so much had happened since we had been apart. I couldn't help but ask him a question I had been dying to know the an-swer to since that day I first saw him again in the swamp.

"Can I ask you something?"

"Shoot," he said listening curiously.

"What happened to you while you were gone?"

He exhaled a long breath and became somewhat uncomfortable after I asked it. Something swam deep in his eyes that I couldn't understand, and the same wildness I had seen in them before returned in flickers. Eventually coming around to speak, his tone was monotonous.

"You remember what I told you my job is right?"

I nodded in response, but let him continue.

"After I left you that day, I made my way out of the country to South America. I was initiated as a fallen angel there and given that job due to my background and skill set. I was put through a series of tests, making sure I was compliant and then given assignments which I completed. Most of those were spying and gathering information, but others consisted of...eliminating angels that were threats.

"They gave me the details and I got the job done. Nothing more, nothing less. That went on for a while until a majority of us returned to the states on different orders. That's when I ran into you." He stood back from me, distressed, and let me take in the information as he ran a hand through his hair.

I nodded, wrapping my head around what he had just divulged. It was true then, he had killed angels.

"What have you been ordered to do now?"

He paused for a second and then opened his mouth to reply. The presence of an angel made me stop him abruptly and I pulled him to the ground, yelling for him to get down as a bullet whizzed through the window and shattered a cabinet. Several more shots rang out as we shuffled on the floor against the cabinets.

"Who is that?!" Nathaniel yelled above the sound of the bullets.

"Jared. He's been ordered to kill you, too. Do you have a gun?!" I yelled back.

Nathaniel nodded towards the direction of the bedroom. I moved towards the bedroom and Nathaniel grabbed a hold of my arm firmly.

"No! He could shoot you!" he yelled as his eyes turned from an icy blue to a colder, darker navy.

I shook my head.

"Trust me, he's not here to hurt me."

With that, I freed my arm from Nathaniel's grasp before he could protest further and made a dash for the bedroom, slamming my body through the doorway. Inside, I shuffled though several drawers until a knife and gun came up. The knife I had brought that was meant to kill angels and fallen angels, along with Nathaniel's Glock and my pack with the other gun. I grabbed all of it, sticking the knife in the small of my back and checking that the Glock was loaded.

Sliding back into the kitchen from the hallway, Nathaniel smiled when he saw his gun.

"I'll draw him off while you get out of here, he's not going to hurt me;

he's here for you," I said crouching and peering around the kitchen to the front door.

A crash sounded down the hall by the bedroom as Nathaniel protested, but there was no time. We stood as Jared's body emerged from the hallway. He was holding one of the pistols we had been given and he already had it directly pointed at Nathaniel.

"Get out of here Alex. This doesn't concern you." Jared's tone was menacing and he was by no means playing. He was there to kill Nathaniel.

I moved in front of Nathaniel slowly with my arms raised, still holding the Glock, but with the barrel pointed towards the ceiling. He shifted uncomfortably as I moved into the gun's line of sight.

"Jared, what are you doing?" I demanded as his brows furrowed.

"He's going to get you killed or worse! And I'm not going to let that happen," he threatened.

I felt Nathaniel's hand move to push me aside and I looked back at him confused.

"He's right Alex, you should go. We'll handle this." But his tone and the look in his eyes were dark.

I shook my head angrily and moved back in front of Nathaniel.

"No! Jared you're not going to kill him!"

Jared glowered at me.

"Get out of the way Alex! You're going to protect this asshole!? He left you, murdered angels, and is going to get you killed!" He shouted angrily, bewildered by my actions as his trigger finger itched to squeeze back.

"That's my business Jared! Now I'm warning you. Put the gun down." My voice lowered as the heat in the pit of my stomach began to rise violently up my chest.

A moment passed and Jared did not move. Not wanting to wait any longer, I let the fire envelope my body and sent a searing shock wave, throwing Jared back several feet and breaking his concentration from Nathaniel, at least momentarily. Jared cursed and raised the gun again toward Nathaniel.

"No! Jared!" The sound of two gun shots pierced my ears.

Several painful shouts and curses followed and I dropped the gun and rushed to Jared's aid. I grabbed a dish towel and applied pressure to the two wounds now pouring out blood.

"Damn it!" I cursed. "Why didn't you put the gun down Jared!?" I yelled, frustrated and flustered, removing the towel and placing my hands over his wounds to try and help heal him.

I had never healed anyone before and my hands shook as I tried to concentrate.

"You shot me?" he said somewhat amused and shocked and forgetting all about Nathaniel.

I looked back at Nathaniel expectantly as he rolled his eyes and stormed off to find the first aid kit.

"What were you thinking?" I asked Jared. I was exasperated, but I was finally feeling energy reach my hands to begin healing him.

He shrugged his shoulders some and coughed up another mouthful of blood as his body began its own healing. A glow of energy seeped from my hands and I continued to concentrate, flowing healing energy into his wounds.

"I followed you last night. I thought you were going to go through with it so I waited till this morning, but I realized you didn't do it. So I figured I'd give it a try. Better that, then you dying for him," he said as his hand found mine.

He squirmed for a moment as one of the bullets began to push its way out of his skin, making me cringe. I felt remorse for shooting him, but deep down I knew he would have killed Nathaniel right then and there had I not intervened.

I shook my head at him.

"Jared..." I began to say, but he cut me off waving his hand as his body tensed once more then relaxed.

"I really don't want to know why, Alex, don't worry. I'm not gonna kill him... yet..." He looked irritated as he glared at Nathaniel who entered with a first aid kit.

Nathaniel tossed the first aid kit to me and I quickly tore it open and bandaged the wounds. I had helped heal him as much as I could, but the consistent pressure on the wounds would help his body heal completely, especially now that the bullets had pushed themselves out. I helped heave Jared up off the floor and moved him to the couch so he could rest and regain some of his strength.

Moving past Nathaniel, I grabbed a new glass and filled it with cold water, giving it to Jared. He stretched out on the small sofa, his feet hanging over the edge, and took the glass gratefully before closing his eyes and resting. Guilt spread through my body and I couldn't help but shake as I watched him.

A few minutes passed and Jared was sleeping; he wouldn't need much time to heal, but a half hour of sleep would do him wonders.

I needed some air. Stepping outside, I walked to the lake and stopped at its edge. I peered into the crystal clear water trying to gather my thoughts; slowly my shaking subsided.

I could hear Nathaniel's footsteps and felt his vibrations as I waited for him to approach. He stood next to me, arms crossed, peering out at the lake before us, but did not say anything for a moment.

"He's right you know. You really should kill me." He spoke evenly, but continued to gaze out at the lake as I turned to look at him.

I huffed out a breath.

"Like you were supposed to kill me years ago? You two should really stop trying to tell me what to do. I can't kill you the same way you couldn't kill me, and I won't. We're just going to have to figure something else out," I said as the weight of my words sank in.

I wouldn't kill Nathaniel and I knew exactly what that meant. Truthfully, I wasn't ready to die either. We had to figure out another plan and quickly. We had six days left to bring Abraxos what he wanted and the clock was ticking. I needed to talk to Luther. Where was he in all this? Surely his eyes were on me somewhere.

Chapter 20

The three of us sat unmoved in the living room of the cabin. Jared had completely healed and we had gathered to try and come up with a plan. Instead of coming up with ideas, however, Nathaniel and Jared sat silently, neither willing to look at the other, let alone, work with one another.

"Does anyone have any ideas?" I asked half-heartedly, desperate to break the awkward silence and tension that filled the air.

"Yea, it's simple. Kill *him* and be done with it," Jared spat suddenly.

"I'd be happy to go outside and let you try." Nathaniel's face darkened.

A headache had creeped into my forehead and I rubbed my temples.

"Seriously you guys? Can we please come up with some useful ideas? No one is killing *anyone*." I was getting annoyed.

I sent Jared an *'I dare you to make another comment'* look before he could muster up a witty reply.

"Now..." I said, staring at the photos of the men Abraxos had ordered us to kill. "Abraxos wants us to take out the leaders of fallen angels. Why? What could he possibly gain from it? Fallen angels would never follow him even without a leader. They would never follow a full blooded angel. So he can't be doing this to gain their allegiance."

I may have been a newbie to the angel world, but even I knew that fallen angels wouldn't listen to an angel. The words of Ezekiel rushed through my head again as I started to piece things together.

"Ezekiel, the angel who carries out most of the Council's orders, came to see me the other night. He thought at least some part of the Council had been corrupted. He asked me to help him find out who's at the bottom of the corruption. Abraxos is the only logical choice, right? He's the one ordering the killings and is on the Council." I looked to Nathaniel and Jared for feedback.

Nathaniel nodded his head in contemplation. Jared spoke up.

"Ezekiel said this to you? Why didn't you mention anything before now?" He sounded irritated.

"He told me not to trust anyone, but I'm telling you both now because I trust you both, and we're all we've got."

"Alex is right," said Nathaniel. "We can't trust anyone else but each other if Abraxos is behind this. He has way too much power and influence, and no one would believe us even if we did tell them. He'd get wind of it and we'd all be dead. We should follow *him*. Start watching his movements and see if we can find out who else is involved in this. There has to be others involved; fallen angels wouldn't follow Abraxos, you're right. We're looking for a group of angels."

Jared chimed in. "What if it's just one guy? A fallen angel coordinating this that wants to be in power?"

Nathaniel shook his head. "I don't think so. Our... their... my leaders would have sniffed him out by now. We've known about something the angels were planning for a while now after intercepting a few of them. That information would have come out," Nathaniel replied coolly.

"You mean the angels you *murdered*? Got it," Jared spat.

Nathaniel was silent for a moment, but his eyes were cold and dark as he stared at Jared.

The tension was becoming thick again. So thick you could drown in it.

"Guys, let's focus. Jared, don't be so quick to judge. Yesterday, you were willing to kill this handful of fallen angels, though admittedly by direct order from the Council. So please leave some room in your brain to understand that maybe Nathaniel could have been held under the same kind of pressure.

"Ok. So we follow Abraxos and see who else is involved in this thing. What if we don't have enough time? What then? Abraxos is expecting the orbs of all of the leaders in six days."

"We don't kill them. We fake it," Jared said reluctantly.

I gave him a dumbfounded look and Nathaniel spoke up.

"He's right. They're not responsible for this just like we're not; we can't kill them. That's exactly what Abraxos and whomever else is involved wants. For some reason, they want to change who's in power and we can't let them do that."

My mouth hung agape for a moment as I looked down at the pictures of the men who had changed my life forever. The men who had kidnapped me and made me a part of their science experiment.

"They're not good," was the only reply I could muster as my insides boiled with anger.

Nathaniel nodded his head.

"It's true, they're not good, but they're not all evil either. We can't kill them and start another war Alex."

I swallowed a lump in my throat at his words. How could *he* above anyone else say that? I knew deep down he was right, but it angered me that I would never be able to seek my revenge.

"Fine."

"You both should return to campus. Start keeping tabs on Abraxos. When he goes off campus, I'll follow him and see if I can find out who he's meeting with. He'll have to meet with them eventually. He won't risk a phone call," Nathaniel stated looking back at me.

"We'll work on getting the orbs. I may know someone who can help us," Jared finished.

We all nodded in agreement and our plan was set. Now I just hoped we would have enough time. Jared grabbed some of the belongings he had stashed outside when he was staking out the cabin the previous night and Nathaniel pulled me aside. The touch of his skin sent hot trembles down my spine.

"You alright?"

I nodded, but he could tell it was forced.

"Everything will be fine, don't worry." His hands met my hips trying to comfort me.

"I can't imagine where I've heard that before," I stated sarcastically. He furrowed his eyes, a grin appearing.

He slowly bent his neck and kissed me. His lips were delicate, but greedy, as they pressed for more, leaving me longing as we parted.

"Have a little faith love," he said with a wink before turning to leave.

"One more thing," he said. "I'll find a way to contact you and let you know what I find out on Abraxos. And you," he motioned toward Jared, "keep your hands to yourself or I'll remove them." He paused making sure the weight of his threat was understood before leaving the cabin and grinning back at me.

Jared rolled his eyes after Nathaniel left.

"So..." I began slowly, still feeling a little guilty for shooting him.

"I just made a call to a friend of a friend who may be able to help us get some orbs," he said slowly.

"That's good right?" I noticed he was uncomfortable.

"Yes and no. The guy who has them is... a little crazy, but agreed to meet with us. He will want something in return for his services though. He always does."

"Ok..." I wasn't sure if I liked this plan after all, but we really didn't have any other options.

"When do we meet him?"

"He said he'd send someone to us who would give us details on where to meet him." He continued when my eyebrows raised. "I told you he's crazy. And paranoid."

"I need to see my family. I'll plan on meeting you back at Crest later, k?"

"We should stick together, Nathaniel said..." But I cut him off before he could finish.

"Listen, I'm going to see my family and if you see Nathaniel before I do, you can tell him that. Besides, I'm a big girl, I can take care of myself."

He rolled his eyes unwilling to argue with me further.

"So I'm learning. Fine, but be ready if I call," he said, defeated.

I made my way to a department store and made some purchases, then changed out of my angel uniform. I figured I had made a good decision when I walked in and received stares from just about everyone. I looked like I should have been on the set of the new Terminator movie or something. In the dressing room, I shoved the *defensor lucem* knife into the new bag I had bought and jostled my angel uniform in there as well before paying up front and leaving. I had just stepped out of the store and had begun to make my way down the street to a bus stop when I heard my name being shouted and a ruckus of car horns. I turned back to find Kate practically hanging out of her car window waving me over.

"What are you doing here!? You didn't tell me you were coming down! Get in!" she screeched as several upset drivers behind her honked their horns.

I darted for the car and jumped in, glad to see her.

"What are you doing down here!? And where is your car?" she asked as she stomped on the gas pedal and peeled through a red light.

It made me wonder how she had managed to skillfully negotiate her way out of all of her tickets when it was evident that traffic laws were merely taken as suggestions to her.

Snapping my thoughts back to her question, I came up with a quick explanation. I had flown here from the cabin using the pendant, but told her I had carpooled with someone from the campus.

"I figured I'd just catch the bus to my parents. What are you doing here?" I asked quickly, diverting attention back to her.

It was great seeing Kate, but I still wasn't ready to tell her what I was. I wasn't sure how she would take it to be honest or if she'd immediately un-friend me forever, and with everything else that was going on, I figured it was best if she was kept in the dark for now.

"I was at Jesse's parent's house for a BBQ, but thank God that is over!" she exclaimed.

"His grandma kept preaching about safe sex practices and I almost died!" she laughed, embarrassed as her cheeks flushed.

"I was on my way back to my house, but I can take you to your dad's if you like?"

I nodded and we proceeded to talk the rest of the drive about her and

Jesse, what was new, and about Trey. She mentioned she hadn't really seen him or heard from him since my birthday and that she was worried he'd gotten in with the wrong 'crowd' at Crest. I told her he was probably just trying to get his bearings, but inside the guilt and anger from the words he said to me at our last encounter hit me.

"You two have acted super weird since you guys started going to that school. Are you going to tell me what's up or what?" she pressed as we pulled into the farmhouse driveway.

I hesitated for a moment knowing there wasn't much I could tell her, only lies and excuses for now, but she piped up again before I could say anything.

"I get it! I'm not going to the same school, but when you two want to divulge what the hell's up lately, I'd love to know," she yelled sarcastically, throwing her arms up in the air in defeat.

I laughed at her outburst, but knew deep down she was genuinely concerned about both of us.

"Seriously though! Don't forget me!" she exclaimed, hugging me before I could get out of the car.

"I promise I'll tell you everything soon, there's just...too much to say right now."

She seemed to accept this answer and I hopped out of the car and told her I'd call her soon. I noticed my dad's car was in the driveway along with my mom's and made my way to the house. I stepped into the doorway hearing shouts coming from my dad's study. It sounded as if they were arguing over something about the divorce.

Great timing Alex.

I reluctantly rounded the corner and stood in the entrance to the study.

"Hey guys! Uh...bad timing?" was all I could muster as both of my parents turned, shocked to see me standing in the doorway.

"Oh my God! What are you doing here?! Did you know she was coming?" my mom turned and asked my dad.

He remained silent, smiled at me and got up to give me a hug.

It was awkward for a moment as the two of them put their argument on hold. They did their best to pretend everything was OK, but deep down I was saddened to know they were still having problems. I knew nothing would be 100% peachy between the two of them after the divorce was final, but I never realized it could get so ugly between two people who had once loved each other so much. I didn't pry into what the fight was about and did my best to move it from my mind as I focused on why I was really there.

"I wanted to spend time with my parents. I miss you guys" With all of the changes I had undergone recently, family was the one thing I wanted to remain constant. It was probably one of the only ways I would be able to get through everything that was to come. I temporarily put my crazy angel/fallen angel problems on hold and visited with them.

I was shocked to realize about three hours had gone by when I looked at my phone again. We had dinner, reminisced on family memories with Derek and me, and even gave Derek a call at the marine base where he was stationed. It felt good to be home with the people I loved, but for some reason it felt extremely foreign as well. Our home would never be as it once was, with Derek and my parents and all of our friends visiting frequently. Those times had passed. Derek was in the Marines, it seemed, for good and my parents were remaining separated, Renee was in the picture now, and here I was, the freak show, hybrid fire manipulator of the family.

Even during the visit with my parents, I couldn't hide the blatant fact that somehow we all were going our own separate ways in life. Was there such a thing as the Constance family anymore? One cohesive unit that went about together and faced problems together? I wasn't so sure anymore.

I had turned my attention to just being in the moment with my parents and relishing in whatever time we all had left with the entire family. And it was clear I had to find a way to tell them sooner rather than later what I really was. That could turn out to be the thing that might connect us again. Maybe.

Evening eventually made its way across the farmhouse, leaving it cloaked in blackness except for the lights from the porch and barn. I finished saying my goodbyes to my parents and reassured them that my ride back to campus was just down the street having difficulty finding our house. Stepping off the creaky wooden porch I made my way across the gravel drive and down the dimly lit street, eventually veering off towards a tiny dirt trail that led in between several houses towards the forest that lay beyond. There, I figured I would adorn my clothing with the angel pendant so I could fly back to Crest and no one would detect me.

Stepping across into the shadowy tree line of the forest, I began to let some of my guard down. The coos of owls in the distance caught the wind and were carried to my ears. The smell of pine and sap filled my nostrils. My feet snapped several twigs as I walked along a path thickly coated with pine needles.

The moon shone brightly, illuminating the darkness. The snap of a branch in the distance made me pause and I stopped to listen. I waited patiently for several seconds as my senses honed in on the noise. Much to my delight, a female deer stepped from behind a tree several yards away. The doe's ears pricked forward as she locked eyes with me.

We each remained still, staring at one another. The doe had wanted to remain concealed as much as I had, and yet, in each other's presence, a certain peace filled the air.

A branch snapping behind me broke the moment and the doe fled in the opposite direction. I hadn't detected anyone else in the forest with me, human or angel, so I chalked the noise up to another forest animal and continued to make my way further into the woods. I was a bit perturbed at having a moment like that be ruined.

Eventually, I stopped to get the pendant. I dropped my purse onto a boulder and dug blindly through it in search for the angel pendant. My fingers brushed against the metal and I gripped it firmly, pulling it from the bag. I held it in the palm of my hand for a moment and examined it.

Up until this point, I hadn't noticed the slight heat that it emitted. It felt as if I was holding an item that had been baking in the sun and that had only recently cooled enough not to burn when touched.

"I told you to stay with Jared." Nathaniel's voice echoed smoothly from above. He dropped down in front of me.

"Jeezus Nathaniel!" I yelled. "You nearly knocked me over." I smacked his arm as I regained my composure, rolling my eyes at his childish antics.

"Still having balance problems – even being an angel?" he chuckled, clearly pleased with himself that he had startled me.

"I'm a hybrid actually," I said sarcastically, "and I have great balance thank you."

Now I was aggravated by his sudden appearance out of nowhere and feeling completely flustered. He continued to stare at me.

"How did I not sense you?" I questioned suddenly, picking up the angel pendant I had dropped and turning it over for a look. I pinned it to the front of my t-shirt.

The devious smirk remained as he leaned his shoulder against the base of a pine. His blue orbs flickered brightly as though the moonlight came from them, but there didn't seem to be a pupil – the same way a predator's eyes look when shined with a flashlight.

"I'm impressed; these pendants still work brilliantly, even against you," he said, motioning towards the flash of metal on his black t-shirt.

"How did you get that?" knowing fully well he was not given one by Abraxos. Was it possible their side had them too?

He stared back at me for a moment before he answered.

"I picked it up this morning, off of your buddy Jared."

"You stole Jared's pendant?!"

I gave him an *are you kidding me* look, rolling my eyes and pressing my palm against my forehead.

"Can you try to not make this difficult? I mean, aren't we all after the same thing here?"

"I'm sure we are."

When I didn't respond he continued.

"I needed it more than he did. If Abraxos finds out I'm following him our whole plan will be ruined. And I wasn't about to take yours either, you need it more than ever. His was the easiest to confiscate and the most ideal." He stated it evenly and it made sense. But that left Jared without a pendant and he sure wasn't going to like it when he found it missing.

He continued to watch me intently.

I put my hands up in defeat.

"Fine, but you guys really need to figure out this whole macho thing you have going on between you two before all of this is over," I said zipping my purse and looking back at him.

His devious grin returned.

"Love to."

"Can you not be sarcastic about this?" But I knew he meant every bit of it. "Jared is a good friend who is trying to help, so can we just drop it?" I was irritated by the jealously I was picking up from him.

Our gazes broke momentarily and it was quiet.

"Anyway, what are you doing here?"

"I wanted to make sure you were OK. I stopped your buddy, excuse me, Jared, outside of Crest and he mentioned you were seeing family. I figured the farmhouse would be the best place to look for you first. Abraxos left Crest, but only visited a coffee shop up North and that was it. It was short, but no one met with him from what I could tell. Any luck tracking down some orbs yet?" he asked, pushing up off the tree.

I sighed.

"Not that I've heard yet."

Thunder cracked in the distance indicating a storm was headed our way. I took a seat on a small rock and undid my pony tail, running my palm through my hair.

"You look like you could use a drink."

I huffed for a moment.

"That actually doesn't sound half bad right now. Too bad I am under age and can't get a drink anywhere besides Club Echo. Too young to drink, but not too young to become a hybrid fire manipulator. Oh, the irony."

"We should probably avoid being seen together at places like that right now.... an Angel Interceder can't be seen hanging around someone like me." He forced a small smile, but I knew his feelings mirrored my own on the subject.

Nodding, I chewed the inside of my lip. I hated the way things were between the species. How much hurt had been caused because two people could not be together? The human side of me could not understand any of it, and Abraxos's words haunted my memory. *Our species will never mix.*

He held his hand out to me. "We should go, rain is going to hit soon." His words were soft as they left his lips.

I took his hands and felt a warmth flicker inside the pit of my stomach.

"Where to?" I asked, not really caring. I just wanted to forget about everything for a little while.

His grip tightened around my hand as a mischievous grin spread across his face. I smiled and rolled my eyes, knowing he was up to no good. Instinctively, my wings unfurled and I relaxed as they stretched outward. To say it was soothing would be an understatement. It was overwhelmingly peaceful.

"Wow." Nathaniel whispered almost to himself.

I opened my eyes and looked back at him, feeling somewhat saddened as I realized he could not fly. As punishment for not carrying out the orders to kill me, his wings were stripped from him and he became a fallen angel.

"I'm sorry." I said quickly as my wings reflexively folded down.

I couldn't help but feel guilty that he had lost his wings for me. After having my own, I couldn't imagine having them taken away. They were a part of me, another appendage. I could only imagine how Nathaniel felt knowing he would never fly again. His hand dropped mine as he stood back from me. It was not anger nor envy that etched across his face, but awe. He seemed literally blown away.

"May I?" his voice whispered huskily as he moved behind me, closer to my wings.

I nodded and kept still.

His warm hand delicately brushed against my right wing and automatically they extended outward from my body once more, welcoming his touch. His hand started from the upper middle of my wing and followed the feathers down towards my back and shoulder blades, investigating each individual black and white feather. My body shuddered and trembled under his touch as his fingertips found my shoulder blades. Goosebumps sprouted across the tops of my arms and a rush of pleasure ran through me. I was vulnerable, but knew Nathaniel would not hurt me, he never would.

Thunder cracked above us as lightening flashed. Tiny droplets of rain began to hit the forest floor around us, picking up in intensity. I felt Nathaniel's hand slide down my spine before he grabbed my hand and began to lead me through the forest. I snatched my purse and we began to run, my wings furling back into my shoulder blades. We ran until we reached a black sedan parked on the side of the road. Jumping inside, Nathaniel wasted no time in coaxing the engine to life. I laid my head back on the seat and watched the pellets of rain hit the window before turning my head to glance at Nathaniel. I had felt euphoric under his touch, and it scared me how much I knew I needed him. My pocket chimed, drawing my attention.

Jared: *"Need cake baking assistance when you get back...2nd cake a bust..."*

Me: *"Be back soon...any news yet?"*

Jared: *"Nothing. It'll be when we least expect. He'll show up though...*

...Oh and tell Nathaniel I want my pendant back."

Me: *"Easier said than done...but I'll try."*

I clicked the screen to black and shoved it back into my pocket.

"Who's that?" Nathaniel's voice hummed.

"Apparently I'm baking tonight. Oh, and Jared wants his pendant back."

Nathaniel smiled playfully.

"Interesting. And 'no' on the pendant."

I rolled my eyes and knew he wasn't about to bend on the pendant issue yet.

"I don't really even know how to bake, I should hardly be giving lessons," I thought aloud.

"That's not true, you used to cook with your grandma. She'd let you select the recipe and help you make it. You'd pass the time playing cards while the food baked. Hearts and slap jack."

I perked up, my mouth agape as Nathaniel finished speaking. The memories of cooking with my grandma when I was little flooded back into my mind. Hearts and slap jack.

My eyes locked with his. I wasn't angry that he knew about a private moment in my life. But I wondered how many of those moments I had where he had been watching over me as my guardian. His eyes shined as he looked at me softly. There was so much those eyes were still shadowing me from, and I wondered if I would ever be able to know him and his past as much as he knew me and mine. Those icy blue orbs hid pain and so much of his past, like an endless sea of emotions too vast to sift through in one lifetime.

The car quietly pulled to a stop and we sat silently staring at the iron gates that lay ahead of us.

"Call me if anything comes up. I won't be far," he said gently.

A small smile slid across my face as I turned back to him one last time, struggling for the right words to say before giving a final nod and turning for the gate, stepping to the other side as the sedan drove away.

Chapter 21

"See you CAN cook after all!" I announced joyously after nearly two hours of step by step instructions on how to bake a cake. Jared gleamed proudly over his chocolate butter-cream master-piece as I checked my phone nonchalantly, hoping that Nathaniel had texted me. No new messages. I bit my lower lip.

"My sister's not going to believe it." I batted my hand at him and tossed the phone into my purse.

"Of course she will. She's going to love it. OK, I think my work is done here," I stated. I was unable to take my mind off waiting for either Nathaniel or the man with the fake orbs to contact us.

It drove me nuts counting down the amount of time Jared and I had left before we had to meet with Abraxos, and on top of that, the amount of time that passed between Nathaniel and me. I couldn't help but feel he would disappear again. Poof. Gone, and not coming back this time. It was merely by pure accident that we found each other before. He had said he'd be near, but where? And could I trust that? Thoughts swarmed and I could feel the heat in the pit of my stomach flow through me wildly.

"You OK?" I heard Jared ask.

I turned to see him standing across the room watching me. A hazy smoldering radiation was coming off my body. I wasn't on fire, but it would be noticeable to anyone, the heat that permeated from my pores. I huffed.

"I hate waiting," I admitted.

He nodded and I could tell he was just as tired of waiting as I was, but there was nothing he could do to fix it. We were in a waiting game.

"Maybe all I need is some sleep."

"Yeah, it's been awhile since either of us really slept. You could always sleep here if you want, you know?" A quaint grin crept over his mouth causing his sea-green eyes to sparkle.

"Smooth, real smooth." I could feel myself regain control and my nerves softened as I relaxed.

"Hey, you can't blame me for asking."

Part of me wanted to stay, I couldn't deny it. I loved how comfortable and safe I felt around Jared. He had a way of calming me down and almost making me believe that everything really was going to be OK, but my thoughts swarmed around Nathaniel. Kissing his cheek goodbye I made the trek to my dorm room alone. Maybe sleep really was what I needed. I would be mentally clear afterward and hopefully my emotions would be in check again.

I plopped my limp body roughly onto my mattress and tossed the comforter over my head, blocking out the entire world and welcoming sleep.

"Parking garage on 5th and Blake. There you will find the answers you seek."

A black silhouette stood in front of me, statuesque. The figure was inhumanly tall and unnaturally slender. The voice was not one I would have expected from such a strange looking creature. It was high pitched, and male, resembling that of a squeaky toy.

"What is this? Who are you?" But no matter what question I asked, the figure repeated the same thing over and over until everything went black.

My eyes opened to the sound of thunder cracking outside my dorm. Buckets of rain began to dump shortly afterward as I stared up at the ceiling wondering what the hell I had just dreamed. *'Parking garage on 5th and Blake, there you will find the answers you seek'.*

Twenty minutes passed before I found myself getting dressed and cursed myself for what I had to do. I couldn't be sure if the dream was real or fake, and calling Jared or Nathaniel would just complicate things. I was apprehensive as I pulled my boots on and grabbed my phone. If it was nothing, then at least I wouldn't look crazy for having brought it up.

I placed the pin on my sweater so I wouldn't draw any attention, grabbed my keys and I was gone. Once off campus, I tossed the sweater adorning the pendant on the seat next to me. After driving all the way downtown from Crest, I pulled into an empty parking garage off of 5th and Blake. The fluorescent lights helped to confirm my fear as I parked in the center of the garage. Nothing. Just an empty one level parking garage that I was stupid enough to drive to alone.

I glanced at my phone. Two in the morning. I squeezed my eyes shut for a second and got out of the car, scolding myself, pacing and palming my forehead. But I was here now, so I decided to wait around awhile to see if anything - or anyone - showed up.

I was also stupid enough to not think about bringing a weapon, but I did have the pendant. If it could shield Nathaniel from my hybrid senses, surely it could shield me from... who... what?

I reached back into the car to grab my sweater and the next thing I knew was pain, lots of pain. Then rough wool against my cheek... and a bed?

Groggily, my eyes opened to inspect my surroundings. I wasn't sure what I remembered. I tried to sit up and was pressed back down by two gentle but calloused hands.

Pain and confusion surged through me and my hand immediately went to the back of my head where it throbbed. A wet substance matted my hair and caked my curious fingers as I began to slowly piece together the events. Alarm flowed through me realizing I had been hit in the head and attacked.

I threw the hands off me and stumbled to my feet, opening and closing my eyes to look for my attackers.

The blood I had felt on my head just moments ago ran down my neck in a stream. I was weak, but that didn't seem to stop the heat from rising in my stomach. Before I could do any damage to anyone or myself, the stranger blew a peculiar purple powder delicately across my face. Immediately, my body relaxed and I unwillingly drifted off to sleep, feeling my body go limp as the purple sedative filled my nostrils and lungs.

"Alex."

I woke to the sound of my name being called, but not by any voice that I recognized. My eyebrows furrowed and I squinted my eyes open. A small, older man sat before me on a wooden stool, eagerly leaning forward with wide eyes and an equally wide smile.

"What... what is this?" I stammered, shakily raising my body until I was in a sitting position.

My back met a cold concrete wall as my fingers reached for the back of my head.

"You've already healed." The stranger was still smiling broadly.

"And this should help with the aftertaste," he said handing me a cup of water. I could feel the grogginess begin to fade and my senses heighten.

"I suggest you start explaining yourself." My skin began to simmer as the heat rose.

The man seemed enthralled with my threat.

"You are Alexandria Constance, are you not? I've been told you and Jared have been looking for me."

I was quiet.

"You're the man Jared called? The one with the orbs? Do you have them?" I questioned, quickly standing.

His smile faded and he waved me off, sliding open a door and leaving the room.

"Wait!" I called desperately.

Woozily, I chased after him as the effects of the purple powder began to wear off. I was met with stern eyes in the small corridor.

"Well, I'm not just going to give them to you! Hybrid or not, you *must* be deserving of my help first." The man sounded irritated by my audacious assumption.

I tilted my head in confusion.

"Then, why did you bring me here?"

He rolled his eyes and motioned for me to follow him.

"And don't look around too much. It disturbs me," he said leading the way through the corridor.

Jared was absolutely right about this guy, he was extremely paranoid.
A tall metal door opened and the man motioned me inside.

"What is this?" I questioned, warily staring into the darkness before me.

"A test. Should you pass it, we can talk about what you came for."

"And if I fail?" The man's eyes glistened for a moment.

"If you are you, you should have nothing to worry about." His tone
was low and un-trusting.

I stepped forward, letting the dark cloak my skin. I heard the door being roughly slammed behind me. I shuddered. Regardless of my abilities,
I tried to avoid dark rooms these days. Nothing good seemed to come
from them. I turned towards a hunched over figure seated in front of a
pile of burning coals.

"Come, come now. Aren't you curious?" the elderly woman questioned.

"Curious about what?" I asked, remaining where I was.

"About who you are of course, and what lies ahead of you," she
cooed.

"What do you mean? How can you know that?" The woman motioned for me to sit next to her and, curiously, I obliged.

I could see that her brittle hands were covered in ash as she placed
several more stones in the burning coals.

"May I touch your face dear?" Her voice shook slightly as she turned
towards me and I realized she was blind.

Outstretching her hands, she grabbed hold of the sides of my face taking the breath from me. The woman held me in a trance like state. I was
awake and extremely aware that I was now at her mercy, but I could not
fight her, nor did I want to.

"Mmm...so many emotions just under the surface...pain, guilt, affection, a longing to belong. Fire. So much heat within you my dear..." She
trailed off as her fingers twitched and my eyelids rolled into the back of
my head. She searched deeper, deeper through my thoughts and memories for what lay inside me. Flashbacks raced across my eyes at lightening
speeds as she uncovered what she was looking for.

"Awe, Alexandria Constance, you are her. I see a clouded mixture of light
and fire...promises made cannot be kept for long. They will be undone,

bringing about challenges in the days and months to come. Yes. All of who you are will be challenged and tested. A dark shadow looms over all of us...wanting to unravel all that we know, and all that is good. It will try and steal what is dear to you, it will try and turn you. You cannot let it win." She exhaled loudly and sucked in her breath.

"...this is only the beginning... you must be ready. Redemption is upon you." She gasped and her hands released my temples.

I fell backwards catching myself and scooting away from her in the dirt until I was standing on the other side of the coals breathing heavily.

"What the hell was that!?" I asked wide eyed.

The old woman knelt and began to rummage through the coals still burning at her feet. Clutching something in her palm she held out her hand. I hesitated then stepped towards her as she reached for my hands. A small, oval, hard, brown stone dropped into the palm of my hand. I searched her face for an answer to why she gave me this... rock? What did it mean? What did she see that caused her to draw away from me completely? I opened my mouth to speak, but she interrupted me.

"You are who you are, you have passed the test and you may go now." The door opened revealing the calming light that I had wanted, but my feet remained planted.

"What just happened? What does this mean? Please tell me what you saw, I beg you."

"The stone is a gift. In a time of need it can be used to save. To protect. Keep it close. There are many counting on you to succeed."

"But how do you know who - what I am - all this?"

And as if I had already left the room, the woman turned and began to tend to her coals in the fire. Glancing back at her, I exited. The man I had awoken to earlier was patiently waiting for me.

"You passed!" he exclaimed rubbing his hands together excitedly.

"I had to be certain, you must understand. These days no one can be too careful. It's better to have a psychic decipher the truth. Well, now that we have that out of the way, let's go check on those orbs you asked for."

"What is your name?" I asked suddenly realizing that I had not asked.

The walls narrowed drastically making it difficult to do anything but follow as he led me towards a dead end. Gently his fingertips slipped into the space between two of the stones and by memory found what they were searching for.

"You can call me Nuri."

The stones compressed against one another, grinding momentarily. The man pressed both palms against the wall and it gave way, groaning until it was fully open. Unsurprisingly, inside it was only slightly wider than the corridor we had just come from, with no more room than a small walk in closet. Large shelves and small makeshift cabinets lined the wall from the floor to the ceiling. Strange items were strewn about in no apparent order in jars, cans and jugs. I tried making out many of the hand-written labels etched on the jars, but nearly all were caked in a thick brown dust or were otherwise illegible.

"What are these for?" I asked curiously.

"Eh, it depends...healing, protection, defense... many are concoctions I have thrown together in the hopes that they do what they are meant to. Here we are now," he said, opening two cabinet doors opposite me.

The light caught my eye – dim, flickering at first, then growing brighter in our presence. As if it had been dormant before our unexpected intrusion.

"This is what you came for, is it not?" he asked, a small smile on his face as he placed a glowing blue orb in the palm of my hand.

"Is... is this...?"

"Course it's a fake orb! Gorgeous, isn't she?" he exclaimed, examining his work proudly.

"This is what they look like," I said aloud, but more to myself.

"Mmhmm. Well, the angel ones anyway, I've got orange fallen angel orbs for you to take," he said, pulling a black metal suitcase out from another cabinet. He began loading the orbs.

I couldn't take my eyes away from the small bowl-sized brightly lit ball in my hands. A brighter orange light emanated from the outer layer and looking at the center there was an oily mixture that churned constantly and seemed to emit a little bit of heat as I held it.

"What's the difference between this and the real thing?"

Taking the orb from me he began to demonstrate.

"Although they look nearly identical, the key way to determine if an orb is fake or not is to feel its heat. You see, a real orb, fallen angel or angel, emits an enormous amount of heat for such a small object, similar to that of a small ball of fire. Most people will run their hands over an orb and as long as it gives off this heat, they won't know if it's fake or real. There is one flaw though. If any of the orbs are separated from one another, they all begin to lose their heat. They become colder the farther apart they are from one another. In order for this to work, you'll need to keep all of the orbs inside this suitcase. As long as one isn't removed, it should fool anyone."

"Including someone with a lot of experience in this sort of thing?" I asked.

Latching the briefcase shut, he told me I could take them to the hand of God himself, and as long as they stayed together, they would be accepted as the real thing.

"Ok, maybe that's a bit of an exaggeration," he chuckled. "Maybe God himself might have a way of knowing they're not real. I'm not privy to that sort of knowledge." He led me out of the potion room and back into the room I had woken up in.

"Before you go, I want you to know that I did not agree to help you because it was right or wrong. I am doing this for what I may need in return. I cannot trust many people these days and the ones I am able to help will owe me a favor. I'll be asking you for that favor one day. It is not a request though. It must be done, no questions asked. Do you accept these terms?" He eyed me questioningly.

"Yes, I understand."

He handed me the briefcase and motioned for me to exit through a door.

"Oh, and sorry about this again," he said, "but policy is policy." As I turned to see what he was talking about, a hard object collided with the back of my skull once more and everything went dark.

My eyes tightened and I groaned, feeling the throbbing of my skull as I steadily regained consciousness.

"I swear you're not watching her anymore. You're not good at it." A familiar voice bellowed.

"I don't see how this is my fault at all! She said she was going to bed! Had I known... And why weren't you watching her too?" another voice accused.

"I had to take care of something. And you're training to become a Guardian Angel? Huh, you need practice," the second voice indicated.

I felt a palm on my forehead.

"Were you too busy killing angels to keep her safe Nathaniel?"

I could feel their vibrations thick with anger and intensity, and grudgingly, I tried to sit up and open my eyes.

Nathaniel had risen from his seat and had turned to face Jared and his accusation. I could see Nathaniel's jaw line tighten from the corner of my eye.

"I'm warning you. Alex considers you a friend, but I do not. Speak to me like that again and you'll likely be added to the list." Nathaniel's tone was dangerously low.

"Ss...stop it. Both of you," I choked as two hands suddenly pushed me back down.

We were still in the parking garage.

"You're just lucky I was able to find her in the first place," he growled.

I heard the engine start and reluctantly fell back into a deep slumber.

When I woke, the cool silk comforter felt rejuvenating against my cheek, but the tension in the room made me fight the urge to close my eyes again.

Nathaniel sat back in the chair close to my side as Jared leaned over me. Concern, frustration, anger and relief all rushed through their faces as I slowly sat up again with Nathaniel steadying me. At first, I was confused as to what happened. Had I fallen? And just as before, slowly, the pieces began to put themselves back together.

"The orbs. The briefcase! Where is the briefcase?!" I exclaimed stumbling out of the bed as a massive head rush whooshed through me causing me to sway.

"Easy." Nathaniel's velvety voice thrummed, catching and steadying me.

"You got her?" Jared questioned as he grabbed something off of a nearby desk.

Nathaniel rolled his eyes irritated by the question.

"Alex, are the orbs in the briefcase?" Nathaniel questioned. His cool blue eyes peered through me and I nodded as Jared set the briefcase on the bed and opened it. Silence took over the room as the two men gazed at the contents of the briefcase. Five glowing orange orbs beamed back.

"How did you get these?" Nathaniel's jaw tightened and the way he gazed at the orbs gave me the feeling it wasn't the first time he had seen one.

I nodded towards Jared.

"Your contact came through, in a very unorthodox way."

I felt the back of my head. The wound had healed again, but I was exhausted, hungry and felt exactly how I'd imagine anyone would feel after taking two massive blows to the back of the head. Sore. Extremely sore.

"Do they work?" Jared asked placing his hand over one of the orange orbs.

"I mean, will they work?" he pressed.

"Technically, yes, but there's a catch. You can't separate any of the orbs. If you do, they lose their ability to emit heat, and anyone, especially Abraxos, would know they aren't authentic."

Nathaniel only slightly relaxed as Jared handed him an orb to test. Sure enough, not only did that orb quickly lose its heat, but the others did as well, and the farther away the orb was from the briefcase, the colder all of them became. Nathaniel's eyes darkened as he held the orb at eye level.

"How much time do we have left?"

Jared checked his watch. "About 72 hours. Give or take."

Nathaniel nodded.

"What do we do now?" I asked.

"We wait. Abraxos will schedule the meet with us soon. I've got to get back to Crest.." Jared turned to me. "Will I see you later?"

I nodded.

"Get better and stop wandering off." He gave me a wink then left the room.

Nathaniel placed the orb back in the briefcase and turned towards me folding his arms. A slight smile played at his lips, but I could tell troubling thoughts loomed in his mind.

"You really must stop wandering off without anyone knowing where you're going."

"I know, I just knew... I got a feeling someone was sending me a message about the orbs. I had to see for myself."

"What do you mean? Who gave them to you?"

"I had a dream... sort of, at least I think it was a dream. Anyway, a cloaked figure said I could find the answers I was seeking at 5th and Blake. Turns out it was Jared's contact who led me there. He said I could call him Nuri, and after passing a test confirming I was me, he gave them to me," I said, quieting some as I remembered the stone in my pocket and the old blind woman.

"Nuri, as in Nuriel?" He came towards me and placed his hands gently on either side of my shoulders, but his uneasiness frightened me.

"What did he ask from you in return for the orbs? And what sort of test did you pass?"

"He said he would call on me for a favor one day. He didn't say what. You know him?"

Nathaniel remained still before responding, trying his hardest not to let his facial features reveal his true thoughts.

"I met him a few times when I was a Guardian in training. He helps each side, but only to advance his own needs, which is why the Council has tried to find him for years. He went into hiding a little over a decade ago. And what about the test he made you do?"

"A psychic had to read my mind," I replied.

His thumb brushed against my cheek softly, sending a wave of heat through me before he turned and ran his hand through his hair. A moment of silence passed between us.

"What's wrong?" I asked standing up, ignoring the throbbing in my head and wishing he hadn't turned away.

"You should eat." he said abruptly, and left the room.

"But..." My protest went unanswered.

I wanted to grab the nearest pillow and scream into it out of frustration. Why did he never tell me what he was thinking? I huffed in frustration and realized Nathaniel and Jared had brought me to the cabin. Funny that this old, modest, wooden cabin was oddly significant to me. Perhaps it was because of the moments Nathaniel and I had shared here. A trivial fire awakened in the pit of my stomach as gentle memories of Nathaniel and I flooded back into my brain.

I brushed off the trip down memory lane. I couldn't let him keep me in the dark now, and why would he need to? Did he think I couldn't handle it? Either way, I stormed out of the room and towards the kitchen with one intention – to get some answers.

"Seriously? Are you ever going to tell me everything?"

Nathaniel was stirring scrambled eggs. His back was to me and he didn't respond at first, but instead, finished stirring and added the eggs to a pan on the stove before wiping his hands and turning to me.

"You're weak and slightly temperamental. Eat and then we'll talk."

I knew he was right, but that didn't stop the rising heat within me from softening any, it just made me even angrier.

"No, you're going to tell me what you know now. I'm not a child and I'm not waiting."

He exhaled slowly and tossed the towel on the counter.

"Alex... I need you to calm down. Eat and then we'll talk about it."

"No! I'm done waiting for partial answers from you Nathaniel. I'm different now, I can handle this, and even if I can't, you can't keep trying to shelter me from everything. I want to know everything." My tone was high-pitched as I became more upset.

"No."

"No?" I was stunned. And then livid.

"No. You don't want to know. I have been keeping you from the wicked things in this world nearly the entire time you've been in existence. There are some things, Alex, I will always shelter you from. Besides, you're not ready to fight yet. You've been on some missions sure, but you're still a novice."

"So keeping me in the dark is best? And I'm the top in my class thank you!" I was getting angrier by the minute, and heat began to evaporate from my pores.

"You're the only one in your class. Of course you're the best in it. I'm still not telling you anything."

I used to just laugh when my mom would preach to me: *Only the people you love the most will know how to push your buttons the most. It is only those people who can get you to a point where you lose your mind and do stupid things.*

Now I understood what she meant more than ever. I felt it, and I had, in that moment, completely... lost it.

My emotions surged and I burst into a ball of thick blue flames that rushed towards him. Expecting my reaction, Nathaniel defended himself, dodging and blocking my punches and any hits I threw.

"Just tell me!" I screamed at him.

"No. I told you you're not ready. You can't even hit me," he stated as if we were just talking and not physically fighting.

I let the heat extend through my fingers and watched as his shirt caught fire. He ripped what remnants remained off, and tossed it on the floor.

"Close," he egged me on.

I took a deep breath in and my wings burst outward almost filling the entire room. Seeing he was distracted momentarily, I jumped and spun, kicking him in the jaw and thrusting my wings forward sending a blast of heat towards him that tossed him into the wall. The room was still for a moment. The only sound came from the toaster announcing the toast was ready as it popped upwards. Nathaniel was on one knee, his head towards the ground with his fists curled on the wooden floor.

"Nathaniel?"

No response. I could hear his breathing had increased and was deep and ragged. A few more minutes passed and I was beginning to really worry, or worse... if I had awakened something frightening within him. Slowly, I walked towards him. I reached a hand out to touch him and it was then that I noticed the scarring on his back. The scars were large and appeared as though they had been done with a blade of some sort. I leaned in closer to him and reached out to touch his back. Suddenly, Nathaniel's hand wrapped around the back side of my neck and he stood, pulling me into a kiss. My eyes widened in shock until I felt his grip loosen completely. His hand moved towards my lower back loosely as his other arm wrapped around my waist and pulled me close.

"Always be ready my love. You did good." he said, kissing my lips gently again and turning to butter the toast.

I stood dumbfounded, processing what had happened as my wings relaxed and fell at my sides.

"What...the...hell. Please tell me that wasn't just a test?" I asked, appalled.

Nathaniel finished buttering the toast and placed it on the plate with the eggs.

"Everything is a test. You're the first of your kind Alex, you're going to be tested more than anyone. I was speaking with Jared about you. I know you have been through some training and I wanted to see what you can do and where you still need some work."

"Oh God." I was suddenly ashamed by how ugly I had acted.

"You're telling me you didn't mean anything you said?" I asked, feeling my wings retract once more and slinking into the wooden chair at the table.

He chuckled a little and placed the plate in front of me before taking a seat across from me.

"I didn't mean most of what I said."

I furrowed my eyes at him, grabbing a piece of toast and biting into it, unable to resist food any longer. I had used so much energy and I couldn't remember the last time I had eaten. He was right, I was weak. I devoured the piece of toast and moved onto the second, still needing more strength.

"What does that mean?" I asked with a semi-glare. Nathaniel may have been testing me, but our fight wasn't over nothing. He had to start telling me the whole story. His story.

"I've always tried to keep you from wicked things; that, I meant. I don't want to tell you everything, not because I think you can't handle it, but because I want you to be happy; sometimes knowing everything doesn't make things better."

"True, but this is what I am now. There's no changing that. I can't pretend I'm a normal teenage girl anymore. I'm an angel hybrid and I live in a world I know nothing about. I have to know in order to stay protected. I'm not scared."

Nathaniel was quiet as he took my statement to heart. He may not have wanted to divulge everything to me, but I think he finally understood that sharing everything would somehow help.

"Fair enough. Just don't be disappointed with what you hear. I'll answer what you want to know when you ask. Just keep eating."

I rolled my eyes.

"OK sensei, for starters, how did you think I did?"

He leaned forward and rested his forearms on the table.

"Good, better than the average Joe, but Jared has only scratched the surface on uncovering your abilities. With my help, you can be better than everyone, including me. You've got the potential, but you still have some work to do on harnessing your abilities."

"Mhmm. You weren't giving it your all? And now I have two trainers?" I asked, toying with him.

He smiled.

"The point was to see what you've learned. Not hurt you. I would never hurt you." His ice blue orbs sent a heat tremor through me.

I swallowed and regained my focus.

"And yes, you'll have two trainers. I've already talked with Jared about it."

I nodded and began eating my eggs.

"You two think you can be civil with one another after all?" I stated, raising an eyebrow and glancing at him.

He huffed, sitting back in his seat.

"What happened to your back?" I asked casually trying to switch gears to some of the other questions I had while he was in a cooperative mood.

"Initiation as a fallen angel, punishment for disobedience, and fights."

"What did you disobey? And what type of initiation?"

Nathaniel turned to show me the scars and I moved around the table, half-sitting on it so I was closer.

"This one," he said reaching towards a jagged quarter sized scar on the back of his left shoulder, "is from one of my first missions as a fallen angel after I was initiated. I went to intercept an angel and just before I let him go, I asked him about you. After a quick fight with a screwdriver, I persuaded him to tell me where you were. That's how I found out you were at Crest."

"That's from a screwdriver!" I exclaimed with a look of horror.

He nodded.

"And that?" I asked touching a deeper slashed scar on his right rib-cage. The blade had gone in clean, leaving behind a smooth pure white mark on the surface of his skin.

"Knife fight. Most of my wounds from those healed. During initiation, each fallen angel goes through a series of tests. Someone with my background is best suited for certain things like fighting. I did what I do best. I fought my way up in rank. That one got me good."

"Who were you fighting?" I asked as I traced my pointer finger along the scar.

"Cassius."

My fingers stopped at the mention of the name.

"Don't worry, he's got one to remember me by as well." I didn't have to read Nathaniel's face to know he was telling the truth. I could picture it.

"And this one?" I asked as my fingers gently caressed the second largest of the scars. It was a symbol, that I knew, but none that I had ever seen before, oval and diamond-like in shape with vines wrapped around a mixture of what looked to be squiggly lines in the center.

"What does it mean?"

Nathaniel shifted slightly.

The marking was carved deep, multiple times in his skin and lay directly over his spine between his shoulder blades seeming to signify something.

"They marked me as one of them. As if I could forget." He huffed more to himself than to me.

"Not every fallen angel is marked. Only those whom they believe need *reminding* are permanently marked with the symbol."

He turned to face me, still seated in his chair, and pulled me close. I leaned into him instinctively and let him rest his head near my abdomen as I embraced him and ran my hands through his hair.

"I'm sorry," I whispered, the feeling of guilt poring over me for what he had gone through.

"Don't be," he said pulling his head back and standing.

He grasped my waist and I looked into his frosty blue orbs.

"It was my decision from the beginning. I knew the consequences. None of this has ever been your fault Alex. And even when I was gone, I looked for you. I never stopped trying to get back after I left." His eyes glistened as he drew me closer to him and pulled me in for a kiss, scooting me off the table and onto his lap.

Smoldering heat surged through my lips and my body. Fervently, I returned his kiss, entangling my fingers through his hair, pulling us ever closer. He loved me. And I loved him. That I knew. I let the world fade as I melded into him.

"Brrriiinnnggg! Brrriiinnnggg! Brrriiinnnggg! Brrriiinnnggg!"

My phone began to sound off in the kitchen.

Nope. I was not going to...

"You. Should. Get. That." Nathaniel stated in between kisses.

"Mmummm." My response was muffled as his hands held me firmly.

The simple fact of my phone going off was not going to ruin it. Whoever was calling could go straight to voice-mail.

"Seriously. Could be. Important." He repeated smiling but continuing to kiss me back.

I groaned and pulled away, running to grab my phone on the counter, utterly irritated by the intrusion.

"Yep." I huffed into the phone, not caring who it was that was so rudely interrupting.

"Alex! Honey! It's me! You know, your mother?" My mom joked over the phone.

"Hey! Mom! Of course I know it's you, what's up?" I said as Nathaniel moved closer to me and leaned against the counter.

I couldn't help but notice his slightly more muscular and slim build since he'd returned, and a hint of a tan at that. I grabbed a glass of water and filled it as I held the phone up with my shoulder and eyed Nathaniel again.

"Alex! Honey did you hear me? You seem distracted." I heard my mom say on the other end of the line.

Nathaniel chuckled as I almost dropped my water setting it down.

"Um, no, sorry. I'm working on a... paper. For class, sorry," I blabbed out as Nathaniel did his best not to laugh and threw me a thumbs up.

I sent him a death glare and covered the mic for a moment.

"Do you mind?"

He chuckled again.

"Seems like you're really into your paper."

I tossed him his shredded shirt from the floor as my cheeks flushed.

"Sorry Mom, I can talk. Go ahead." I continued.

"Well, I was calling because your brother comes back into town this evening. We were all going to go pick him up from the airport tonight and wanted to see if you were coming. You're still planning on coming home for the weekend, right?"

Shit. I had completely forgotten that technically it was Thanksgiving break and I had promised my parents I'd stay with them for the weekend and visit with everyone. Especially since my brother Derek was coming home again and I missed him dearly.

"Yes! Absolutely! Um when are you going to pick him up?"

"His flight gets in at seven tonight so if you want to be at your Dad's around 5:30 just in case, then that should be good."

"Perfect! I'll see you at Dad's at 5:30, Love you!"

"Love you too, hon!"

The dial tone sounded on the other end of the line and I hung up.

I checked the time. It was still relatively early, so I had plenty of time to get my stuff ready at least. I trotted down the hall to where Nathaniel had wandered and found him freshly clothed.

"I forgot its Thanksgiving break, my family's picking my brother up from the airport tonight. He gets to come home for a bit again," I said leaning in the doorway.

"That's good. How is your brother?"

"Pretty good I think. He's been on a Navy ship for months visiting different ports and training with other Marines. It'll be nice to see him."

Nathaniel moved towards me and gently pulled me into him.

"Spend the weekend with your family. It's moments like those that you can never get back. What time do you need to be at your dad's?"

"5:30. Which means we have plenty of time for you to answer the rest of my questions," I replied triumphantly.

He sighed in defeat and we headed outside.

Chapter 22

The dock creaked as we walked towards the lake. Part of me was excited with the thought of finally unveiling who Nathaniel was; another part of me was apprehensive. The connection I had with him was undeniable. Stronger now in fact since I became a hybrid, but the fact that he wanted to almost protect me from himself is what made me slightly uneasy. All I knew was that whatever I had been led to believe about Nathaniel, now was my chance to finally get some truth.

He seemed to be in deep thought, miles away as we slunk down at the end of the dock. I scooted closer to the edge allowing my bare feet to skim and dip into the cool water below creating ripples across the surface. Nathaniel leaned back onto his elbows. The muscles in his shoulders and biceps flexed under his weight and I couldn't help but notice his perfection even as a fallen angel.

"So... I know you grew up in a small town in Europe... when dinosaurs roamed..."

I watched his mouth curve into that perfect smile as I continued.

"What about your parents? What were they like?"

"My mother was gentle and beautiful. I remember she always used to sing to me when I was young. She was smart and had a family that was well-off, but she fell in love with my father against her father's wishes.

Consequently, she never spoke with them and I never knew much about them apart from what she divulged here and there. I guess you could say they never saw eye to eye after that.

My father was a hard man. He hadn't had the most loving upbringing when he was a child and it hardened him to his core. He was a strong worker and always wanted to make things better for us. He would always tell me that I had to live my life, no one else would live it for me; to go after what I want most and to never let my position or status keep me from it. In his heart though, I think he was devastated when he knew Uvall and I didn't want to become farmers like him, even more so when I told him I could see angels.

My mother was religious, but my father never was. He never spoke of it and it was a subject that you'd do well with not bringing up around him. My brother Uvall began to see angels too, shortly after I had, but he never told a soul. My parents were under the assumption that I was the one with the 'problems', but Uvall and I became close because of it. At the time, it wasn't safe during the Reformation period and my family and I fled to the Americas to avoid the chaos that seemed to engulf our home. My father left everything he'd ever known to give us something better, and hoped all of the visions of angels would stop as well.

We settled here, but he never forgave any of us for leaving, and when the angels appeared again... well, let's just say he tried to get his point across in other, more direct, ways."

Instinctively, I reached for his hand and covered it with my own, only imagining what he had to have gone through. The thought of his father hurting him made my stomach tighten and twist, but I remained silent, urging him to continue.

"The night before my father was going to get me alternative help, Uvall took me and we fled. He had managed to stash some food for us and got me out before they could take me. That's when Ezekiel led us to the church. My brother and I both made a choice that night and we've never looked back."

"So that's when you became an angel?"

He nodded.

"I never saw my parents after that, training commenced for each of us almost immediately. My skills grew and I graduated to Guardian status.

Uvall fell in love with Beth around that same time, a human he'd met by chance, or fate if you'd like to call it that, and... well, you know the story from there. I hadn't seen or heard from Uvall until he found out who you were after I fell. Now, this is who and what I am." He finished, gazing across the translucent lake, then looked back at me.

His words were unemotional and matter of fact, like he had shared his story thousands of times with others so that it had become memorized, but the weight it bore was unmistakable in his eyes.

I was only one out of a mere few who knew his upbringing or where he came from. A realization splattered across me. Nathaniel's past wasn't something I needed to hear or know, my feelings for him would not have diminished any less if I had not heard it from his lips. I was so incredibly drawn to Nathaniel that I wanted to appreciate all of him and understand him just as he did me. His silky voice broke me from my epiphany.

"I may not have pictured we'd be where we are now, but I would have done it all again knowing how I feel about you Alex. You're what I want most. I'm yours or I'm no one's."

His words sent waves of heat licking at my skin as his arctic orbs held my gaze. He wasn't perfect, but in the most incredulous way he loved me. Me. Our lives were far from normal, but somehow through my transformation, the horrid and the astounding, he was my constant. My craving; the addiction that I couldn't get enough of; the one person who seemed to know me better than I knew myself and still loved every dysfunctional part.

In a swift moment I moved towards him. I felt his arms draw me on top of him, our lips hungry, but never satiated. His tongue slid swiftly over my lower lip and I eagerly parted my lips allowing our kiss to deepen, flowing into an abysmal need for his lips against mine. My fingers grew audacious and greedily tangled around his neck drifting to his chest. His arms tightened around my waist, his hands firmly steadying me as we tried to quench our need for one another, knowing it would never be enough.

Eventually, his hand moved to the side of my face, delicately brushing the hair behind my ear to peer into my eyes without interruption. Our kissing slowed and stopped as we breathed heavily from the euphoria.

I smiled down at him, sinking my cheek deeper into his warmth, never wanting to be torn from this moment. His grip never loosened, holding me securely to him. Listening to the strong thud of his heart beat through the rise and fall of his chest I finally felt what I had longed for since my transformation. I felt *home*.

I couldn't convince Nathaniel to go with me to pick up my brother, he made sure I took the briefcase with the orbs, just in case, but he seemed to struggle before remaining steadfast in his decision that it was best if he stayed behind on this one. Although it was most likely for the better, given that my parents and everyone still thought he wasn't good for me and had no idea he was even back again, I couldn't help wanting him to be near after our intimate moment on the dock.

I beamed as my dad drove us to the airport, exultant with seeing Derek again and elated from the tingling sensation lingering on my lips.

"Who has got you all smiles back there?" my mother said, closing the visor mirror as she peered back at me.

I noticed my dad's eyes glimpse in my direction through the rear-view mirror, but he remained quiet. My cheeks flushed, yep my enchantment was obvious and I tried to play it cool, knowing they would not be duped.

"Why is it *always* a guy?" I questioned, trying to avoid their question, but failing to hide the smile on my face.

"When it's *that* look, it's *always* a guy. Is it... what was his name? Hottie-Mc-Hot-Pants?" she pried.

"Mother! No, it's not him!" She giggled.

"Who's Hottie-Mc-Hot-Pants?" My dad couldn't hide the disdain that dripped off his words as he looked to each of us for answers.

Mom shrugged nonchalantly giving me a wink.

"Not sure... but seeing as it's not him..."

"Oh look we're here!" I exclaimed from the backseat, opening the door before the car could pull to a complete stop.

I could hear her laugh before I exited, but was thankful when neither of them meddled further.

Inside, I was indebted to Jared for the lessons he and I had done together. Teaching me how to control the vibrations I sensed so they

234

weren't completely draining and overwhelming as they used to be. The atmosphere was thickly muddled with the sensations of human vibrations. Thousands of humans moved about, and although honing in on my vibration skills wasn't fully seamless yet, I could tune out much of the movement around me now. We waited until the familiar, yet unfamiliar, outline of my brother formed in the crowd ahead of us.

He had changed considerably since we had seen him last. He looked to be twice his size, with the majority of his mass in his shoulders and arms, but he was basically still slim and agile.

He'd slung his forest green pack over his left shoulder as he approached us. Beyond the changes we noticed immediately, there were the familiar distinctions that separated him from just another body in the crowd. The way he carried himself, a steady, yet long-gated stride that dipped slightly right, his large brown eyes that beamed and seemed to hold so much life as he smiled, and the same crooked grin he always wore. Yep, my brother was home again.

"Derek!" I swung myself towards him and we laughed as we embraced.

"Look at you! I leave for boot-camp and you're all grown up when I get back." His eyes assessed what I knew his brain couldn't comprehend, that I was definitely his sister, but... different. Not like a child growing into adulthood, but like a well-known family member suddenly becoming unfamiliar, like a stranger.

I smiled, avoiding his gaze for a moment as both of my parents rushed for their hugs.

"How about you! What were they feeding you out there? You're like really... buff." I decided as we all appraised him, his grin spreading wider.

My dad heaved his bag and we made our way back to the car as my parents began throwing questions at him left and right. They were curious and anxious to know where their son had been these past months and what he'd done and experienced along the way. I relaxed back in the leather seat and let the presence of my family and my brother's stories envelope me.

It was some time later that my parents eventually succumbed to sleep, my mother left for her apartment and Derek and I were left in the den at the farmhouse lounging across the sofas. The feeling of being home seemed to be surreal to Derek.

"How are you and Jessica?" I asked staring up at the ceiling, curious as to why she hadn't been at the airport with us to pick him up.

I saw his hand raise and give me the 'so-so' expression.

"She's struggling with the fact that I have to go back. Doesn't like seeing me come and go so quickly."

I stayed hushed but nodded my head. It had to be hard. I decided not to inquire further and he seemed content and relieved with not divulging more.

"So what's new around here? You seem like you've been going through some big changes."

I pondered my response, not knowing really what to say, or what I could say for that matter. 'Big changes' could be the understatement of the century.

"Just a new school, new friends, you know how that goes..."

"Yeah, Mom and Dad told me about that. You sure you're OK though? I thought Mom and Dad were overreacting in some of their letters, but you seem a little different. Everything good with you?" he meddled, knowing I wasn't relinquishing all of the truth to him.

I wanted to tell Derek. If there was anyone in my family who might understand me at all, or at least not alienate me, it was him. I could trust him, right? We had always kept each other's secrets, from him skipping classes and me covering for him to him paying to fix the ding I left in my dad's car door so that I wouldn't get in trouble. We each still held each other's secrets.

I sat up in the sofa and realized Derek had already scooted himself so the pillow was propping him up to eye level. I chewed the inside of my bottom lip, maybe it wouldn't hurt. After all I'd kept my secret safe for so long it would be fulfilling to finally get it off my shoulders and share it with someone.

"Listen... what if... if I told you something, would you promise to keep it between us? Like FOREVER between just us?"

He watched me carefully and gave me one nod of his head.

"I mean it Derek, this is a *'take with me to my grave FOREVER and then some'* type of thing."

"I get it. What's up?" he said holding his hand up for me to stop procrastinating and just spill it already.

A lump in my throat formed and I swallowed unsuccessfully trying to dislodge it.

"OK... I, I'm not like everyone else... I mean I'm not like you or anybody we know..."

His brows creased as he tried to understand what I was getting at.

"I'm not explaining this right... OK, here goes. I'm a h-y-b..."

An unexpected vibration made me close my mouth abruptly as I turned my attention towards the door. Derek followed my gaze as one soft knock sounded. He stiffened as I made my way to the door. I knew five angels awaited me on the other side, and although I didn't know all of them, I had a pretty good idea just who was waiting for me.

I cracked the door wide enough for me to get a good look at everyone as Derek slid off the couch and made his way over to me. None of them said a word as I gauged them. The man in the suit who had given Jared and I the weapons as well as three other husky looking angels I didn't recognize stood on the porch with Jared in between them.

I could feel the apprehension seeping from him pelt me like hail. They were here for the orbs, this was supposed to be our arranged meeting. One of the men nodded for me to go with them. I closed the door just before Derek could pry it open fully. *Great, these guys had impeccable timing.*

"I forgot, I've got something I've got to do tonight. I'll be back a little later OK?" I said still blocking the door from Derek, hoping he'd let it be, but knowing he was not about to back down.

"What thing? Alex, get out of the way, who's at the door?" He pushed past me against my protests and flung open the door revealing an empty wooden porch.

I felt the vibrations of the angels; they hadn't left, but they had moved towards the barn and were waiting for me. They'd probably sensed Derek there too and didn't want to reveal their presence. I had a feeling they wouldn't wait all night for me though. Derek turned to face me and closed the door, locking it.

"Did someone knock?" He seemed to wonder if he was going crazy, but the fact that I had opened the front door kept him holding onto his sanity; that there actually had been someone there.

"Kids doorbell ditching I bet. It's been happening a lot around here lately," I added keeping my voice even.

He watched me carefully as if he was contemplating sitting me down for that brotherly-sister talk where he would tell me he was worried about me and that whatever I was going through that it would be OK. As much as I was pressed for time right now, that talk sounded much better than what I was currently dealing with.

A moment passed and he brushed it off and scratched the back of his head heading to the fridge.

"What do you have to do tonight?" he asked as he grabbed some cheese and a tortilla.

I shrugged.

"I've just got to go meet a friend, they're on break too, but I forgot to get the class notes from her before each of us left campus."

He heated the tortilla and cheese until it bubbled, then wrapped it in a paper towel stealing a bite as it cooled.

"OK, I'll let Dad know that's where you went if he wakes up." He looked up at the ceiling as each of us heard the slight snoring sound cascading down from the second floor.

I smiled and turned for the door.

"Thanks."

"Oh, I almost forgot, what were you going to tell me before?" he asked before swallowing what was left of his tortilla.

I played dumb.

"Oh, it's nothing big, I'll tell you when I get back, k?" I crossed my fingers hoping he'd leave it at that.

"Sure, sure. See you later," he said waiving his hand at me and getting a glass of water to rinse the food down.

I braced myself against the front door after leaving and took in a deep breath.

I was frozen for several reasons: first, I couldn't believe I had nearly just revealed to my brother what I truly am. It was the closest I had come thus far to telling any human, aside from Trey that is. Second, the fact that the meeting with Abraxos and everyone was apparently going down now.

You've got this Alex, just meet with Abraxos, give him the orbs, and go back home. It's that simple.

I rejected the negative thoughts in my brain and pulled my car out of the driveway, driving it down the street and parking it off a dirt path so it was fairly hidden. Whipping out my cell phone I sent a text to Nathaniel.

Meeting with Abraxos happening now in forest behind house. They have Jared.

Impatiently, I waited for a response, but I could feel the angels like beacons in the night pressing me to make haste. They had moved to the forest beyond our house, but I knew that they sensed me too, and if I didn't find them soon, they'd surely come find me. I clicked my phone on vibrate and slid it into my back pocket before heaving the briefcase with the orbs, ditching the car, and making my way towards them. Nathaniel would come. He was wearing the pendant so I wouldn't be able to tell where he was, but he'd be there.

Chapter 23

The forest was noiseless aside from the crunching of twigs and branches under my feet. My heartbeat began to quicken and the dryness inside my mouth increased as the forms of angels appeared in front of me.

"Where are the orbs?" the same angel from before asked, getting right to the point.

I glanced towards Jared and back at the man before holding up the briefcase.

He smiled wickedly.

One of the husky men grabbed the briefcase roughly from my hands and set it on the ground in front of us as a familiar voice sounded.

"I knew you wouldn't let me down, Interceder." Abraxos's voice sent needles into my spine as I tried to calm my nerves.

He moved towards the briefcase from the shadows, a black pendant adorning his business jacket.

Kneeling by the briefcase, he stroked his hand across each orb before returning to his feet with a smile.

"How did you do it? I'm curious." He looked to Jared.

I could feel Jared tense, remaining stiff and short with his words.

"It wasn't easy."

"I'd bet not. Still... there's one individual that was on the list that I'd like to know how you *surprised*."

My stomach roiled knowing he was referring to Nathaniel as his eyes met mine.

"I did it." The words felt like sandpaper in my mouth, as I watched the pleasure spread across Abraxos's face. I thought I could vomit.

He was testing me. I knew it. I'd have to play along with his sick little game if we were going to survive this.

"Awe, but how I wonder? I must know," he compelled.

My insides recoiled, but I couldn't let him see through me, I did what I could to make my words sound convincing.

"He trusted me, that's how I got close enough." Abraxos stood mere inches from my face, analyzing my every breath and word. His eyes searched for something I wasn't sure they found.

Several minutes passed in an anxious stillness before he walked back towards the briefcase.

"Well then! It's seems you've both done what I've asked of you," he said beaming proudly as he knelt one last time in front of the briefcase.

He ran his hand over the orbs until he gripped one and lifted it out of the briefcase for further inspection, as if to say his own cruel final good-bye to whomever soul he thought was clutched in his grasp. I couldn't tell if my heart skipped a beat for a moment or if it was Jared's that I felt, but with each passing second I became more restless and fearful that our secret would be revealed.

My back pocket vibrated soundlessly.

"Are we done here? I'd like to get home." I asked impatiently, trying to break his attention from the orbs and knowing Nathaniel had finally sent me a text.

His head jerked my way.

"Just one more thing... there's someone who doesn't seem to think you've done what you say you have."

Trey was hauled from behind a nearby pine by a lanky angel, their pendants cloaking them in the darkness.

Our eyes locked and the fear that permeated from each of us hung like a thick cloud of smoke in the air.

"What better way to ensure the deed was truly done than by asking someone who's sworn to the fallen? Someone who cannot lie about it." Abraxos proudly patted Trey's shoulder.

Trey scowled under Abraxos's hand.

"Well? Are they as she says they are? Dead and gone?" The impatience turned his tone sharp and unforgiving as he shoved Trey forward to look at the orbs.

Trey's head lowered and he glanced at me painfully.

"No."

"With that single word, any hope I had crumbled to my feet and fear completely overtook me."

I turned to Jared and he shook his head as dread swept across face.

Abraxos studied the case once more, knelt and fingered one orb before sweeping it into his hand promptly and holding it. I knew the orb as well as the rest of the orbs had begun to lose their heat. Unexpectedly, Trey shoved one of the angels behind him.

"Run!"

Jared and I freed ourselves from the distracted angels around us and took off into the trees. They would catch Trey, but if Jared and I were able to get away, we could come back for him with Nathaniel. We had to go back for Trey.

Not moments later, I could hear Abraxos and his men calling for us as Jared and I dashed through the forest. Abruptly, I remembered the pendant in my pocket.

"Jared! Catch!" I tossed the pendant to him as we ran. One of us had to go get Nathaniel, one of us had to get help.

Before he could interject with my plan we were ambushed from each side. The first two angels were heavily built, but momentum was on my side. I plowed through them like a linebacker, knocking one of the angels unconscious, but only stunning the other.

"Use it and get out of here!" I called to Jared who refused to put it on at first.

Several more agile angels surrounded me as my body became inflamed in blue fire and my wings outstretched.

"Go!" I yelled as I watched the outline of Jared's body disappear and eventually his vibration as well.

One of the angels lunged. I caught his wrist and moved behind him swiftly, using my other hand to break his arm and kick him aside. Another tried to attack and I sent a flame ball at his face knocking him to the ground. More angels surrounded me like sharks circling a bleeding victim in the water, waiting for their chance to strike.

"Alex, Alex. I thought we had agreed? You do what an Interceder is told to do and all is well. Such a waste." Abraxos was there shaking his head in disappointment.

"Was that before or after you take control over fallen angels and the council? Why'd you do it?" I spat.

He laughed.

"A mixture of our species will never happen. But when you came into the picture, it's all anyone could ever talk about. I'm putting an end to that, and my partner share my interests. Besides, who could say no to unlimited power, money and resources?"

My skin boiled at his words. Trey's body was slumped against the ground. He was alive, but he'd taken a beating for trying to help us.

"I'm going to kill you."

He smiled.

"Afraid it doesn't end that way for you. You've broken the rules Alex. Broken your oath. We've already got plans for what we're going to do with you."

A shadow moved behind him catching my eye and I watched as the hollow, murky eyes of Corson came into view. The blue fire emitting from my body flickered against his sickening sneer and lifeless cold eyes. A shot rang out and I felt my wings ripped roughly against my back, bashing me to my knees. I attempted to burn the netting holding them, but was unsuccessful.

"Steel. No burning through that I'm afraid,"

Another shot, this time it sent me writhing in pain on the forest floor. An electric pulse shocked my body repeatedly. Through the painful jolts I ripped the excruciating square device from my chest, crying out as it took a patch of flesh with it and tossing it as far from me as possible. They advanced, and with every cell in my body that I could muster, I sent a fiery shock-wave towards them, attempting not to target Trey in the process.

My vision blurred as boisterous screeches echoed through my ears, screams of angels and my name. A sharp blow to my skull sent a wave of pain through me and my consciousness dimmed to blackness.

Nathaniel's soothing hand caressed the side of my cheek delicately. I sighed against his touch, tingling my nerves and sending a surge of comfort and longing through me.

"Where are you Alex?"

His words faded in and out like a soft song playing in the background.

I choked from the icy wet spikes suddenly hitting my skin, taking the vision of Nathaniel away. Coughing, I was jolted back to consciousness. The air was thickly decayed and muggy; my eyes flickered open and closed, attempting to get a visual of my surroundings and feeling my restraints at the same time. The backside of my skull ached, but the tender throbbing was an incessant reminder that I was still alive and in serious trouble.

I longed for Nathaniel's touch, wishing my vision was my reality and this was all just a dream. But my nightmare was my reality.

A rush of adrenaline coursed through my body and I welcomed the heat from within as it helped fade the grogginess.

"She's awake."

"Good. Let's get started."

I glowered towards Abraxos and the man who had tossed the bucket of ice water on me. The heat rose and glided naturally through my veins, but a presence behind me caught my attention, followed by a sharp puncture in my left shoulder.

"Ow!" I attempted to look behind me to see what had just been shoved into my skin so roughly, but the culprit had already been removed.

"That should do it."

"You sure you gave her enough?"

"Oh yes. Any more and it could be deadly."

"What did you do to me?" The panic in my voice rose as I felt a thick foreign enemy traipse its way into my veins and all visions of being in Nathaniel's arms once more vanished.

Fire burst from me and began to dwindle rapidly. The substance I had been injected with slowly ate away all of the heat in my body until I could no longer feel or control it. My fire was gone, my biggest source of protection, gone in an instant.

"What did you do!?" I coughed, feeling clutched in its alien frostiness. Abraxos smiled.

"Doses of the doctor's good drug here will keep you docile and easier to handle. Interestingly enough, this stuff actually suffocates fire," he said pleased with the vile liquid.

I squirmed in the chains, distraught and frightened.

"What do you want!? You've already won haven't you?"

"Not yet, but I plan to."

Another presence entered the room.

"Has she testified to the crimes yet?" Ezekiel's frame appeared in the doorway, face stony, eyes sullen.

"She's guilty."

"The proof?"

Abraxos straightened, clearly agitated, and then turned to me.

"She disobeyed her oath, she lied and attempted to protect a fallen angel over those she vowed to protect first. She was conspiring with him and God knows what else." Abraxos's words demonstrated how disgusted he alleged himself to be, and he continued to conceal his true objective.

"I never broke my oath!"

Ezekiel studied Abraxos.

"Those are some strong allegations Abraxos. You'd better hope you're correct."

"A picture's worth a thousand words. I'm sure the Council will agree with me after they've seen the pictures I have."

I shook my head fervently, why wasn't Ezekiel helping me?

"Ezekiel! I'm innocent! Help me!" I pleaded, fearing the so-called pictures Abraxos had against me.

Were they of Nathaniel and me together? My heart sank at the thought of what the Council would do about my so called 'betrayal'.

"The Council will want to see her at first light to determine if these allegations are truthful or not."

Ezekiel's gaze lowered to the ground, pausing before he exited the room.

"Ezekiel! Wait!"

My shouts fell on deaf ears and went unanswered. He was gone. I couldn't understand it. Why wouldn't he help me? He'd hardly acknowledged I was even in the room. Couldn't he see what was happening? Ezekiel's indifference enraged me. It was clear his help would not be given. I'd have to find another way out of this place.

"As I was saying," Abraxos went on, "I want soldiers. Soldiers that have your abilities, but unlike you, answer to me and my associate only and don't have the ability to disobey. I give an order, it's fulfilled, and there's no mixing of our species. Nothing more, nothing less."

"Soldiers?"

"I wouldn't worry yourself too much about what the future holds Alex, you won't be a part of it for much longer." His words sliced through me as he shifted uncomfortably in the room. The four concrete walls seemed to give even him the chills, only adding to my fear and hopelessness.

If this place gave Abraxos the creeps, how would I survive here?

"It's time I'm off. Doctor." He gave one nod of his head and turned on his heels for the door.

The lights flickered and a scream sounded from somewhere in the distance then ended abruptly. My breathing caught and I fidgeted with my shackles, completely unnerved. The doctor still hovered over the table behind me. Every horror movie I'd ever seen flashed through my mind agonizingly. I had to keep it together.

"What are you getting for all of this?" I asked trying to peer over my shoulder to get a better look at the doctor and what he was so focused on.

"Science my dear, science! I've never had an opportunity like this one, nor the funds for that matter." He remained hovered over the table.

"So innocent lives don't matter to you?"

"Innocent is a strong word to toss around these walls, but just think, with your donation to science, it could further everything we know about genetic modification and the human genome." He seemed pleased with himself as he grabbed a syringe with an empty silver base to it.

I had a pretty good idea where that syringe was going and it made my skin crawl. I had thought the days of needles and being poked against my will were behind me; little did I know they were still very very real. I had no idea how Abraxos planned to create soldiers, but something told me I was happily unaware of what really surged through my veins on a daily basis.

"What's that?" Hoping to get a better idea of what the hell was going on, I played on the doctor's love for science to explain things further and motioned towards the syringe in his hands.

"With your blood, we're hoping to unlock a few secrets and re-create your abilities in another subject, either an angel or fallen angel."

"I'm not sure I follow. I thought that would kill the subject? Trying to mix the species, that is," I said, remembering what Nathaniel had previously told me.

"It would. This would be a temporary solution only. The effects wouldn't be long lasting, but they would be quite effective for a short period."

The door slammed and a shadowed figure stood near the concrete wall.

"Chit-chatting with the prisoner? I'd hold my tongue if I were you, that is, if you want to keep it." The figure snorted.

The hairs on the back of my neck stood on end; he was an angel, but not like any I had met thus far and his presence was disturbing at that. His vibration was darker than an angel's, but not of a fallen angel.

"She ready yet?" he questioned, uninterested, fiddling with a blade and picking at his finger nails.

I noticed the doctor hurry his pace as he mixed several vials of a smoky concoction, when I realized he intended on using me as a pin cushion once more, I threw my head and body backwards knocking the doctor into the table behind me as the vials crashed against the floor.

"A little help!" The doctor seemed agitated as he collected the strewn vials from the floor.

I smiled as I watched him.

"I don't like needles," I affirmed, but was startled by the angel who had moved swiftly in front of me at the doctor's request.

The small hanging light in the room illuminated his features to reveal a hardened, rounded jawline, disinterested light chocolate eyes, and short, military buzz-cut styled dark hair. The most shocking feature was the left side of his face, which appeared to have been severely scorched long ago. It had healed, but the charred lines of his past remained deeply etched.

"Don't move," he said firmly, his eyes revealing that he could care less about what was happening, only that he had a job to do.

"Our eyes moved to the doctor's needle that pierced my skin filling the vile with crimson. I watched as the angel flicked the knife in his left hand over each end repeatedly. I decided to heed his warning about not moving. I wasn't in any position to argue, well, that and it seemed like it didn't matter to him one way or the other if I remained in one piece.

The doctor waved his hand, dismissing us as no longer being needed, as his eyes fixated on the vial.

The angel didn't hesitate to unchain me and drag me out of the room. His stride was long and swift making me quicken my pace along-side him as we walked through the damp, cold cave-like hall. It was dark and disorienting, with flickering lights appearing sparingly, revealing shadowed cells here and there where veiled inmates mumbled uncontrollably to no one, laughed hauntingly or sought refuge in the blackness of their cells silently.

I could feel their lingering stares creeping across my skin as I passed, their angel and fallen angel vibrations as dim as the sparse lights surrounding them.

"What is this place?"

"Prison," he replied, bored with the same question everyone always seemed to ask him.

"Prison?" My expression was one of confusion. This was not like any prison I'd ever been led to believe existed.

"Seems more like..." But I was cut short.

"Hell?" he guessed, passing a glance my way.

"Yeah... so... you work here?" I asked trying to keep my nerves calm and the shakiness from my voice.

He looked at me like I had asked the stupidest question imaginable.

"Um not exactly."

"What then, exactly?"

He stiffened and shot me a shut my mouth look, irritated with my questions.

"You don't like talking, do you?" I was not taking the hint with his silent response so I proceeded to ask more questions. Truthfully, I needed answers. This was some serious shit and I now I knew I would need to go all the way, live or die. I mean, I was kind of hoping to see the light of day again. I was beyond the point of thinking about what I had to live for.

"So do you have a name?"

He stopped walking abruptly and gripped the sides of my arms firmly.

"I'm not your friend. I move inmates and I execute inmates, got it?"

"But you have to have a name at least. They have to call you something." For a second, I thought he was going to break my arms right there; I was pushing.

He proceeded to drag me again, down another hallway, but I'd gotten under his skin.

"Why does it matter?" he nearly shouted.

"Just want to know who's executing me when the time comes I guess." Saying the words out loud made my situation even more real. I think, in my mind at least, there should be a reason for me and this guy to sort of be allies or something. He was all I had right now. And he was a new player so I had to be ready for the unexpected. What if I did die here? And now it seemed like it was going to be more of a 'when' than a 'what if'. I wanted to cry, but something in me knew I needed to focus on 'this' more than anything else.

"Sam."

"Really?" I asked shocked.

He glared at me. "What!?"

"I would've never pegged you for a Sam. A Max maybe, but not a Sam." He rolled his eyes.

We rounded a corner with a dead end and a set of five cells, one with the door open. He tossed me inside the cell and closed the door. I caught myself from falling and turned back towards the front of the cell.

"See you later Sam!" I yelled as he ignored me and disappeared in the darkness.

I laid my head against the cold steel bars and let out a sigh. The foreign liquid I'd been injected with earlier traipsed through my veins again, reminding me of my weakened state. Bruises on my arms already formed where Sam had hauled me through the hallways. Just another sign that it would take me awhile to heal now.

"Alex! That you?!" My eyes shot open as I cranked my head to the right wondering if I'd actually heard that voice or not.

"Alex?!"

"Trey?"

"Oh thank God!" A hand shot out of the cell one down from mine and waved frantically.

"I thought you were dead! I'm so sorry! They were going to kill my parents. I had to do it. But I thought I got YOU killed afterwards. I swear they told me they weren't going to hurt you, they promised! Bastards!" He sounded franticly panicked.

"Trey, Trey!" I interrupted his rambling. "I'd have done the same thing, it's OK, they had your parents, what were you supposed to do? Do you know if Jared got away?"

"I'm not sure, I didn't see him except before with the orbs."

My heart sank a little.

"You know where we're at? You got any ideas?" he called, hope filling his voice.

I looked down at the floor.

"Yep, and... not exactly."

Chapter 24

I wasn't sure how much time had passed since Sam had brought me to my cell, but time ticked slowly by as I threw pebbles towards the stony cell wall and watched them bounce off. I had attempted to contact Nathaniel and Jared through my dreams in hopes that they could figure out where I was, but whatever the doctor had injected me with earlier prevented me from doing so. It was like a giant mental block or a dead zone with no reception. No calls out and no calls in.

After I realized connecting with the outside world was impossible in this place, I paced the cell looking for ways to get out, even attempted to break or bend the bars, but nothing budged. For the first time since my transformation, I felt as weak as a human again. Trey and I spoke sparsely, eventually tapering off to mostly silence. Neither of us really knew what to say to console the other. I knew I wasn't leaving this place, and he, well, he knew it too I think.

Footsteps sounded in the dark ahead of my cell and Sam's figure appeared out of the shadows moments later. I stood, but to my surprise he passed my cell without so much as a glance and opened one several down from me. Trey's voice echoed in the dark as I attempted to peek my head through the bars to get a better look. Sam motioned for Trey to leave the cell.

"What is this? Where am I going?"

"You're being released, humans don't belong in here. Your father's waiting for you."

Trey was quiet for a moment.

"What about her?" He motioned towards my cell.

I dropped my gaze to the floor when it was silent.

"Trey, don't worry about me, get out of here while you have the chance."

Sam didn't respond to Trey's question and impatiently motioned for him to start walking.

"Trey! Get the hell outta here! I'll figure something out, it'll be OK. Promise."

Trey walked over to my cell with Sam close behind and hugged me through the steel bars.

"I'll try to help you from the outside," he whispered.

His face was pained as Sam prodded his back forward again with the blunt end of his knife.

I managed a bleak smile attempting to believe him as he was escorted away. I watched as the darkness swallowed them and a cold shiver ran up my spine. At least Trey was out and safe.

It felt as though hours had passed again. I couldn't fall asleep. Sure, I was exhausted, but each time the pull of slumber whispered to me and drew me in close, the inevitable startling shriek or cry of another prisoner in the dungeon threw my blood-shot eyes wide open again. I shivered against the stone floor, shifting my body weight unsuccessfully trying to find any sort of comfort against the sharp edges in the stone floor. Sighing, I wiped a tear that had escaped my weary eyes. I just wished I was home again; anywhere but here.

A long eerie whistle sounded in the cell next to mine, opposite of where Trey had been held. Several moments later it sounded again.

"Don't tell me the hybrid is already giving up?" a curious male voice insinuated.

I perched forward in my cell, my senses told me the voice belonged to a fallen angel. When I didn't respond, he continued.

"Ahh, they've weakened you somehow? Tsk tsk. All alone now. Waiting for the Council to decide what to do with you." The word *Council* came out like a fowl taste in his mouth, making fun of their supposed superiority.

"Awaiting the impending doom soon to follow you no doubt," he continued.

"Oh and I suppose you've got a better idea don't you? Tell me, how long have you been a guest here?"

I could sense the smile on the stranger's face widen with my response.

"Maybe a few decades... but I'm experienced, I know certain things now that make someone like me invaluable," he cooed.

I walked towards the bars, pressing my head against the cold steel to get a better view of the stranger. Nothing.

"And I suppose you want me to take advice from someone who's been prisoner for that long? If you're so invaluable, why are you still here?"

"Let's just say I've been waiting for the right cell mate nearby to make my escape."

"Let me guess, that cell mate is me."

"If you don't believe me you're more than welcome to stay put until they decide it's time to kill you. I think we both know that's not too far off in your near future, hybrid."

"How do you know me – know who I am?"

But before he could answer, a bloodcurdling screech in the distance made me swallow hard. I wasn't fond of strangers, or trusting them for that matter, but this stranger was right. If I didn't take a chance and trust him I'd be dead for sure.

"What exactly do you have in mind?" The words forced themselves out of my mouth, making me reluctantly cave, but with no way of contacting Nathaniel or Jared, and my impending demise from the Council and Abraxos, this stranger may very well be my only way out.

I heard the shifting of several bricks and boulders and was surprised to see a hand reach into my cell and wave.

"Name's Ely." The hand shook wildly as I watched it. "This is only going to work hybrid if you trust me."

My hand reached for the winged pendant around my neck for a moment. The heat it emitted gave me comfort and I thought about everyone I could very well be leaving behind once again.

Reaching down, I shook Ely's hand.

Sometime later, I was pacing my cell trying to understand what exactly Ely wanted me to do.

"I'm sorry, it sounds like you want me to wait for the Council to come get me. Are you insane? How are we supposed to get out of here then? I don't have the strength I used to, and I'm pretty sure I'll be dead if we wait till then."

"Tsk tsk. It's the only way to get out, trust me. After three decades in here, I think I know," Ely said, irritated I wasn't buying his idea.

"You need to convince the guard to help you, otherwise we have no chance. He's the key to making this whole thing work. Only the guards know how to escape this place; only the guards know where we are."

"*Sam* is the key? Now I know you're crazy, he's not going to help us!"

"Shhh! These caves have more ears than you know! And yes, you must convince him. Guards here don't choose to work here, they're sent here as part of a punishment for something they've done. Our guard has been here since before I arrived. My guess is his sentence is for a lot longer if not permanent; with enough convincing he may want out just as much as we do."

Footsteps sounded down the corridor and I could make out Sam's distinct vibration.

"Convince him hybrid or you can kiss your life goodbye," Ely whispered quickly before shifting a boulder back in place and returning to the silence of his cell.

Great.

Sam walked to my cell and unlocked the door, letting the bars slide open and creating a boisterous clanging noise in the process.

"Sam! So great to see you again!" My enthusiasm was met with stern eyes.

"I mean, not so great the fact that you're basically leading me to my death, but good to have someone to talk to I guess." I mentally slapped myself. *What the hell was I saying?*

Sam just shook his head and, with his knife, motioned for me to leave my cell. I had no doubt I was the kookiest person he'd ever met.

I stepped out of the cell as Sam went to take off in stride. I clutched his arm for a second and let go when I was met with both of his blistering pupils.

"Can we just walk a little bit slower?" I asked giving him a half smile and wanting to procrastinate the inevitable.

He didn't reply, but his pace slowed some as we walked down the dark hall and left my cell and Ely behind.

"So is there anyone waiting for you outside of here?"

He was silent.

"There's a family outside of here waiting for me," I thought aloud.

"Should have thought of that before you broke your oath then hybrid." His response was cold and calculated.

I stopped him, but he brushed past me.

"Broke my oath? According to whom? Listen to me, the Council has been corrupted, are you telling me *you* deserve to be here?"

Eying me, he kept walking.

"I'm serious! My only crime is that I care for someone who's different from me, and because I promised to protect angels somehow I'm a criminal for doing both?"

I was getting more amplified receiving no response from him.

"You'd have to do more than just care for someone who's different from you to end up here hybrid," he said, matching my gaze.

I stared back at him.

"What did you do to get here?" I said breaking my gaze from Sam's and staring at a pair of glowing eyes as we passed a cell, making me pick up my pace.

"None of your business."

I could feel the vibrations of hundreds of angels coming from up ahead and my pulse radiated with fear.

"Fine, enjoy being used for the remainder of your life. I'm done trying to save someone who won't save themselves."

He stopped walking and the tip of his blade met my throat, backing me into the stone hard wall swiftly.

"What do you know?" His eyes blazed, but something else stirred in the back of them, shining with desperation.

"We both don't want to be here. If you want to put things right then help me. We can help each other get out of here."

"Now we shall hear from Alexandria Constance, bring her in!"

Sam looked towards the lit doorway and hesitated.

"If you don't help me, you might as well condemn yourself to living in this place forever. Help me get out of here and I promise I'll give you your freedom too."

"Oh yeah? How exactly do you plan on doing that? You're just as screwed as I am for all I know." His blade glistened against the light dancing under the doorway ahead of us as he contemplated the validity of my words.

"I'll speak with Ezekiel, he'll hear me out, and he'll free you."

Sam lowered the knife to his side and shook his head.

"You know you actually had me going there for a second hybrid. Too bad Ezekiel has already heard me out and sentenced me to life here. You can't save me, no one can. Just more lies," he said shaking his head and tossing me in front of the doorway.

My thoughts ran wild trying to think of something, anything, when suddenly my hand reached inside my pocket.

"Wait! I'll give you this!" I yelled tossing him the stone the physic had given me.

The doorway moved in my presence; smoldering bronze hands grasped my upper arms pulling me backwards into the blinding bronze light away from Sam, and I realized the door was alive. I watched as Sam caught the stone and looked back at me before my body was pulled through the liquid doorway completely.

I was told it could help save someone, if I was lucky, maybe it could help save Sam, and in turn, save me as well.

Voices echoed through the auditorium around me and the shifting of so many vibrations was suffocating. The blinding bronze light made it impossible to see until my eyes adjusted fully, revealing a circular room with angels framing every space.

A white radiance was emitted against the bronze that painted every surface and I realized they were wings. It was a dazzling, almost mesmerizing display of bright light, with all manners of shapes and sizes.

I stood in the center of the room with a smaller circle of seven angels gathered evenly around me, all judging eyes peering out from behind a giant circular bronze desk. A slew of angels arranged evenly behind them appeared to be sitting in bleacher-like chairs. This was it. The Council. The fire I had become so accustomed to felt like ice-bergs crashing inside my chest due to the foreign liquid swimming through my body.

The Council members began to stand and announce themselves. Through ringing ears, I heard several names, Suriel and Remiel. Then came the reiteration of their vow as they monotonously announced, "We swear to uphold our oaths, seek out goodness and truth, to enforce as necessary and to uphold balance on this earth above all."

I could feel the bile rise up my throat, it was all I could do to hold it at bay, wishing the bronze door that had swallowed me here could spit me back somewhere else. My face turned to one of disgust when my eyes fell upon Abraxos, one of the Council members.

"Announce yourself and what you are." The angels looked back at me awaiting my introduction.

"Mm my name's Alexandria Constance. I'm a hybrid." The fear beginning to hollow out my insides.

"And?..." One of the Council member's spoke up impatiently.

I leaned forward clueless as to what they were still searching for.

"I'm an Angel Interceder..." I finally said after a few awkward and terrifying moments.

"Do you know why you've been brought before us Alexandria?"

I was deathly still.

"I have an idea why, yes."

"Curious, why do you think you've been brought here?" One of the council members questioned sympathetically.

"Enough." Another Council member spoke up harshly. "Alexandria Constance, you've been brought before the Council on traitorous charges of breaking your oath."

"With a fallen angel no less," another Council member pressed.

"What say you?" a third demanded.

"I... it's not true. You've been misled."

"What proof do you have that these allegations are misleading?"

I peered down at my feet and bit my lip, knowing I didn't have anything to prove my innocence.

"Nothing other than my word. I don't have any reason to lie."

"You would to avoid this place!" I heard an angel scream in the bleacher-like chairs.

Suriel surveyed me.

"No, she couldn't have had much knowledge of the consequences, I don't believe fear was a motivating factor here."

"What evidence is there against her to prove she is lying?" Ramiel questioned.

"This looks compelling enough." Abraxos flicked his wrist and sent a string of pictures to all the other Council members.

The men and women reviewed the pictures carefully, some moving in their seats upon viewing the pictures and my heart dropped wondering what they were observing.

What did Abraxos think he had on me? My stomach reflexively tightened again holding the sickness at bay.

"What is your affiliation to Nathaniel Archais Corvix?"

"You know my affiliation to him. He was my guardian angel before he fell."

"These pictures show us otherwise."

"Those pictures show you what you want to see," I interjected.

A cacophony of angels erupted behind the Council.

"Traitor!"

"Innocent!"

"Guilty!"

"Death!"

I flinched as the vibrations stirred, feeling vulnerable.

"Do you love him?" one of the members asked, silencing the crowd of angels everywhere with the raise of his fist at the same time.

I caught my breath as all the eyes in the room fell upon me.

I didn't answer.

"I'll repeat the question. Do you love him?"

A clamminess met the palms of my hands and I couldn't help but begin to sweat. I couldn't lie my way out of this and if I tried, it would only stir them into believing I had lied about everything else. The room grew so silent I could hear my own jagged breathing.

"Yes..." I said hanging my head lower. "It's why I couldn't kill him when I was ordered."

But the uproar from the stadium surrounding me made much of my answer unheard by almost everyone.

"Her love for him is in direct violation as an Angel Interceder. She cannot be in love with him and fulfil her duties. It's preposterous!" Ramiel boomed.

"It's true, her decisions could be swayed if orders were given, just as Nathaniel's decision was swayed when he was ordered to eliminate her before she became a hybrid. Imagine if the balance was to shift like that again?"

"Balance must be kept. I agree, and you?" Abraxos sent a motion around the table to the other Council members.

"Aye".

"Yes".

"Keep the balance, yes."

"Sadly, yes".

"Mmm aye"

Suriel did not speak, but nodded his head.

The shrieking and booming of the crowd echoed around us. "Judgment! Strip her wings! She's not one of us!"

A tear escaped my eye as the shouts came flying from every direction.

"Wait, did you say..." One Council member began to speak up, but was cut short by another.

"Alexandria Constance, I hereby strip you of your title, Angel Interceder!"

"Wait!" I heard Suriel yell, but it was already too late.

A cold spell came over me. Like someone removing a cozy warm blanket from my shoulders leaving me naked and exposed to the elements. The family I felt I had won over had been stripped from me as quickly as it had been given. I was no Angel Interceder, I did not belong with angels nor with fallen angels, but was left as I had been, adrift. The strange creature even angels knew should only be a bedtime story.

Clutching my sides, I felt my body slide to my knees and the feeling of belonging disappear as if it had never existed for the slightest moment.

This was their judgment. A familiar friend welcomed me into its cold outstretched arms once more, clinging to me like a sickness I couldn't shake, and I felt alone.

I let out a scream, quieting some of the yelling around me.

"Repeat what you said before," Suriel asked me curiously.

"It doesn't matter now!" I heard the same man yell that had given me my judgment.

The cool liquid that had been traipsing its way through my veins uninvited was beginning to fizzle. I could feel it burst forth and then slow to a trickle as if it mysteriously was losing its hold on me and my fire.

"What? That I love him? What do you want me to say again? That you've banished anything that ever made me feel normal or whole? Or that even though I'm not an angel or fallen angel, apparently loving both of the species is forbidden?! You can sit behind your desks as judgmentally as you want, but I'm not the enemy for not killing someone I love! Don't you see how wrong all of this is? I'm both species, as hard as it is to believe, and I *love* both species. There's no crime in that. I never asked to be changed into this. *This* wasn't my choice." I rose, anger and hollow sadness filling me.

Several Council members exchanged looks uncomfortably.

"We never ordered you to kill him."

The room was so silent you could hear a pencil drop; I could almost hear their hearts beating out of their chests.

A slow appreciative grin tried to emerge on one side of my mouth as I began to wrap my head around what Abraxos had done. He had acted on his own, with his few select cronies. *He* was the 'bad seed'. Perhaps this was my chance. I smiled.

"You're right. He did." My finger landed on Abraxos who had, up until now, plastered a smile on his face.

"That's ridiculous!"

"Is it? Jared Macomb knows the truth as well, that is, if you haven't already killed him for not following through with your orders to kill fallen angels."

"You were ordered to kill fallen angels by Abraxos?"

I nodded.

"What did Abraxos say to you?"

"That if I didn't follow through and bring you their orbs that I'd better find another profession."

The grimace on Abraxos's face made me smile. I had him. Or at least I'd peaked the Council's interest so they could investigate my accusation further.

"Why don't you tell everyone what you're planning..." But before all of the words could leave my mouth Abraxos had snatched a sword from underneath the desk and stabbed a Council member next to him.

The entire room shifted making me woozy and I caught myself before I fell. The uproar Abraxos had caused had sent all of the angels reeling towards us. It was a few moments before I realized they would be no help at all.

The Council members and I were encased in a giant glass dome that couldn't be penetrated from on-lookers. My guess, to prevent any judgments from not going through if someone in the crowd disagreed.

The downside, Abraxos was single-handedly eliminating the Council members with the help of several other Council members he had corrupted. The screams and shrills of those around me had me trembling at my knees as I tried to force the remaining arctic liquid out of my body. I could see Ezekiel on the other side of the glass desperately trying to punch through to no avail. Ours eyes met briefly, and I knew what I had to do.

I stood, catching Abraxos's attention and, smiling, he made his way towards me.

"I've been looking forward to this; didn't think I'd get to execute you myself though." He seethed, wielding the blade effortlessly in his hands.

My wings unfolded sensing the danger and rage building inside me. I threw my hands forward at Abraxos sending a flaming fireball towards his face. Dodging it by only millimeters he closed the remaining gap between us as I attempted another fireball attack, with only a simmer of smoke escaping my fingers.

"Shit." I whispered as Abraxos's sword came barreling towards me. I ducked, moving out of the way just in time, and attempted to use more fire, but the trace amount of liquid that flowed through my veins made the fire come out in spurts, unreliable and sparingly. I didn't have full control of my fire yet.

"Something wrong with your fire Alex?" He mocked, licking his lips like a rabid dog about to seal its next victim's fate.

I dodged another attack from Abraxos kicking him away from me so I could gather myself. I had to focus solely on the training I had done with Jared, without my fire and without a weapon.

"Alex!" I heard my name being called and turned towards the owner's familiar voice.

Seraphina called wildly from the other side of the glass dome. "Seraphina?"

But my slight distraction caused the tip of Abraxos's blade to slide cleanly across my forearm from my elbow to my hand. I hollered as my brain registered the searing pain. A second later, Abraxos's boot met my jaw and threw me across the room. Dazed, I looked up at the advancing Abraxos and then back to Seraphina.

"Alex! I'm coming, just hang tight!" She screamed before disappearing into the chaos of wings and angels above.

In the next moment I felt my ribs crack from a kick Abraxos landed, reeling me on my back. Gripping my sides, I managed to kick the sword out of Abraxos's hands. He pressed towards me, grabbing my neck and dragging me atop a desk.

"I'm really going to enjoy this," he sneered, pure hatred and fury flashing in his eyes.

Terrified, I stared back at him feeling my breath become quiet with each passing second. I closed my eyes and Nathaniel was there. A longing, burning sensation tore at my insides shaking me awake. I looked around and saw one of the other corrupted Council members was still standing along with Abraxos. His hands clenched tighter around my throat and with my last breath I released forth all of the energy and fire I could muster letting out an uncontrollable torrent.

I screamed feeling my insides scorch away the remaining icy liquid that still lurked, discharging all of the heat, resentment and wrath I had. I opened my eyes to see the entire dome was encased in an impressive sapphire glow. My fire and scream diminished as I looked down to where Abraxos lay. A pile of ash and soot scattered at my feet.

I looked up fearing that I had killed everyone, but found that only the corrupted Council members had been burnt to ash. The surviving members remained untouched from the fire.

Ramiel and I locked eyes. He said nothing and only watched as a tear fell from my eye.

The room was silent. No one had ever seen anything like this – this display of fire, not in all the annals of angelic history. But the vastness of the universe is commanding in its awesome beauty. Surely God himself created it.

Momentarily, voices sounded close by and bodies began filling the interior of the dome with Ezekiel leading the charge followed by throngs of angels assessing Council members and attempting to revive those less fortunate.

Seraphina's voice filled my ears as she embraced me, dashing us through the crowd amidst the confusion and carnage. I couldn't make out what she was saying, the ringing in my ears had silenced my world completely, making only my jagged breathing clear, and the amount of fire I'd used had sapped my last store of energy. Hands seized my arms and I was surprised when the liquid doorway had spit each of us out of the dome room and back into a cave-like hallway.

"Alex!" Seraphina shook me vigorously.

"You need to snap out of it! We're getting you the hell out of here!" she yelled, pulling at my arm.

"What?" I questioned, confused and sluggishly coming to from my shock.

"Sam found me. I don't know how, but he told me how to get you out of here."

"What?" I asked, my awareness slowly returning.

"Sam! He told me how to free you!"

My eyes shot open at the sound of his name hitting my ears.

"Is he free? Did the stone work?"

"Whatever it was worked, but it won't for us if we don't hurry." I nodded, following her as fast as I could.

We dashed down another corridor passing the hollers of inmates.

"Wait!" I screamed, finally feeling the blood rush back to my head.

"We can't go! We need to get Ely out!" I shouted, dragging her to a stop.

"No, Alex we don't have time!" she pushed ignoring my plea.

"We have to! Seraphina!" She finally halted, breathing heavily and studied me wide-eyed.

"Do you know where he is?" She exhaled, but fear flashed behind her pupils.

I nodded and burst into a sprint in Ely's direction, gaining a burst of adrenaline.

I wished the caves hadn't been so narrow, flying to Ely's cell would have been much faster, but then again, I wasn't sure I had enough juice in the tank for flight at the moment either. We eventually reached the long-darkened hallway where our cells had joined.

"Hybrid? That you?" I heard Ely's voice in the dark, different from how it had sounded before, almost hopeful.

I engulfed my hands in flames and went for the lock, inadvertently lighting the area around me in the process.

Ely slipped from the shadows nearing the blue flame and I finally got a look at my neighboring cell mate for the first time.

What were left of his clothes were tattered and torn from the many years he'd spent as a prisoner. His skin had taken on an ashy-gray color and it covered a skinny body with blood shot eyes and matted brown hair with red undertones.

Seraphina pushed me aside briskly and using her knife snapped the lock with a force that surprised both Ely and I. The lock fell and none of us wasted any time. We fled, weaving back through the catacombs, we could almost taste the freedom we so craved.

I could feel my body pleading internally for us to slow, attempting to retain the last energy reserves it had, but I pushed forward, overlooking the cry for oxygen my veins begged for. Voices shouted nearby as we rounded a corner to a dead end.

"Did we take a wrong turn?" I asked.

"No. It's here. There's a doorway here somewhere," she said letting her hands glide briskly across the chilly damp rock.

I could feel my heart beating violently, fear transfixing my entire body as the voices and shouts became more audible, inching closer to where we stood. We weren't going to make it.

Ely and I ran our hands over the rocks on either side of her, desperately trying to help identify the hidden doorway. Seraphina's hands suddenly went through a section of the rock, disappearing entirely as a hoard of angels and guards made their way around the corner towards us.

"I found it!"

Ely smiled and jumped through without a second's notice as Seraphina waved for me to follow.

"Go!" I shouted shaking my head.

"What!?"

"They'll follow us! We'll all be trapped here, now go!"

Bewildered, she refrained from arguing, knowing I was right. I saw her mouth the words, 'I'm sorry' as her eyes watered and she vanished into the rock.

I turned back to the mass of bodies running my way and smiled as fire encased my body. Moments from releasing the fire a shot rang out dropping me to the ground forcefully. I gasped and reached for the dart that had burrowed its way into my hip. Pulling the vicious dart out I held it at eye level examining the now empty vile it held as I gasped for breath. A shiver seeped its way into my pores, cooling me and my fire entirely and I gathered it was the same liquid the good Doc had injected me with. The difference was, this felt like a shot to the heart versus a liquid filling my veins. And through the bodies of angels, the last face I saw before blacking out was Ezekiel's.

Chapter 25

I didn't know how much time had passed since I'd almost been tran-
quilized to death, but the chatter of voices stilled as I came to.
Groggily, I cracked my neck and opened my eyes, fearing I was right
back in my pitch black cell left to rot. I was intrigued to find I was sitting
in a chair in an empty, clean, room no bigger than a classroom with seven
angels standing before me. I recognized Ezekiel as well as some of the
Council members, those who had survived, and a few guards, and I
straightened wondering what was happening.

"You're OK Alexandria," Ezekiel said. Everyone's attention turned to
me.

I stilled.

"What's going on?" I asked, grimacing from my wounds; wounds that
were not healing thanks to the second dosage of that vile liquid.

Someone had attempted to bandage my forearm, but it was now a
bloodstained wrap. I fingered the cloth, delicately resting my arm on the
table, favoring my side where the several broken ribs made the act of
breathing difficult, courtesy of Abraxos.

"We're sorry about the tranquilizer. It was the only thing that would
keep your fire at bay long enough for us to talk to you civilly.

I snorted.

"You could've just asked."

"We had to take necessary precautions after the attack, we hope you understand."

"If I wanted you dead, I'd have killed you in the dome with my fire like I did Abraxos and his followers," I snapped, annoyed that I was still feared.

"We know. What you did, Alexandria... you saved us, you saved Ramiel from a besmirched angel who would have surly killed him."

I looked at the man standing on my right, who nodded his appreciation.

"It seems that during the attempted coup we also lost a guard and inmate as well." The Council member spoke aloud, more to himself and the other members.

"So what does this mean?" I asked looking towards Ezekiel who was fighting a glow himself and ignoring the indirect acknowledgement of Sam and Ely escaping.

"It means you've redeemed yourself. It means Alexandria Constance, although your job as an Angel Interceder was already rescinded, you're free to go."

I stayed seated briefly letting his words fill my ears and my mind. Somehow I really just didn't believe it.

"I'm free to go?" I repeated in astonishment, remembering flashes of what the psychic had proclaimed. *'Redemption is upon you.'*

"What happens now? What about my family? My friends? My life?"

"Things will move forward as they should, you have nothing to worry about between us and your friends and family. There are several items we must let you know of though.

"Firstly, the revocation of your title as Angel Interceder does mean that your place at Crest has been removed. You can still visit, but you will not be allowed to stay there permanently.

"In addition, we'd like for you to retain an open line of communication with the Council from here forth. You tend to have an insight that we feel is valuable to add to the group on certain matters. Like the insight you had about Abraxos. Do you agree to these terms?"

I nodded, part of me crushed that I would not be able to remain at Crest, but the other part of me elated that I would not be killed or thrown into a cell for the rest of my life either. I'd at least earned my redemption from that.

The members nodded, confirming our agreement and, closing the meeting, exited, leaving Ezekiel behind to escort me home.

"Ready to go home?" he glowed as he helped me from my seat.

"That's the understatement of the century." My eyes widened as we left the room.

We were quiet as we walked the catacombs, but I could tell things were on his mind. I did not know Ezekiel all that well, but he seemed to be unable to hide much of his emotions.

"What is it?"

"You proved them wrong." He smiled warmly looking ahead of us.

"About what? That I'm not some kind of hybrid monster?" I joked.

"No," he said shaking his head. "That you can love both species."

I smiled fleetingly with him and looked down at the ground.

We came to a halt eventually reaching the dead end I had come to previously with Seraphina and Ely, and I observed Ezekiel as he stepped ahead of me allowing part of his body to disappear. He held his hand outstretched towards me and I took it willingly leaving behind the shadows and screams of the catacombs.

My eyes were blind, feeling ahead with my other hand and being led by Ezekiel. I followed uncomfortably forward into the abyss. Raindrops scattered atop my fingertips, then my hand, followed by the rest of my body. The smell of rain filling my nostrils was euphoric; anything was better than the smell of death and decay. Breathing deeply, I welcomed the rich earthy smell.

I opened my eyes thinking we were outside, but I was wrong. We stood under a small cavern opening in the earth, water creating small pools around us from the rain above. Ezekiel unfolded his wings and reflexively I did the same. It seemed the only way in or out was to fly.

Leaving the rocky cavern below, we ascended skywards to freedom. Exhausted from my ordeal underground, I was beyond grateful when we had almost reached the top, fearing my beautiful wings would not be able to carry me back to safety. I was startled when my vision was blinded once more as we reached the top of the opening. Ezekiel grabbed hold of my wrist to guide me and my nerves settled as my feet touched down on something soft.

Blinking my eyes open, I surveyed my surroundings to discern our whereabouts. A stunning landscape lay before me. Towering trees speckled the land, their branches and bodies twisting together with mosses and ferns layering every inch of the forest before me, creating a rain forest masterpiece of every shade of green. The wet air was thickly caked in mist and fog making the climate even denser and wetter as raindrops fed the already drenched scene.

"Where are we?" I asked, awestruck by the forest's natural beauty.

"Hoh Rain forest. Stunning right?"

"I'll say," I whispered to myself.

My brain struggled to understand how this beautiful place could be sitting atop a literal hell hole of caverns and tombs below. I turned around to see where the cavern entrance was, but was stupefied to find there was no cavern or hole in the earth. Ezekiel answered my question before I could ask it.

"The opening is hidden, for good reason as I'm sure you can understand, but the barrier also acts as a two-way mirror, you can see out, but no one can see in. A human or animal wouldn't be able to fall into it either, only the nonhuman, and only angel guards and Council members know its exact location."

My feet stayed planted where they were, terrified one wrong step would send me free-falling back into the endless tomb below. He continued.

"Pretty clever location too, this place is one of America's most preserved and treasured national parks."

"Where exactly is the Hoh Rain Forest?"

"Washington State."

I turned towards him with raised eyebrows.

"Any chance you have a car... or a phone?" I half smiled, half laughed, clutching my broken ribs. I wouldn't make it home in my condition flying. Hell, considering how dense this forest is, I'd be lucky if I made it out of the woods.

"I don't, but I know someone who does. They'll be meeting us at the forest's edge."

My stomach fluttered as Nathaniel entered my mind and I was eager to leave the enchanting forest to get back to him. I matched Ezekiel's pace through the pain, striding over tumbled moss covered logs, rocks and fallen trees as we made our way out of the forest.

"I still can't understand why Abraxos would throw his entire life's work away, why he would turn so dark." Ezekiel murmured more to himself than to me as we sidestepped a small creek and boulder.

Searing pain shot through my torso making me light headed.

"Seems he became buddies with a pretty dark friend and followed suit," I said, sucking in a breath and deeply wishing my body would heal itself already.

"What do you mean? Who was it?"

"Corson, the worst of the worst. Somehow he got into his head and made him think he'd have it all if they worked together."

Ezekiel did not answer but the way his muscles flexed under the weight of that name made me think it wasn't the first time he'd encountered the name or the man behind it. He seemed to have as much disdain for the person behind the name as I did.

"So what are we going to do about him?" I asked when Ezekiel said no more.

"We will not do anything, because we cannot do anything. For now."

"What do you mean? We've got plenty to go on. Abraxos, the Council members? We should hunt Corson down and finish it. Why give him an opportunity to strike?"

Ezekiel held his hand up for me to let him respond. Apparently, I'd been increasing in volume and intensity. I quieted my mouth, but my heart beat madly.

"Whatever Corson is up to, Abraxos and his plan didn't work. Once he finds that out, he'll be back to the drawing board. We need to be patient and find out what his true intentions are before we do anything. Besides, with Abraxos dead, he'll be warier about his movements now."

"And once we find out?"

Ezekiel turned to me monotonously, as if I had to ask. Acknowledging his meaning without speaking, we continued our trek to the outskirts of the rain forest.

My boots squished through mossy water and I was astonished to learn how sound-deadening the mosses in the rain forest were. Aside from the occasional babbling brook or creek, the noises in the forest seemed to be nonexistent.

"And Nathaniel?" I asked after we'd trekked for some time in silence.

"What about him?"

"Well... can I... I mean can we...?

"Be together?" he finished for me.

I was quiet but my gaze was entirely focused on him and his response.

He shrugged. "Don't see why not. The Council didn't confirm otherwise, especially since you are no longer an Interceder, and after what happened, I think you've earned a place in their good graces. People get accustomed to rules and traditions, they don't like change, so I wouldn't expect others to be too keen on the idea. You'll still need to be careful, but yes."

My feet stopped moving forward.

"Is something wrong?"

I shook my head silently looking back at him and smiling. The sound of his approval and the word 'yes' was not what I had been expecting to hear, and yet hearing the words gave me hope. Nathaniel and I could be together, actually together.

I could feel a warmth spread through my chest cavity, filling my emptiness. A new eagerness filled my stride knowing I could be in Nathaniel's arms without any fear of what would happen to him, or to us, if anyone found out.

"You know, I actually think everything is going to be OK," I said, moving forward with a renewed vigor.

The rest of the way went by grudgingly sluggishly. I'd made the first five miles with no help, but appreciatively accepted Ezekiel's helping hand the remaining distance. I'd slowed considerably, and with late afternoon approaching, we needed to make it through the rain forest with better pace.

My legs quivered under me, making my steps jagged and misplaced. I leaned further on Ezekiel for support, thankfully he didn't seem to mind, or at least never mentioned it.

"The clearing should be just up ahead." Ezekiel's words made whatever adrenaline and energy I had left spring forth and I pushed through the last bit of distance to the edge of the rain forest hastily.

Reaching the clearing, my breathing stopped when I saw him. He paced in front of the SUV rapidly, anxiously rubbing the back of his neck. It was only the second time I had seen him this way, so vulnerable. A swelling built heavily in my throat when he stopped pacing and looked at me and I couldn't fight back the tears. We bolted for one another's embrace.

The comfort his warm arms gave as they wrapped around me only deepened my emotions. I truly had thought I'd never see him or anyone else again. He squeezed me tighter, tucking me into his chest as I breathed in his presence, euphoric that he was here.

"I'm here. God, I thought I'd never see you again." His voice was a desperate whisper and his breathing erratic. It took me a moment before I realized he had cried too.

"Get her some rest, it's been a long day. Take care, you two. I'll be in touch," Ezekiel said before nodding and smiling at our gratitude; then he disappeared.

I hadn't even noticed we had company till Luther stepped out of the SUV with a smile on his face. The tears kept flowing, but I smiled, embracing him.

"Thought you could use a driver, it's good to see you Alex," he said smiling and opening the door for us. "Caim and Lahash send their apologies too, they're halfway across the country, but were ready to bring the cavalry when they heard Seraphina made it out but you didn't."

I smiled wearily, "It's ok," Climbing into the SUV with the help of Nathaniel, I settled in, burrowing myself into him once more after he slid next to me, his grip around my waist never loosening.

"Take me home," I whispered as I let my eye lids mercifully close and rest. The agonizing ache of my injuries began to thrum through me as the last of the adrenaline escaped causing my body to go limp and slump against Nathaniel. I was finally out and he was here. That's all that mattered now, and I would heal as I always did after some sleep and time. I drowned out the engine and road noises; the only audible sound was Nathaniel's heartbeat against the rise and fall of his chest.

Epilogue

I don't remember dreaming. I don't remember getting out of the SUV or where or when Luther left us. I wasn't even sure of how long I had slept, but the tender stabbing discomfort across my mid-section, legs and face was real. Its rawness jarred my memory quickly to the previous events.

I scooted to the edge of the bed rubbing the sleepiness from my eyes and viewing an array of trays and beverages covering a nearby coffee table. I blinked a few times and a feeling of uneasiness crept its way into my bloodstream. I didn't recognize where I was, and although there was a smorgasbord of food in front of me that I was dying to devour, I needed someone, preferably Nathaniel, to fill in the blanks first.

I began dressing, favoring my ribcage as I slid my jacket over my tank top, taking note that someone had kindly removed my pants so I could sleep in my lacy underwear. I'd be sure to let Nathaniel know my thoughts on undressing me when I am unconscious. I glanced at myself in the mirror noticing the bruising that remained heavily on my abdomen. The rest had seemed to fade, aside from a darker hue near my left eye and the bloodied slash on my forearm that seemed to be healing at a snail's pace. Hopefully my super human healing abilities would get a kick start here shortly and finish the job, otherwise I'd have to come up with a convincing story for my parents and especially my brother, who wouldn't believe me anyway.

I stole a few pieces of bacon from a tray and headed towards the door adjoining the next room.

The voices had risen an octave as I opened the door causing Nathaniel and Jared to abruptly cease their argument in my presence. Nathaniel strode over and kissed me without hesitating. I pulled back, slightly surprised and feeling a bit better about the whole no pants thing, but still needed some answers. Jared rolled his eyes and brushed past Nathaniel so he could hug me. I groaned when the pressure squeezed my ribcage and Jared let go, giving my injuries a once over.

"I'm OK, really."

"No you're not, you haven't healed yet," he said, lifting up the corner of my tank top and revealing a ghastly black and purple bruise.

His hands reached for my side; a warm tingling sensation began fighting its way to the source of the wound and I knew he was trying to heal me.

"Don't bother. Healing won't work on me until this crud is out of my system." I gratefully smiled at his attempt, feeling the heat of his hand on my side and the warm smell of vanilla and rain drawing me in closer.

He seemed to acknowledge his hand was lingering and he kissed the top of my forehead before stepping back.

"Glad you're OK."

I smiled at him and my eyes widened with the welcoming greetings I was receiving.

"Well! Good morning!" I said, blushing from all of the unexpected attention and finding a table to sit at as my angel and fallen angel emotions teeter-tottered everywhere.

Nathaniel's glare toward Jared diminished and he went to the other room to bring me a tray of food.

"You should eat. You need all your strength."

"Don't worry, I won't fight you this time." My grin was returned with a sly wink.

"So!" I said propping my legs onto the chair next to mine. "What's the story this time? It's going to be a little hard to hide all *this*," I joked, waving a hand over my bruises, "even with a good one, so fill me in on what we're doing.

Jared shifted anxiously causing me to look towards Nathaniel for clarification.

His face was stern and resembled a hard exterior similar to the one he was wearing when I'd first met him.

"Why don't you fill her in Jared?" His tone was sarcastic and had an edge to it I didn't like.

"Tell me what? What's going on?" I asked feeling my ribs ache as my body went rigid.

A faint muffled sound tickled my ears and I zeroed in on the location in the room, the hallway closet. I slowly rose from my chair and followed the sound to the closet door.

"Listen, Alex, don't freak out, just let me explain," Jared said hastily, attempting to block my path.

I pushed past him and opened the door to find my brother staring back at me, hogtied, and with a serious amount of duct tape over his mouth.

My eyes widened as Derek looked both relieved and pissed.

"Derek! What the hell are you doing with my brother!?" I yelled as I began untying him and removing the duct tape, tossing a perturbed stare towards Nathaniel.

Nathaniel put his hands up and plopped himself down on the sofa to witness my implosion.

"Don't look at me! Wise guy over here was the one who hogtied him and brought him here in the first place."

The shocked expression on my face turned to anger as my widened eyes became slits and fire raged through my veins.

Derek finished untying himself as I advanced on Jared.

"Start explaining." My voice was low and dangerous.

"Alex, listen, after you helped me get away I bumped into him on my way back. I was so distraught from Abraxos taking you and I wasn't even paying attention, but he followed you and saw me. I admit, I may have panicked, but I couldn't let him go!"

I felt Derek's presence behind me, free of all restraints.

"You're screwed now." But Derek would have to wait his turn. Jared was mine at the moment.

"Alex, just calm down. I didn't mean any harm."

"I am so sick of everyone telling me to calm down! You kidnapped my brother and dragged him into this!"

I could feel my fire erratically spurting through my bloodstream, but refusing to come forth. I was still weakened, but the rage I held and the internal battle inside me made my wings reflexively burst forth knocking the table over in the process. Everyone froze. Nathaniel jumped up from the couch but it was too late. The cat was out of the bag.

"Alex?" What the hell!

I held my breath, closing my eyes and wishing that I had the gift of time travel instead of fire so I could go back and reverse what I had just revealed to him. I turned ever so slowly as I took in his dazed and shaken expression.

"Hey..." I said giving him a tiny smile.

"What...?" But his sentence was cut short by a whack to the back of the head.

Luther helped ease Derek to the floor before breathing out an exhausted sigh.

"Well. Thought I told everyone to keep the excitement to a minimum until I got back," he said lighting a cigarette and taking several extra-long drags, seeming oddly relaxed about the situation.

"My credit card is on file for damages," Jared said suddenly as he looked at the broken table, causing me to give him an 'are you kidding me' look.

"I'll pay for it, it's fine," he said hurriedly.

I looked back towards Derek's unconscious body.

What had I just done?

The cloaked figure remained hidden in the shadows while Corson's rage filled the room.

"How was he so stupid! Revealing himself at a Council judgement hearing! We should have killed the hybrid when we had the chance!"

"Enough!" The figure bellowed. Its shape was fragmented as wisps of black-

ened air and smoke shot out of the darkness towards Corson. Corson's breathing caught and he remained planted where he stood, but his expression hardened.

"It's because of the hybrid's blood that we are where we are now..."

The figure's decayed greyish-black hand reached for Corson's face menacingly, as if it had trouble keeping itself from attacking. Then it shot back towards its own body as the figure hovered in front of Corson, its face remaining cloaked in darkness.

"The soldiers are ready, we've got the hybrid's blood. What do you want us to do?" Corson questioned, trying to force the smell of rotting flesh out of his nose. He'd made a deal with death itself, and he was holding up his end of the bargain too, even if Abraxos had failed. He just needed to give them what they wanted and he'd have unlimited power; no more bending to the rules of his father or to the balance.

"Take several subjects and test the serum on someone close to you, we need to know the full strength of it power before this war begins."

The Next Book in
The Awakening Series

readersfavorite.com/book-review/absolution-the-awakening-series
facebook.com/AshleyLucero.TheAwakeningSeries

www.ingramcontent.com/pod-product-compliance
Lightning Source LLC
Chambersburg PA
CBHW051416170626
46809CB00006B/2188